THE Edge OF Always

Rebecca Ryan is the author of *My (extra)Ordinary Life*, *The Philosophy of Love*, *The Next Chapter* and *The Edge of Always*. She left a career in teaching to pursue writing, and now mostly spends her days making up stories and dreaming of the impossible – a completed to-do list. Rebecca lives in Bradford with her partner and their five children, five guinea pigs and twenty-seven sheep. She also owns no small number of notebooks and an expansive collection of scatter cushions. And she wouldn't have it any other way.

Also by Rebecca Ryan

My (extra)Ordinary Life
The Philosophy of Love
The Next Chapter

THE Edge OF Always

REBECCA RYAN

SIMON &
SCHUSTER

London · New York · Amsterdam/Antwerp · Sydney/Melbourne · Toronto · New Delhi

First published in Great Britain by Simon & Schuster UK Ltd, 2026

1 3 5 7 9 10 8 6 4 2

Simon & Schuster UK Ltd, 7th Floor,
199 Bishopsgate, London, EC2M 3TY

Simon & Schuster Australia, Sydney
Simon & Schuster India, New Delhi

www.simonandschuster.co.uk
www.simonandschuster.com.au
www.simonandschuster.co.in

The authorised representative in the EEA is Simon & Schuster Netherlands BV, Herculesplein 96, 3584 AA Utrecht, Netherlands. info@simonandschuster.nl

A CIP catalogue record for this book is available from the British Library

Paperback ISBN: 978-1-3985-3882-5
eBook ISBN: 978-1-3985-3883-2
Audio ISBN: 978-1-3985-3884-9

Typeset in Bembo by M Rules
Printed and Bound in the UK using 100% Renewable Electricity at CPI Group (UK) Ltd

FSC www.fsc.org
MIX
Paper | Supporting responsible forestry
FSC® C013604

For Dan

Prologue

THEN

'So, this is it? You're really leaving?'

Emmett nodded, his eyes full of tears. Luna's too. She thought it might have been the wind, the way it whipped around them, making their eyes water. Luna thought it could have been the wind, but really, she knew that it wasn't.

They stood together on the edge of the cliff – their cliff. Below them, the sea battered against the rocks, sending big foamy froth into the air. For one halfway hysterical moment, Luna wanted to laugh. It was a plenty dramatic place to be dumped by.

Emmett had his duffel bag by his feet. That's how Luna knew that this was a proper goodbye – the sort where you pack all of your worldly goods into a bag because you know for certain that you're not coming back. Luna knew, on some rational level, that it wasn't the bag's fault that Emmett was leaving. The bag was a symptom of his leaving, not the cause. But still she hated it.

'I have to go.' Emmett shouted a little louder because of the wind.

Luna had imagined this moment of their last tragic goodbye a thousand times. They had a love as intangible and flighty as the wind, something that was impossible to grasp; that was impossible to hold onto. But this wasn't at all how Luna had imagined their last tragic goodbye would go, with both of them having to shout.

Emmett held tight to the lapels of her denim jacket, his head bent forward. It stole almost all of her breath, how much Luna wanted him to stay in this place. This place where she longed for them both to belong.

'I just . . . can't.' He looked at her straight and Luna knew what he meant. He meant that he couldn't forgive her, for the secret she'd kept.

Which, maybe, was fair enough, since Luna was sure that she'd never forgive herself either.

'I'm sorry,' she said. It was the truth. She really was sorry.

'I know,' Emmett answered, finally letting go of her jacket, leaving her untethered in more ways than one. 'I'm sorry, too.' He turned to walk away, and it struck Luna how wrong this whole thing was. She was meant to be the one who leaves. Not Emmett, never Emmett. Her whole life was wrong now, falling apart and ruined, and Luna knew that this moment on the cliff would haunt her. That it would charge through the rest of her life like an electric current, leaving a trail of destruction in its wake.

She had the strange sensation of wanting to shiver right

out of her skin. Just shrug it off and leave it on the ground like a snake. Possibly, being dumped was turning her insane.

'But Emmett,' Luna called. 'You can't . . . because . . . because . . . I love you!'

Words she'd wanted to say so many times were finally free, only to be stolen by the wind. Words that had formed a thousand times were now out there, living and breathing with a life of their own in this world where everything was wrong.

He didn't turn around.

Art flashed into Luna's mind, a collage of colour and form. It often did when she felt so emotional. *Weeping Woman* by Munch. *Ophelia* by Millais. It struck Luna that Millais, Munch, and all the others, had never fully captured it – what it was to have your heart broken.

'Emmett,' she shouted, one last time.

But the wind took her words, lifted them to the sky and blew them away.

'Art is a protest against death.'

AUBREY FLACK

Chapter One

NOW

The Edge of Always: Oil on canvas. The most impressionist of Spencer's work, *The Edge of Always* incorporates loose, visible brushstrokes to create a dreamlike quality and sense of movement. The figure appears to be in motion, caught in a fleeting moment as opposed to frozen in time. Date unknown.

'Hello, Deathers, and welcome back to The Art of Dying, the blog where we connect you, the living yet slightly morbid public, with art inspired by death. Today, we're going to be diving head-first into the paintings of Ernst Ludwig Kirchner who was a nice guy, if a bit weird. Kirchner was one of the founders of the Expressionist movement. Expressionists were great with decay, and Kirchner himself

loved a bit of death art. He painted a self-portrait as an amputee despite having two excellent hands. He'd had a bad war though, poor thing . . .'

My phone is on the coffee table (read dumping ground) in front of my laptop, vibrating constantly. I'm not meant to turn it off, just in case, but it's an annoying distraction. I've spent all week planning this script on Kirchner and now I can't get through it without being distracted.

It's bound to be Mum with another round of reels about the benefits of bovine collagen. The woman never rests.

It vibrates again.

I hit pause, annoyed. I'm always annoyed these days. Mae thinks that it's a result of my being depressed, which I refuse to accept. Still, I reach to snatch my phone from where it's balanced on top of a pile that's mostly art history books and magazines. Mum would (and has) described the cottage as 'squalid'. I'd describe it as homely.

Nine messages, all of them from Mae.

Mae: Look what I found!
(There's a link to an article.)
Mae: Did you read it yet?
Mae: Actually, I only sent it ten seconds ago.
Mae: How about now?
Mae: Are you there?
Mae: You're not cutting your fringe again, are you?
Mae: STEP AWAY FROM THE SCISSORS.

Mae: Seriously, can you reply now?

Mae: HELLLOOOOOO

Mae's my younger sister. She's the most brilliant yet annoying person that I know. Ironically, she's probably the only thing in the world that doesn't annoy *me*. Or not really.

Me: I'm here, I was recording.

Mae: Shhhiiittt. Didn't even think of that. The Kollwitz one?

Me: He's next week. I was doing Kirchner

Mae: Cool. Cool. Dude with the hand. Well have you opened the link yet?

Me: I've literally been messaging you the whole time. Give me a second.

The last link Mae sent me and insisted that I read was a spicy Adam Brody fanfic. She thought I'd like it since he and Emmett look a bit alike, with dark curly hair and green eyes. The main character transformed into a dragon, and much was made of his dragon-sized penis and how, and I quote directly here, 'it hurt so good' – which is irrelevant, but it means that my expectations aren't exactly high.

Still, my phone is vibrating with messages from her, so I scroll back up and hit the link that she's sent, sinking back down between the couch cushions as I do. Kirchner will have to wait.

Mae: I'll be home in five.

It's the middle of the day. I've no idea why Mae is coming home.

The article loads, and something deep in my chest lurches.

'UNE VIE EN COULEUR' EARL JOSEF SPENCER – Nouvelle exposition temporaire au Musée d'Art Moderne de Paris.

'Fuck me,' I say, even though there's no one here to hear it. Blood starts pumping around my ears. A persistent thud. *Dum. Dum. Dum.* I click the little Union Jack flag to translate the article to English and keep reading.

> The MAM in Paris is hosting a new exhibition of the late, great expressionist Earl Josef Spencer. Spencer's work, has yet to be exhibited in Paris, and Rise Art understands that this temporary exhibition will incorporate several pieces from his final years, including:
>
> *The Weight of Light*
> *Portrait of the Longing for Human Connection*
> *Montmartre in Motion*
> *The Juxtaposition of Life and Death*
> *The Rubicon*
>
> Mari Marigold, the curator responsible for the show, told Rise Art, 'It is a true honour to display the last works of Earl Josef Spencer. He's an artist I've wanted to

bring to our space since my tenure here began. His *The Juxtaposition of Life and Death* and *Portrait of the Longing for Human Connection* are two of my favourite pieces.

'There's no doubt about it; visitors are in for a treat. Spencer's work combines the emotional intensity of Expressionism with the objective clarity found in post-Expressionism, creating a masterclass in colour and form. At least that's what we believe here at Rise Art. And if a Spencer exhibition isn't exciting enough, we can exclusively reveal that MAM has acquired a new work which will take centre stage in the exhibit.'

Spencer died at age eighty-seven, almost twenty years ago, and so the mystery of a new piece is taking the art world by storm.

Madam Marigold remained tight-lipped on the whole thing and refused to be drawn on where precisely the new painting had been found. But Rise Art understands that it's a verified Spencer titled, *The Edge of Always*. And if you can't wait to see the real deal, we have an exclusive first look here.

The exhibition is set to run for the whole of September. This isn't one to be missed, art lovers!

I feel . . . confused. So much confusion. It spreads like mist on an autumn evening, clouding my thoughts and darkening my outlook.

How? *How* can there be a new painting by Earl? It's impossible.

I click the link to see the painting, but the WiFi is dodgy and it won't load.

I put my phone down. Pick it up again. It still hasn't loaded. I hit back, confusion making way for frustration. I jab at my phone.

Work, goddamit. The article loads again, so I re-read it, trying to take it all in.

A new painting by the late artist Earl Josef Spencer has been unearthed.

It's being exhibited in Paris throughout September.

No one knows where it came from.

It's almost September now. Three days away.

My heart is still beating a persistent beat in my ear.

Why didn't anyone tell me?

I dismiss the thought right away. Why would anyone tell me? I'm a no one. Before I gave it up, my own art had become so unprofitable it was just a hobby. Turns out people don't want dismembered hearts all over their walls.

And who would connect my Art of Dying blog with Earl? So few people know everything that happened back then.

There's Emmett. He'd know.

As thoughts go, it's an unwanted one. I never even think about Emmett. And I'm certain that he's not thinking about me. He probably doesn't know about the new painting. I'm *in* the art world, and I might have missed it if it wasn't for . . .

Mae.

'I'm here!'

The door to our cottage bursts open with so much force that it whacks the wall behind it.

It's a tiny cottage, just five rooms. To one side of the main door, there's a small kitchen with the same round dining table we've always had, the only bit of furniture we kept. On the other, the living area. Then there are two bedrooms and a bathroom.

We've never needed anything bigger as it's not like we have people over very much. Zadie sometimes comes, and Ahmed the couple of times he's been back to visit. Mum has come for dinner precisely once, when Mae took the opportunity to announce that she was in a throuple, and Mum had broken into a literal, visible sweat at this and had never come back. She'd tried to remove Mae from the family WhatsApp.

'You didn't need to come home,' I tell my sister.

'What? And let you see that alone, without support? And oh my god, you have cut your fringe some more.'

'I like it short.'

'It's two inches long.'

'I think it makes me look interesting.'

'You're wearing a waistcoat – you are interesting.'

Truth be told, my fringe is a bit shorter than I'd hoped it would be. I was going for edgy. I'm guessing, however, that edgy is rarely achieved on a steroid high, armed with a pair of blunt scissors late one Thursday night.

Edgy people have a team. I don't have a team; I barely have an anyone. I have a Mae, some vaguely peripheral friendships that are hanging on by a thread, and a couple of hundred strangers, known as Deathers, who subscribe to my blog about death. And it's the way I like it.

Mae flops down on our charity shop acid green couch; a little plume of flour puffs into the air as she does so since she's still in her white uniform.

She works in the local café as a baker. I swear she could bake sawdust into a cake and it would still taste great. 'I can't believe that Earl had another painting.'

'I know.' My mind is racing now. Earl. Even just hearing his name brings back so many memories from then.

The time before.

Mae is still talking. Like me, her hair is red. Strawberry blonde in summer, more rust-like in winter. She absent-mindedly blows a strand that's escaped her hairnet. I've tried to capture it so many times, the colour of her hair. There's a whole wall in the living room of the cottage that's red, different shades and textures too. Sometimes I feel this overwhelming urge to commit it so deeply into my memory that nothing could ever dislodge it.

Those are the days I have to adjust my meds.

'Have you seen the painting?' she asks.

I shake my head. 'It won't load.'

'Well, you just wait till you see it. *The Edge of Always*. Great title. He was always good at coming up with titles, wasn't he? Fucking smashed it out of the park Earl, my man.' She looks up at the (also painted) ceiling as she says the last part.

'Yep.'

I'm only half in the conversation. Less than that, even.

A part of me is looking to the past, remembering. You'd think that so long ago, it'd be like looking through a murky window, but it isn't. Looking back is like seeing the person I was in the time before under a spotlight. Everything is in technicolour.

'Obviously, you need to go and see it,' Mae says.

That makes me laugh.

'Of course, I'm not going.' It's such a ridiculous notion and it makes my heart rate pick up even more. I don't want to overwhelm myself; I'm not meant to. So, I steady my breathing, count to four over and over to match my inhale and exhale, and once I'm done, I answer Mae. 'You know that I can't.'

Mae completely ignores me. 'Do you think Emmett knows? I wonder where he ended up. I still can't believe he dumped you. What a dick move.'

I tell Mae everything, but I've never told her that I know something about Emmett's life. I know he trained to be a doctor and works abroad in places that look dangerous, and only very occasionally updates his social media. It's a tragedy of the highest order to admit to still keeping tabs on your boyfriend from two decades ago.

'No idea,' I tell her. 'But did you hear me? I said I'm not going to go to Paris.'

Mae twists her head to look at me dead on and laughs. Her face is so similar to mine; everyone has always said that we could be twins. She's only thirteen months younger than me, but if people looked closely, they'd see that her face is fuller, more joyful. Her features are arranged in a way that's just a bit nicer than mine. I've always thought I was too symmetrical, too ordered. It annoys me, but then like I said already, what doesn't.

'You have to go but you could wait a bit, miss the opening if you like. I'd understand that with your fringe, the selfies will be appalling. But either way, you're going.'

I have no idea why Mae is pushing this.

'We'll call it The Paris Plan,' she says, sitting on her hands. 'Aren't you just a bit curious to see the new painting?'

'Yes, of course I am. But that doesn't mean I can go. I just can't . . . You know that I can't.'

'You could blog while you're there, do a Spencer special. Be honest, there's literally no one better placed than you to do a Spencer special.'

She's talking so fast she's barely breathing at this point.

It's the most ridiculous thing I've ever heard.

'Stop saying the words Spencer Special. What about my other work? Earl's stuff isn't exactly my bag these days.'

It's the first objection that springs to mind. The first, but far from my last.

'It's an art history blog. You're not contractually obligated to *only* talk about death art. Plus, no one will die if you don't turn up to work for three days.' Unlike Emmett – who I definitely never think about – people would actually die if he didn't turn up for work. 'And anyway, you can finish and edit the Kirchner episode today if you work late – I'll help.'

It's a stupid idea. In a lifetime of questionable ideas (she has a tattoo of a pigeon on her thigh), this has to be one of Mae's worst. I don't want to go to Paris. Too many people, too much stuff.

Mae isn't done. 'Plus, you're the one who's always droning on and on about the difference between seeing and looking at art.'

I start biting my nail.

'Dr Dave would never agree to it.'

'Dave loves me. I'll ask him.'

Mae has swivelled round to face me and has one leg tucked under her on the couch.

'You can go to Paris,' I tell her, 'if you're so desperate to see the painting. I like it here.'

'Trust me, I would. But Gemma said I can't have any more time off.' She sighs dramatically.

'Now look at that painting. That painting will make you want to go to Paris. Trust me.'

Mae reaches out and laces her fingers into mine. We've been like this for years. Trauma bonded, she calls it. I'd just say we're close. Best friends.

With my free hand, I reach for my phone and try to open the link again.

Mae squeezes my hand as the page loads, slowly, clunkily revealing the painting.

'This is going to change everything,' she tells me as it loads.

I go to say that she's ridiculous, way too dramatic, that

nothing, not even a painting from Earl, could change everything.

But as the painting fills my phone screen, I see what she means.

It's beautiful, so beautiful.

But it's not the beauty of the piece that's making my eyes fill with tears.

No, it's the fact that there's a girl in the painting, and well, that girl, it's me.

Chapter Two

'What about your vibrator? Which one are you taking? Should you take two? Sex toys are obligatory in Paris. The French carry them around like lip balm.'

Mae, a woman who has never been to Paris, or France for that matter, is in my bedroom, 'helping' me to pack. By which I mean she's rifling through the drawers of my bedside table and throwing things onto the enormous pile of stuff already taking up the bed.

I'm in a state of suspended animation, frozen with something that feels like shock, or fear, or possibly good old-fashioned overwhelm at the speed at which Mae had booked me a trip to Paris.

But she was right in one respect. Once I realised that I am in the painting, I can't not go and see it.

As a general rule, I don't *do* things like this. I don't go on last-minute trips to Paris to see a mystery painting of myself that's about to be on display in one of the most famous art museums in the whole entire world.

I think I'm hyperventilating. What is happening? I don't even go into cafés where they play the radio too loud.

My shock has rendered me incapacitated, which is why Mae has taken control of the packing situation. From what I can see, a turquoise bra has wound its way around a hairbrush. She's trying to ram my entire wardrobe into a little wheelie case.

'So do you think two will be enough?'

Shock aside, at the news that I'm about to take a plethora of vibrators on a three-day trip to Paris, I decide to become more actively involved in the packing process.

I, too, start to rifle. It's chaos. And usually I'm fine with chaos. The whole cottage is chaotic – like this room. Possibly, I'm just a cliched artist till I die, but I'd painted every corner of it, I even put a mural on the ceiling before it became a thing that home renovators did online. I'd once had a quick fling with a man who described the room as like waking up in a fever dream. He'd messaged me weeks later to tell me that the taxidermied squirrel I have on my bookshelf was his new sleep paralysis demon.

Mae let me paint her room, too. She's in the one we used to share. She says that it's karma for Mum that I turned out like this. Earl used to say that we could be anything we wanted in life, as long as we weren't dull. 'Live a life of colour, Luna.' I'd told Mum what he'd said, and she'd called it a load of leftie nonsense. But I'd taken his words to heart. I was different then.

I wonder what Earl would think if he could see me now.

'I don't need *any* vibrators,' I tell Mae, hobbling over to where she's still in my bedside table. She throws half a packet of tissues on top of the mountain of stuff.

'But French people are so horny. And you're going to see art. Art always makes you horny.'

'Not a painting of myself.'

She pauses for a second.

'I turn myself on all the time.'

'No vibrators.'

'Urgh, fine. If you're determined to make this trip as unfun as possible.'

'You're basically making me go.' This isn't exactly true, but it was Mae's idea.

'Yes, yes, how awful, being sent on a compulsory mini-break to Paris. My heart bleeds. And I used my credit card to pay for the hotel, I paid extra for a view of the Eiffel Tower and everything. Even you can't be depressed in Paris.'

'I'm not depressed,' I huff and keep packing. 'I just have a complete lack of hope. Which is realistic and sensible.'

'Oh yeah, that's lovely, that is. A complete lack of hope. Great way to live.'

We pack in silence after that.

'I think that's everything,' I tell Mae, adding the little mic I use to record videos to my rucksack and then, when there's nothing else to do with my hands, nothing else I can do to distract myself from my complete lack of hope, I sit on the edge of the bed and stress. 'Where could the painting have come from? Earl would have told us if he'd sold one.'

Mae pauses and leans on the windowsill. Both of the bedrooms are at the back of the cottage, looking out over the long lawn.

'Maybe Gregor had it but only sold it recently?'

Gregor was Earl's art dealer. He was about a hundred and two, talked about the Russian Revolution as if he lived through it, and consumed an entirely vodka-based diet. I've no idea how he's still alive after all this time.

'Yeah, maybe. It's still weird that we knew nothing about it.'

'Ask that museum curator, the one from the article. It sounds like she loves Earl's stuff,' Mae says eventually. 'She's bound to tell you more than some randomer since you're in it. It's obvious it's you.'

And it is obvious that it's me. My hair is shorter now, but Earl has the colour of it in summer exactly right. Pale red, like the surface of Mars. I'm looking straight ahead in the painting, not smiling; if anything, I'd say that I'm somewhere between sad and resigned in it. My mouth is set, and my eyebrows are straight. It's a look I often wear now.

'She might.'

I don't want to sound miserable; it annoys Mae, and she's obviously excited about this, so I just let it go. I try to fold some of my stuff before giving in and just ramming it in the case.

'I bet being in the painting will get me more followers. Even if it isn't death art.'

I'm trying to smooth the edges of what feels like a frayed conversation and doing as bad a job of that as I am at folding. Mae doesn't say anything, but she rolls her eyes, and I know exactly what she's thinking. I've listened to her lecture on how I need real human connections too many times not to know what's going on in that head of hers.

'You're the one who wanted me to have a goal,' I protest.

'Yeah, but like a real-life one.'

She doesn't get it. And I'm glad she doesn't.

My commitment to smoothing edges evaporates, and I snap. 'Can you please not have a go at me now? You know I can't handle stress.'

Mae's shoulders slump but she doesn't say anything and in return I'm hit with a potent dose of guilt. It's fine for her, with all of her relentless positivity. She's the one who gets to step up all the time – she has no idea what it's like being me. But still, Mae's the only person who manages to make me feel guilty about my being miserable.

We sort in silence for a few more moments until I give in.

'Fine, one vibrator,' I tell her. 'But I'll pack it once you've left the room.'

She claps her hands together really fast, tension apparently forgotten.

'You're going to have the best time.'

We take turns trying to close the small suitcase. Mae has to sit on it to get it to shut.

'You're sure that I should go?' I'm biting my nails again, eyeing my suitcase like it's harbouring an unexploded bomb. Mae looks right at me. She's wearing a baggy jumper with a yellow smiley face on it and leopard print leggings, and I'm 100 per cent certain that every single thing she's wearing is mine.

'I'm sure. You're going to Paris, not Jupiter, and you heard what Dr Dave said. You've got everything else that you need.'

I nod. The truth of the matter is, deep (deep) down, I think she's right. It might be self-involved, and it probably is, but it's been so long since I've thought of myself as the main character in my own life that I have no idea what self-involved even feels like anymore. I have self-pity nailed, but, that aside, I think Earl would have wanted me to go. I let him down once; I can't do it again.

Mae starts to bundle me out of the door – the bus leaves in half an hour.

'Now your train back is booked for Wednesday,' she tells me like I'm literally a child. Mae has assumed the role of eldest sibling with ease. I have assumed the role of younger sibling in need of help with . . . less ease.

'I know.'

'Which means you only have two full days to see the sights of Paris.'

'I know.'

'You're sure you don't need more time? This might be your only chance.'

She means to see the painting, but we both know there's more to it than that.

'I have to come back on Wednesday, I'm running Art Therapy at the hospice, remember?'

'I know, but it's hardly life or death.'

Mae hugs me so hard it knocks the wind out of me.

'It's three days.'

'Are you sure you don't want me to walk you to the station?'

'There's no need.'

I don't trust myself not to cry saying goodbye to Mae at the bus stop, and I won't do that, I've promised myself. I don't cry in public anymore.

'Just be careful,' she tells me.

'I will, I promise.'

'Good, now go and take Paris by storm.'

I was around five when we bought the holiday cottage in Northumberland. Dad had a particular interest in puffins, and Mum wanted to spend the summers on a beach, which is, I think, how they'd arrived at Bamburgh, on the coast, as the perfect place to buy a holiday cottage. To me, though, this part of the world has always been so much more than lovely beaches (or puffins for that matter). It's the place I've always felt hopeful. Even right back to that first time we visited, it wasn't the castles that impressed me (though they seemed especially huge back then), or tales from an impossibly distant history. It wasn't even the sea, which seemed to me to stretch right out to the end of the world. It wasn't any of those things that made me feel hopeful. It was, I suppose, a sense that here, things could be different. That here, in this place that was so different from home, things could be okay.

I've been disavowed of my hope so many times over the years, stripped of it by a series of disappointments, some micro, some massive. Each time, when I've struggled, battled, to find it again, it's come back smaller, with less potency than before. Like a fire that once roared and is now reduced to smouldering embers. Now, my hope is nothing but ashes. I think that's why I stopped creating. You need to feel some hope to create, and I feel so little. I'm nothing. Numb and neutral.

Or that's how it felt before I saw that painting.

I have my head down as I walk through Bamburgh. These days, I never leave my house without headphones, so music, any music, beats away in my ears.

'You have a good time in Paris, Luna pet. Take care of yourself.' Mrs Gimley from the corner shop stands in front of me and waits until I've taken my headphones off to talk. It's the end of tourist season, the final fling of summer.

'I will, thanks, Mrs Gimley.'

'Eat a croissant for me, Luna.' Tony, who sells the *Big Issue* in the market square, calls so loudly that I don't need to pause the song.

'I will, Tony.'

I've no idea why it's easier to talk to strangers online than it is to actual people, but I'm out of breath and looking directly at the ground as I wheel my little case over the cobbles towards the bus stop. The blue and yellow coach that'll take me to London is already waiting.

It looks so out of place. Everything in Bamburgh is old. Old streets, old houses, old everything. Here, more than anywhere else, there's a sense that we're all just tiny dots, part of a much bigger story.

I'm fully panting by the time I make it to my seat. It's only mildly warm outside, but I'm still sweating, and it takes a while for my breathing to return to normal.

I shrug off my jacket – my navy blue velvet shacket, and fold it on my lap.

I check my phone. Three messages.

> **Mae:** Did you get there okay?

And another mere seconds after.

> **Mae:** I should have come with you.
>
> **Me:** I'm fine. On the bus now, just waiting for it to leave.

I add three celebrating face emojis because I don't want Mae to know how absolutely terrified I am.

She replies immediately.

> **Mae:** I'm SO excited for you! Send so many pictures. Love you!!!

I reply with a line of hearts and check the other message.

> **Mum:** Mae seems to be operating under the illusion that you're going on a mini-break to Paris. Call me, Luna.

I don't reply. I don't have the capacity to deal with Mum right now.

Instead, I take out my book, Ahmed's latest, as the bus pulls away from the station, and I think that for the first time in a very long time, that maybe there's still time for the feeling to come back.

Chapter Three

As my train pulls into Paris, a part of me can't believe that I'm here, that I actually did it.

I'm exhausted. And terrified. There's a kernel of excitement in there too, I think, but it's being mostly crowded out by the terror.

Today has been a lot. A lot of travelling. A lot of people, noise, just a lot. But if I think Paris is going to be some sort of a break from the relentlessness, I'm sorely mistaken. If anything, it's dialled up.

Outside the Gare du Nord, I'm hit with such a potent dose of, well, life I suppose, that I think about turning straight round and getting back on the train to go home. There are people everywhere. Horns beep, and the lights of the row of cafés opposite the station are bright in the early evening. It's affronting. People try to sell me cigarettes, mini key rings of the Eiffel Tower; someone tries to hand me a bottle of wine. Everyone is laughing, smiling, and talking so loudly. A woman on a bike almost mows me down on her way into the station.

I can't go home. I wouldn't survive the journey back, so instead I start wheeling my case towards the taxis lined up at the edge of the station, doing my best to dodge people as I go. I run over a woman's foot with my suitcase. 'Sorry, sorry, désolée,' I tell her. She blows smoke from her cigarette in my face and shrugs. Her lips are the reddest lips I've ever seen.

I scuttle onwards, towards a row of taxis lined up by the kerb. A taxi to my hotel won't be cheap, but I need to be on my own, somewhere quiet, somewhere that isn't here. Plus, there's the very simple fact that if I don't get a taxi, I won't make it to the hotel. I'll just collapse on the street, a pique of Parisian drama. Mae will ignore all of my rules and start a GoFundMe to repatriate my corpse.

I pause by the taxis, just for a second, breathing in the warm evening air, full of dust and fumes and so different from home. It's late now and dark, and I might be out-of-this-world exhausted, but I was once an artist, and like a homing pigeon, Paris is my ancestral homeland. I do my four, four, four, breathing, and feel my shoulders drop, just a fraction.

I show the driver at the front of the taxi queue my phone with the address of my hotel on it. I'm staying near the MAM gallery, so I can just walk there in the morning.

He nods and I clamber in the back. We aren't moving yet, but I still feel like I'm moving. That's how much travelling I've done today. It's a bit disconcerting.

I WhatsApp Mae.

Me: Made it!!

I send a quick picture of me in the back of the taxi.

Mae: Are you in a taxi? Why? Are you tired? We never get taxis. Fuck that fringe.
Me: I'm fine, honestly. Just been a long day. I'm excited to be here!
Mae: I'm excited for you!!!

The driver starts the car, and we're setting off; he has the window rolled down and he's resting an elbow on it. He seems to share my feelings when it comes to the need for chit chat, and we drive in silence.

Sweet merciful silence. I rest my head against the window of the taxi and take in the streets of Paris as they pass by.

When I wake the next morning, it takes me a short moment to remember where I am. And then it all comes back to me. I'm in Paris.

I twist my head to get a good look at the room; I can barely remember stumbling in last night. I just vaguely recollect a very chatty receptionist who I was possibly quite rude to, and several flights of stairs that almost finished me.

My case is still propped by the door in the corner of the not-at-all-square room. It's tiny. I fill the space in a way that's quite disconcerting. There's a bathroom, which is also tiny. Despite this, the ceiling is high, and I'm not used to existing in a space where I can't reach up and almost touch the ceiling. It's dizzying, and it only adds to the sense that I'm completely out of place here.

A huge vertical set of doors with windows opens onto a small balcony. You can see the tip of the Eiffel Tower over the top of other buildings. I lay, staring at the tip of that tower and thinking about all of the people who probably died building it. It's a morbid thought, but I find it strangely comforting, the reminder that literally everyone who ever lives will die. I'm not special. It doesn't matter that I feel all displaced here in Paris, because I don't matter. Just saying that I don't matter relaxes me. I feel my chest loosen and my hands unclench. I don't matter. See, there, I feel better now.

After the chaos of yesterday, I revel in the silence as I rummage through the clothes Mae and I packed, feeling nostalgic and missing home already, which possibly isn't that normal as I've been gone less than twenty-four hours, after all. I pull out a white shirt with enormous sleeves that makes me look like I walked straight out of the seventeenth century. I also have a denim overall dress and my Doc Martens.

I set it all out on the bed and take a shower. I scrub away the grime of travelling and rub until my skin feels raw and tingly, and my stomach insists that I get out and go in search of food. I'm rarely hungry these days, so I plan to take full advantage.

I run the hairdryer over my hair. There's so much of it that a full blow-dry takes an absolute day and age, so this will have to do. I get my navy shacket, push my sunglasses into my hair, and pull my boots on. I fill a bag with today's meds and my credit card. The blissful silence is a balm to my displacement nerves. Going through the motions is sometimes everything that we need to do. Going through the motions means that we're still going, after all.

'Madame, madame!' the receptionist calls as I try to leave. It's the same one from last night. She has deer-like brown eyes and a pencil behind her ear. '*Bon matin*, it is good to see you this morning.'

The obvious relief in her tone makes me sure that last night I looked like I was going to die in my sleep.

'Yes, I'm fine now. Thank you, I mean *merci*,' I say, feeling and being as awkward as humanly possible. I remember again that I was possibly rude last night, and I'm not yet so far removed from polite company to feel like that's okay. '*J'ai besoin un croissant.*' I dig deep to remember some school-level French.

'*Ah, oui très bien,* your French is very good.'

I mean, it's a blatant lie, but I appreciate it nonetheless.

'*Merci*,' I say again, smiling stiffly, and wondering if I've done enough to seem like the friendly sociable person I was in The Time Before. 'Well, I'd better . . .' I make a strange hand gesture towards the door.

'*Oui*, say no more. Paul's on the corner is very good. Best croissants,' she makes a kissing sound with her lips.

'Okay, that's good to know. Thank you, *au revoir*.'

'*Au revoir*,' she calls after me.

Outside, I take a deep breath, in and out. I look up at

the weak morning sun and let it soak into my bones for a second. I can do this. Or at least I think (hope?) that I can. I spot Paul's straight away and hurry towards it. The street is everything I would expect of Paris, with tall grey buildings and Juliet balconies.

I'm sure that half of the world is on this boulevard. People push past me, but I use my headphones to block out some of the hustle and bustle.

At Paul's, I order the biggest croissant I've ever seen, with pistachio cream. There's a small park opposite, and I settle on a bench to eat, pleased to have found somewhere quiet already.

The croissant is good. I snap a picture and send it to Mae.

> **Me:** *image attached* I wonder if all my Deathers would be quite so morbid if they were eating pistachio croissants on the regular.
>
> **Mae:** She's alive!! That looks so good.
>
> **Me:** It really is.
>
> **Mae:** Have you recorded anything yet?
>
> **Me:** No, too tired yesterday. I might do a quick intro while I'm sat in a park. There aren't many people around.
>
> **Mae:** Go for it! And send a pic of the painting please.

I also fire a quick message to Mum explaining what I'm in Paris for and reassuring her that I'll be back in a couple of days.

There's only an hour until the exhibit opens. On the journey here, I'd thought long and hard about what Mae said, about doing a Spencer special for my blog. In a way, it makes perfect sense. I did know Earl's art better than almost anyone on the planet. I could let people know about the man behind the paintings. The Deathers would get it; they're the ones who understand.

I want to record right now.

Except I've never recorded in public. Is it a bit of a wanker move? Does it matter?

I pull out my selfie stick from my rucksack and hook it up to my phone. I made some notes, things that I could say about Earl, during yesterday's mammoth journey. It's less prep than I usually do; I typically write and practise a script beforehand, but it's better than nothing. I set a smile on my face and hit record.

'*Good morning, Deathers, and welcome to the Art of Dying. This week, I have something special for you, a mini-series if you will. You see, I'm in Paris and I'm going to be looking at the work of Earl Josef Spencer. I know what you're thinking: what's Spencer got to do with death and decay? But fear not Deathers, I think you'll like this. You see, a new Spencer has recently been discovered, and I'm something of an aficionado on his work. I'll also hunt out some death art, just to keep you all sated. I'll be vlogging daily, direct from Paris. Stay tuned to see why this painting might be especially important to yours truly.*'

I re-record it to smooth out the bits where I stumbled, and again when someone jogged past and I felt too self-conscious to keep talking. I just stared at myself on my phone screen like a lunatic, wondering if Mae was right on the fringe front, but admiring my eyeliner flick.

Once I'm happy, I upload it. It feels good, as if I've achieved something, or else taken some small crumb of control. That's what Mae doesn't understand. The Art of Dying isn't just about hiding in an online world to avoid the real one. It's the only part of my life where I feel I still matter.

The walk to the art gallery is short but beautiful. The pavements of President Wilson Avenue are so wide, there's a market taking place down the middle of them – stalls selling seafood, flowers, cheese, olives, and so much bread that it assaults every sense. The sun is shining and there's a light breeze from the Seine, which should be absolutely perfect, except I'm so nervous, I feel ill. My hands are shaking; it's like I'm having an out-of-body experience. My headphones play Edith Piaf's *Non, Je ne regrette rien*, and while I appreciate the authenticity of the moment, it doesn't exactly help matters. Unlike Edith, I have many regrets, many.

At first, I don't realise that I've joined the back of a queue. There's a hustle of people, all waiting by the entrance to the MAM. It's huge, both the building and the queue. I read about it on the way here. Apparently, the MAM was built in the 1930s and has 15,000 works of modern art. It's only when I hear the words 'Spencer' more than once that I realise that these people are here for the same reason that I am. They're waiting to see the new Earl Josef Spencer. They're waiting to see the painting of me.

I'm full of something that feels like pride, for Earl. I wish he could be here for this; people actually queuing to see his work. He'd have just laughed and tried to make them all a cup of tea. He'd have found a way to find out what each of them needed and taken care of them. Some artists shy away from the real world, preferring instead to operate in some liminal space between life and art. I'm one of those artists, or I was. But not Earl – he loved people, and people loved him.

Mum always thought it odd, that as kids we wanted to spend so much time with an old man. But it never felt odd, or weird to us. Earl felt like family.

I'm ignoring every one of my rules about crying in public. Tears are dripping onto my cheeks by the time the doors open and we lunge forward en masse towards the museum entrance. I'm still crying as I pass my things through the security monitors, thinking of Earl and the fact that he won't get to see this, and all the people who came to admire his work. But also for me and everything I lost back then. For Emmett, too, I suppose.

I'm out of practice when it comes to dealing with all this feeling, but like, it's fine. I suppose if you can't be an emotional wreck in Paris, where can you be one?

No one looks twice at my puffy eyes when I tap to buy a ticket for Earl's exhibit.

Outside, the MAM looks like the Pantheon, with smooth pillars carved from stone. Inside, it's a bright, white space, most famous for the enormous *La Fée Électricité* by Raoul Dufy. I promise myself that I'll stay and see this later. For now, though, I follow arrows directing us to Earl's exhibition space.

It's on the first floor, where there's an enormous picture of Earl on the wall. He's younger than I ever knew him, but wearing the same top hat he always wore. *Earl Josef Spencer*, it says underneath the picture. *'Une Vie en Couleur'*.

My hands are shaking slightly as I take my sunglasses off my head and put them in my bag, as I reach the long bright corridor. It's jarring, since it's so different from how Earl lived, all this grandeur and space. It's overwhelming.

There's a small crowd of people clustered at the end of the exhibition, looking at a single painting on the wall. That must be it – the *Edge of Always*. I make myself walk slowly, recognising the other pieces on the walls, how the colours jump out at you. I can chart the final years of my childhood through these paintings, and it's both miraculous and unbearably hard seeing them again. I had so much hope then. Losing that hope hurts more than almost anything else I've lost.

I can't dwell on that now, though. Not when the paintings are right here, dragging me back to The Time Before. Reminding me, against my will, how colourful the past was. It's like coming home, seeing them again:

The Weight of Light
Longing for Human Connection
Montmartre in Motion
The Juxtaposition of Life and Death
The Rubicon

If I had more time, I could go there, to the places he painted. They're all in Paris. But there isn't enough time. There's never enough time.

I wait at the back of the small crowd, stepping forward only when someone else moves.

It's there, and it takes my breath away.

The Edge of Always.

Oh, Earl.

It is, it's different from his other work.

Gone are the bright, vivid colours that he favoured. Instead, this piece is almost pastel. There are greens and blues, thick brush strokes that sweep across the bottom of the canvas, blurring the distinction between land and water. I'm certain that it's Northumberland, the way the coast juts over the sea, all broken lines, like a jigsaw; the sea and land coming together as one. The greens and blues give way to lighter colours, pastel pinks and pale yellows, white clouds that draw the eye up.

And there I am, right in the centre, my hair blown out in all directions by some invisible wind, red and vivid against the background. My eyes are sad. I thought they were neutral, but here up close, I think I'm sad. It's clear that it's me. My eyes, my hair, the shape of my face. But it's also the fact that I'm in Northumberland, and that's the place that I'm meant to be. I've often felt that I couldn't exist in any other place. There's some symmetry between the land and me.

There's a shadow too, a patch of green only just darker than the rest. You have to look closely to see it.

Great art isn't what you see; it's how much you feel when you look at it. And I feel so many things when I look at this painting that it's impossible to untangle all of the threads.

I'm immortal in this painting, and I can't look away. I stumble backwards and sit on a concrete bench. People don't block my view, so I sit some more, trying to commit every stroke to memory. It's almost whimsical and so beautiful.

There's a line of writing in the bottom corner under Earl's signature. I squint at it.

The answer is always in the art.

I tilt my head to the side, wondering what Earl meant, and catch a couple of people looking at me and then the painting. I ignore them, consider putting my sunglasses on. I'd do it except for the fact that they'd dull my view.

It wasn't exactly true, what I said to the Deathers about Earl's art not incorporating death. Earl might not have painted death overtly, but his work was often inspired by it. He'd said this once when the local newspaper had run an article on him, and they'd asked him what his favourite thing to paint was.

'The moment before death,' he answered simply. 'I imagine that there's an explosion of colour, in the seconds before we die. A last hurrah, if you will, before eternal darkness.' The reporter from the *Bamburgh Echo* hadn't really known what to make of him after that. But Earl had just chuckled at his startled expression and carried on. 'Whatever question you ask, my friend, death is always the answer.'

After that, the other kids on the caravan park had avoided

him for a few months. They'd dared each other to knock on his door, until Mae had punched one of them on the nose.

But this isn't a painting of death.

The answer is always in the art.

What answer? I wonder. *What question?*

I'm absorbed in it. I'm trying to imagine where and when Earl painted the piece, wondering how he could have kept this work secret. No one had any secrets on the caravan park; everyone lived too close together for that. Gregor had managed to sell some of his work during Earl's lifetime, but once he'd been 'discovered' in the years after his death, they'd all reappeared, owned mostly by the same collector in London. How can it be that there was a whole painting just out there somewhere?

I'm so completely lost to my thoughts that I don't notice a person sitting down next to me on the concrete bench.

I try to focus on the painting as the man beside me shifts a little.

I feel light-headed all of a sudden.

I can't look, but I have to. Earl, the painting, me, Emmett, it's all too much.

It can't be. Surely not. Not when I've imagined him next to me so many times over the years. Yet, in all my imaginings, it's never, ever been real.

'Luna,' he says. And when did my face become so wet?

I turn to him – how can I not? His face is the same, just a little more worn. There was a time when I knew his face better than my own.

'Luna,' he says, and it is him, not some figment of my imagination, but the real thing. How can he be here now, not all the times I needed him, but now, when I want time with Earl and this painting?

Emmett is here, though, and I am crying.

I thought I'd feel sad. Or happy, even. I thought I'd be overcome with guilt. After all, it's the guilt that has plagued me for all these years. Weighed me down and broke me before I understood how broken I really was. It's none of those things that I feel. I'm angry. I'm so angry that it lights me up from the inside out, all this anger. I'm surprised at the depth of my own feeling. I didn't think I was capable of that anymore.

'Emmett,' I answer, trying to inject some coldness into my voice. He leans back, just a touch. Good. He should feel bad.

I recall all the other instances when I first saw him. How long I waited for him. How I was always, always happy to see him at the start of each summer. I try to push the memories away, but they assail me, they rain down on me. And no matter how hard I try to fight them, they won't let me go.

Chapter Four

THEN

Luna was 13
Emmett was 14

As they passed a sign declaring that it was a mere twenty miles to Bamburgh, Luna realised that she was fizzing. It was all the excitement, you see, because twenty miles meant that the journey was almost over. They were so close to their holiday cottage, so close. She was desperate to see Emmett.

She wouldn't be this desperate if she had a phone. But Luna's mum hadn't relented on that front. She didn't care that it might make Luna and Mae social outcasts, the only people in school without one. Luna's mum said that phones caused brain rot. And cancer. Brain rot and cancer.

She wouldn't even let Luna have MySpace.

Normally, these things really bothered Luna; she wanted to fit in with everyone else more than she wanted anything else in the whole world. People like Mae, they were made for standing out, but Luna wanted to pass through the world without being noticed by anyone or anything. She didn't know exactly why she wanted to fly under the radar so much, except it just felt safer that way.

It didn't seem to matter so much now, though – the phone thing or the MySpace thing or the becoming a social outcast thing. It didn't even matter that she was wearing a skirt from Tammy Girl, even though all of their stuff was for babies, not now they were very nearly there.

'You look lovely, Luna.' Luna's mum twisted round from her seat in the front. Her mum didn't often tell Luna that she looked lovely. And while Luna wanted to pass through the world unnoticed, her body seemed to have a different plan entirely. She'd grown so much this last year, her body tall and broad, with muscles that were hard to the touch. Her mum said that Luna had her dad's physique.

Looking lovely was their mum's top priority, always. Luna was pretty certain that her mum thought that being scruffy was about as bad as killing someone. That was why Luna wasn't allowed some Miss Sixty jeans because her mum said that they were for tramps, not for people who want to look lovely.

Her mum gave a pointed look towards Mae.

She'd cried when she saw what Mae was wearing that morning – a stretched-out T-shirt with the face of the Frosties tiger on the front. It was more of a wail than a proper cry. She'd thrown her hands up in the air and started shouting. When she was little, Luna would sometimes hide under the bed when her mum started to shout. She'd just lie there, on the carpet that was thicker than the rest of her bedroom, since it hadn't been walked on, and wonder what it would be like just to disappear. She could spend hours imagining how peaceful it would be to not be herself, just some spec of dust floating around, all the things she could see. She'd draw it in her head, the things she'd see and do if she were unnoticed. Except that she wouldn't be able to hang out with Mae. Not Earl or Emmett either.

Emmett.

There'd been no time for thoughts of disappearing that morning, and anyway, Luna wasn't sure that she'd fit under the bed anymore.

Mae said that Luna's mum didn't love their dad anymore because he was scruffy too. And really, Luna thought that it must be hard to live in a house full of scruffy people when looking lovely was all you wanted from your life.

Luna chose always the path of least resistance, which is how she found herself studying maths for almost the whole of the journey. Even though concentrating on the numbers in the textbook she had perched on her lap was making her feel sick.

Their mum clucked her tongue. 'So scruffy, Mae.'

'Come on, Jennie, she looks fine.' Their dad answered.

Mae groaned loudly. They all knew that trying to defend the girls was pointless. It just extended the lecture they'd all get from their mum.

Luna took the opportunity to close the textbook. She sat on her hands to stop them from moving.

'Fine! If you're happy for your daughter to be out in public wearing hot pants and a T-shirt she found in a bin!'

'It wasn't a bin, Mum, it was a charity shop.'

Their mum ignored Mae. 'I honestly don't know what went wrong with her. She's wild, Michael.'

Luna had to bite her lip, since Mae had started roaring like a lion.

Then everyone was shouting, everyone except Luna. In her head, she was running along the beach so fast that she was drawing in big gulps of sea air. She was running faster than she'd ever run before, her hair streaked out behind her. Emmett was there, too, of course. It wasn't summer without Emmett.

Luna let the argument wash over her, imagining each emotion as a colour. At the moment, they were hot and bright, but she could change them. She could water them down and make them light and delicate, a suggestion of colour across a page.

Calmer now, she focused her mind – for the millionth time – on the possibilities of summer.

In Luna's humble opinion, Northumberland was the best place in the whole world. Even their tiny village, Bamburgh, had a gigantic castle right on the seaside. There were beaches and dunes and fields with grass was so long, you could get lost in it. Every summer, a carnival came, and Luna would get sick and sticky from too much candyfloss. Or else they'd go to Holy Island. Holy Island was one of Luna's favourite places, an island you could only reach when the tide was out. The rest of the time, it was lost to the sea. Luna thought it was desperately romantic.

Mae didn't think that Holy Island was desperately romantic. She did think that Luna was desperately in need of a boyfriend, though, if she thought an island was sexy. Luna couldn't quite explain it, but she liked the thought of living on that island, cut off from everyone and everything else half of the time.

Not that Luna wanted to be cut off from *everyone.* Not Emmett, or Mae. Earl too. They could come and visit her on her island anytime they wanted.

So no, Luna didn't think that she was desperate. Except this one time, when she was looking at *The Kiss* by Gustav Klimt in an art book that Earl had given her, the way he was sort of leaning over her, cradling her a little bit . . . Luna thought you called it *yearning,* that look you get when you want to kiss someone but aren't kissing them yet. Well, the yearning in *The Kiss* made Luna feel all warm in the bottom of her stomach.

Mae had taken this as confirmation that Luna needed to get kissing people stat. Any people, according to Mae.

'That's what I did,' she'd said. 'You need to practise so that when you get to kiss someone that you really like, you're already decent. It's all in the tongue action. You don't want to be slobbering all over your one true love.'

Luna definitely didn't want to kiss just anyone. She had

thought a lot about Emmett this year, but that was normal. She always missed him when they were apart.

Their mum had overheard the conversation and grounded them. She had left a book about puberty on Luna's bed, about three years too late in Luna's mind. Plus, Luna's boobs didn't look anything like the cartoon ones, neither of them. And she was sure she'd grown hair EVERYWHERE, not just in the places the book said that they were meant to. Basically, between her muscles and her hair, Luna felt like Sasquatch.

And being Sasquatch, she felt it would be nothing short of a miracle to find anyone who wanted to kiss her.

Plus, she had ginger hair.

Luna's mum was still talking.

'And I don't want you spending all of your time at The Edge this summer. There's so much to see and do, I imagine you'll be plenty occupied.' Her mum hated The Edge as much as scruffiness, maybe. A couple of years ago, Emmett had got into a fight. Emmett got into fights quite a lot, but Luna's mum had found out about this one and turned him into public enemy number one.

Luna had absolutely zero intention of staying away from The Edge, the caravan park where Emmett and Earl lived (next door to each other).

She shook her head at Mae, a warning not to argue with Mum. There was no point. After a few days, their mum always got too preoccupied with Eyebrow Clive – their neighbour who spent all of his time in Northumberland, not just the summers – to really care what Mae and Luna were up to.

'Why do we need to stay away from The Edge?' Mae asked as Luna sank further into her seat.

'It's just not good for you. For your future.'

Luna's mum meant because the people there were poor.

'Poverty isn't contagious, *Mum*.'

'I never said it was, *Mae*.'

A red stress rash began to work its way up Luna's neck. She never knew what to do in these situations. She wanted to stick up for Earl and Emmett, of course she did, since she cared about them. Sometimes, Luna thought she cared so much about them that it physically hurt. Like a band around her chest being wound tighter and tighter.

But she didn't want to argue with her mum either. Luna began to sketch, only in her head. She pictured the pencil, the way it slid across paper, almost effortless and smooth. Luna didn't know if this was the best coping mechanism, but it was the only one that she had.

'Plus, the caravans there are super clean. I only saw like three heroin needles tops last year. Isn't that right, Luna?'

Luna had actually seen needles on the ground at The Edge, but she didn't want to tell her mum this.

So she just laughed really loudly and tucked her hands even further beneath her legs.

Finally, *finally* the car turned into the cobbled path that led to their holiday home.

Luna's mum described it as the 'holiday place'.

That's what she said when she told people what their summer plans were. 'Oh, we're off to the holiday place,' she'd say.

Mae had once mentioned how much of the holiday place Mum had paid for since Dad was the only one of them with a job. She'd been grounded again after that. Mae spent a lot of time grounded.

Luna wasn't thinking about any of that now, though. She wasn't even thinking how relieved she was that the journey was over, since that was always by far the worst part of the holiday. Her family didn't do well in confined spaces. No, instead, Luna's brain couldn't think of anything other than the fact that Emmett was right here.

Emmett, as usual, was waiting on the front step, reading a battered old *National Geographic* magazine.

Luna's seatbelt was unbuckled before they'd even rolled to a stop.

'Luna, we're still moving!'

Luna heard her mum kicking up a fuss but she didn't care. All she knew was that she'd throw herself out of a moving car if it meant that she got to Emmett as soon as possible.

It was a new sensation, this urge to be near him. Maybe she'd think more about it later, when she wasn't marvelling at the fact that he was standing up and smiling and the whole thing was making Luna's brain run a sort of static, as if her thoughts were scattered to the wind.

'You got so tall!' Emmett wasn't as tall as Luna. 'And you

got your braces off.' He was studying her face. Luna wanted to draw him. 'Your teeth are really straight.'

Emmett's teeth weren't straight. Some of his side teeth were a bit twisted. Luna liked it. She thought it made his face more interesting.

Luna was especially pleased to see Emmett's face this year, to see all of him in fact. It made sense. Even though they only saw each other for six weeks of the year, Emmett was Luna's best friend, aside from Mae that is. Her first summer, Luna had seen Emmett on the beach with Earl. She'd walked right up to him and asked if he wanted to be her best friend and that was that.

It's really odd though, because this year she felt especially pleased to see him. And that strange feeling in the bottom of her stomach was back, the same as when she looked at *The Kiss*. Yearning.

Luna looked at Emmett and tried to make sense of it all, but making sense of it felt like trying to finish a jigsaw puzzle with pieces from different boxes. Emmett wouldn't like how long his hair had got. It was black and curly and Luna wished that she too had a nice normal hair colour. Something brown. Not that the rest of Emmett was normal. He had green eyes and long eyelashes. He was interesting to look at but not bad interesting. Good interesting.

'Watch out, coming through.' Luna's dad barged through the middle of them, carrying a box high above his head.

'Afternoon, Emmett, here so soon,' Luna's mum said.

'Yes, Mrs Banks, I wanted to see Luna right away.'

'How lovely,' she answered in a sickly-sweet way that let Luna know she didn't really mean it.

It felt unfair. Even if Emmett sometimes got into fights, he was always super nice and polite to Luna's mum and dad.

'Get a room already, you two.' Mae slid up to the pair of them. Luna was fairly certain that the stain on her T-shirt, which might well be a pyjama top, was dry sick. The Frosties Tiger face was all stretched out.

Luna noticed the red patches high on Emmett's cheeks as he hugged Mae. Another piece of the jigsaw that she didn't know where to place.

'Later losers.' Mae saluted them. 'I'll go keep the Terrifying One occupied for a bit.'

Luna's dad was still going backwards and forwards to the car, his arms full of boxes that he carried easily, so Luna and Emmett moved down the side of the cottage. Even though it was much smaller than their other house, Luna thought of this cottage as home. It was 300 years old, with roses climbing up the wall. She loved to draw it. She'd sketch the stones and wonder about the lives of the people who'd laid them. She'd imagine their hands, their faces, what their lives might have been like. She wondered how they'd died. She'd wondered if this was exactly normal.

By the side of the cottage, Luna and Emmett were protected from the wind. It was always windy in Northumberland, even when the sky was blue like on this day. The wind only added to the appeal for Luna. She liked the fact that it was such a beautiful part of the world and also so wild. It made it interesting. And Luna loved interesting things.

'Hi,' Emmett said again, now that they were on their own. Luna didn't precisely know why she was smiling so wide it felt like her mouth was all stretched. Or how it had come to be that the warm feeling in her stomach was back so strong that it made her feel woozy.

'Hi,' she answered, running her tongue over her teeth because it was quite strange not having a brace. 'I missed you.'

'I missed you too.'

Emmett looked so much more grown up this year. He was older than Luna, despite the fact that they were in the same year at school. He was born in September and Luna in August. Emmett was fourteen and Luna thirteen. So far, she wasn't sure that being a teenager was a lot of fun. It seemed to come with a whole heap of feelings that Luna had to work hard at, if she wanted to make sense of them.

Like the fact that she felt something for Emmett, something that was different to how it had been before.

'How's your year been?' she asked, still studying Emmett's face.

'Fine, you know,' he shrugged. 'Same old, same old.' Emmett looked at the ground, where his trainers scuffed the dried earth. Luna knew that Emmett's life here was hard . . . with his mum . . . where they lived. She wanted to be able to do more. Maybe this summer she would.

She took a step towards him, acting on instinct. She was

about to ask about his mum when her own started shrieking from the front of the cottage.

'Luna, LUNA, where have you got to?'

And then her mum was there, frowning and taking a deep breath as if she were about to start shouting.

'We were just catching up, Mum. I'll see you later, Emmett.'

She twisted round and smiled at him, even though her heart was beating super fast, trying to let him know that everything was okay. Emmett didn't need Luna adding to his worries.

He smiled at her, and she felt woozy again. 'Usual time and place?'

'Definitely.'

Luna's mum was holding her by the top of the arm, digging her fingers into the muscle there. 'What's gotten into you?' Luna knew that she'd be hearing about this for the rest of the afternoon. 'And I don't know where you think you're going later, but you'll be taking Mae. You're not running off with some boy all over the place.'

Luna wasn't sure which part of what her mum said was the most ridiculous. One, that she thought Emmett was just some boy instead of . . . well everything, or the fact that she reckoned that taking Mae would keep Luna out of trouble. Mae, who just last week tried to give herself a tattoo.

As she let herself be led into the cottage by the top of her arm, Luna disappeared into her own head. Sketching, drawing out the lines of Emmett's face. The way his cheeks had a high dimple on them, the way his curls curved around the top of his forehead. It settled her, kept her calm. She felt happy, despite her mum's lecture, and that happiness wasn't some mysterious jigsaw that she couldn't complete. That was tied as much to seeing Emmett as it was to being back here for the summer. So, she let herself continue to sketch in her mind. Emmett. Emmett. And as she sketched, she wondered what, exactly, the summer might have in store.

Chapter Five

'So, are we off then?' Mae asked from her bed. She was playing snake on their dad's phone while Luna set up her sketchbooks in the small circle of space at the end of their beds. Luna and Mae shared a room at home, where they didn't need to, and in the cottage where they did, since there were only two bedrooms.

The cottage, decorated by their mum, was cream. And white. Everything was cream and white. Some of the things had little pink flowers on them, like Luna's bedding for instance. Or else little blue flowers, like the curtains. There was one wall of bare stone behind their beds (this was Luna's favourite thing in the cottage) and an antique chest of drawers by the door (her second favourite).

Luna felt like it was the bedroom of a dainty person. The sort who brushed their hair until it was shiny every night before bed and knelt down to say their prayers. No matter how hard she tried, Luna didn't feel like that person. And Mae . . . well, Mae didn't even try.

It was almost 5pm – time to go and meet Emmett. Luna's

earlier inexplicable excitement at being so palpably close to Emmett that she could reach out and touch him, if that was a thing that they did, had worn off and was replaced instead by worry. Worry that her mum would try to stop her from seeing Emmett as much as Luna hoped to this summer. Worry that she'd be locked in her bedroom with the white walls for the whole summer. Possibly Luna was being a bit dramatic.

'What about Mum?' she asked.

Mae rolled her eyes where she was laid on her bed, a leg draped over her bent knee.

'She's not going to ground us for the summer – we only make the place look a mess, same as Dad. Plus, Eyebrow Clive is here. I saw her heading out into the garden with a cocktail twenty minutes ago. Let's just go ask Dad if we can go out.'

Eyebrow Clive was their neighbour; their cottages shared a hedge. Luna's mum was a Clive fan, a Clive superfan if you like. In Luna's mind, Clive was ancient already, with this sweep of grey hair but the biggest, darkest eyebrows she'd ever seen. They were like slugs. That's how he got his nickname, which wasn't very original, but it was what they'd come up with four years ago when Clive bought the place next door. Eyebrow Clive was rich. He talked about his favourite wine a lot and did this chortly-posh laugh while saying things like, 'Very good, Jennie, very good,' when he and Luna's mum had deep and meaningful conversations over the hedge.

Luna could never remember a time when her parents had seemed as if they liked each other, so she had no real basis for comparison, but it seemed like her mum laughed an awful lot more with Eyebrow Clive than she did with any of them.

'Poor Dad,' she said.

'Yep, totally tragic. Maybe he can get a serum to grow his eyebrow hair, and then Mum will fancy him again.' Mae launched herself out of bed. 'But you know what's even more tragic?' she asked.

Luna noticed that Mae still hadn't changed her T-shirt.

'No, what?'

'The fact that you're thirteen and you've never been kissed. That's way worse than your own wife being repulsed by you. They're going to write articles about you in *Seventeen* magazine.'

'They are not.' Luna stood up too, a little bit worried that that might actually be a thing. She didn't want to be weird, or tragic. She just wanted to be normal, to fit right in. 'There's just no one that I want to kiss. I'm not kissing just anyone.'

There was a chortly laugh from the garden. 'Very good, Jennie, very good.'

'Come on, before her drink runs out and she has to come back in the house.' Mae grabbed her sunglasses from the top drawer. Luna was pretty sure that they were joke ones; they were so thick, but Mae thought that they made her look cool, and who was Luna to argue?

Luna fluffed her already wild hair in the little mirror they had hanging on the wall next to the door.

'You look amazeballs,' Mae said, already out of the room. '*Someone* better snog your face off this summer. Now let's go.'

The girls found their dad at the small dining table, glueing together a model of some old aeroplane. Neither of her parents had ever demonstrated to Luna what a happy relationship might look like, but her dad had instilled in her an almost encyclopaedic knowledge of old planes, which hopefully counted for something.

'Look at this, girls.' He ushered them closer in hushed tones, as if talking loudly might cause the model to fall to pieces somehow. 'It's a Supermarine Walrus mark one.' He held it up so that Luna and Mae could inspect it.

Luna and Mae made a sound to show that they were impressed. Luna mostly felt sorry for her dad, which made her kind of sad.

'Where do the bombs come out?' Mae asked, talking in a normal voice. This wasn't their first rodeo when it came to their dad and his models.

Luna might feel sorry for her dad, but there was no denying that he was the reason she was so big and hairy since he was a big bear of a man. This was what Luna thought when her dad took his T-shirt off at the beach. He even had hair on his back. He was tall and wide and probably quite strong. It was just that his personality didn't match his stature. He was softly spoken and gentle. Most of the time he just seemed confused by his wife.

He was an aeroplane engineer. Her mum once asked why he spent so much time making aeroplane models, since he spent his working life around the real thing, and he'd answered that he admired the fragility of models. Even now, it did look kind of funny, his big hands delicately touching a small, fragile aeroplane.

'This plane was purely for reconnaissance, Mae. No bombers on this one.' He held up his model carefully.

Their dad only stayed with them for two weeks of summer, then he went home to work before driving back to get them four weeks later. It meant that Luna, Mae and their mum were here for six weeks. Six weeks. It felt like a whole lifetime.

'It's a great model, Dad,' Luna said. 'Maybe we could go to the puffins while you're here.'

Mae was making eyes at her since she wasn't the biggest fan of the puffins or their dad's bird talk. But Luna wanted their dad to have a nice time.

'What a fantastic idea, Luna. We might even see a puffling while we're there.' Her dad nudged her with his elbow and winked. 'You always liked them.'

'Hopefully,' she played along. 'Hey, would it be okay if me and Mae went and played outside for a bit? We've been inside all day and in the car. I think some fresh air would do us good.'

He waved them away. 'Of course, go, go, you girls have fun.'

They made a dash for it, only stopping when their dad

called, 'What time did your mum say that you needed to be back?'

'Nine!' Mae answered, not missing a beat, even though it was definitely eight.

'See you at nine then. Have fun!'

They quite literally ran out of the door, down the path in front of the cottage and along the pavement that took them to the centre of Bamburgh. Luna's jaw hurt from smiling. She held out her arms as she ran. Here, she felt taller, unburdened. And in this instance, her extra height felt like a gift rather than something to be ashamed about.

They ran faster still, breathing in the salty sea air and laughing.

Bamburgh was tiny, so it took no time at all to reach the red telephone box. That's where they always met, and there was Emmett.

Luna might come and go from Northumberland, but he was always here. So much so that Luna wasn't entirely sure where Northumberland ended and Emmett began. They slowed to a walk, her smile so big that her face was at risk of splitting in two. Emmett was wearing a faded T-shirt with a small rip by the hem, and his trousers were slightly short, but he was smiling too.

Luna was relieved. All she ever wanted was for Emmett to be happy. It was her deepest desire. She found it almost painful when he'd sometimes have his darker moods. The ones he described as like looking at the world from behind sunglasses, just a little bit dim.

'Hi,' she said, coming to a stop in front of him.

'Hi.' He smiled back.

'And hi to me too.' Mae stood next to them both, almost forming a circle.

'Nice glasses, weirdo.'

'Nice T-shirt, freak.'

And then they were laughing, and Luna felt so light that she could float off into the sky, like a feather caught by the wind. She'd feel this way for the whole summer if she was lucky. She'd try and bottle it and take it home with her.

'Come on, Earl's desperate to see you, and the others,' Emmett said, taking off towards The Edge. Since Emmett lived here all the time, some of his school friends had become Luna and Mae's friends too.

'How's his work?' Luna asked as they walked to the caravan park where he and Earl lived. Her mum had once said that living in a caravan park all year round was against the law, so Luna didn't know how Emmett and his mum and Earl managed it. Or any of the people who lived on The Edge all year. But they did. It was Luna's favourite place in the world.

'He sold a piece in February, to that London buyer. But nothing since then. Gregor says it'll pick up.'

'It always does,' Mae and Luna said together. Mae called 'Jinx!' and punched Luna in the arm.

Bamburgh had a massive castle on the cliff by the beach, but mostly it was just cafés in the centre. A couple of people, putting tables and chairs away at the end of the day, called to say hello. Even though Luna and Mae were only here for six weeks of every year, they knew everyone. Louisa, who ran a bakery, gave them a paper bag of scones with fat, juicy currants. 'They're going off – try and get your mum to have one, eh?' she told Emmett.

'I will, thanks Louisa.' Emmett held the bag close to his chest and then, as they walked away, started eating one straight away. Luna and Mae pretended not to notice the fact that he barely seemed to breathe between bites.

'So, tell me everything about what's been going on,' he asked around a mouthful of food.

'Well, I had my first kiss.' Mae started talking really fast. 'And my second, and third. I think I'm getting way better at it.'

Emmett stopped walking. 'No way, Mae – you're too young to be kissing anyone.'

She pushed on the back of her sunglasses so that they lifted up to look at him directly.

'I'm twelve – it's perfectly acceptable to be kissing at twelve. It's another world of tragedy if you haven't kissed anyone and you're, I don't know, thirteen.' She said 'thirteen' in a really exaggerated way and Luna went bright red, as if she was being filled with cherry aid at lightning speed. Emmett just laughed.

'Plus, I got my period already,' Mae carried on. 'I'm practically of childbearing age.'

It was Luna's turn to laugh now, as Emmett basically choked on his scone.

'Ignore her,' she told him. 'Second child problems. As you know, she's literally always this dramatic.'

They were almost at The Edge.

'Nothing else exciting has happened really,' she carried on their conversation. 'I managed to get Mum to agree to me taking art at school next year. She wanted me to drop it.'

'Mental.' Emmett agreed because he knew how much she needed it.

'I know. She thinks that Earl is a bad influence. Said that I'd end up living on a caravan park my whole life if I tried to be an artist.'

Luna glanced at Emmett quickly. He was frowning.

'Not that there's anything wrong with living in a caravan,' she said and she meant it. She'd rather live at The Edge than her house at home even though it had two garages and French doors into the garden. To her, Earl was living the most perfect life. He got to live here, in her favourite place in the world, surrounded by people he loved, and he got to paint too. For Luna, it didn't get more perfect than that.

Emmett had gone quiet. 'Don't worry about it.'

'What are you taking?' she asked him, forcing her voice to be cheerful.

'Triple Science, Economics, French and Spanish.'

'Mate,' Mae said, 'those are the worst subjects I ever heard in my life.'

He laughed, and Luna's heart soared. There was nothing better than Emmett being happy. 'I like them. Doing Critical Thinking with Mr Stubbins after school too.'

Emmett was clever, like crazy levels of clever. He already knew the name of every single bone in the human body. He got all these science books out of the library in a bus that came around sometimes, just so that he could learn more science, for fun. And every year on his birthday, Earl bought him a subscription to *National Geographic* magazine.

Earl said that Emmett needed to learn to control his temper, though. Because if he didn't stop lashing out, it wouldn't matter how clever he was – he'd get nowhere in life. Luna hated the thought that Emmett might get nowhere in life. It was one of the reasons she wanted him to be happy all of the time.

They made it to the drive that led down to the caravan park. It was on the edge of a cliff – that's why it was called The Edge. Earl told Luna once that the people who built it thought that the views would make all sorts of rich people want to buy caravans there, but the drop put people off, so they just let any old person buy them for really cheap.

There was a sign, 'Welcome to The Edge', in fading white paint over the road that led to the park. Luna thought it looked a bit like that one they had over Auschwitz, the one that said that work sets you free, so maybe that might have also had something to do with people not wanting to buy caravans there, too: the drop and the concentration-camp sign.

The path split once they passed the entrance. They took a left, passing caravans with washing lines hanging between them or toddlers toddling around at the front. They called hello to the people they saw. To Luna, it always felt like coming home, being here.

Some of the caravans were used just for summer. Emmett said you could tell those ones because they weren't as bedded in. The permanent residents had plant pots and satellite dishes. The people on holiday had bikes and tubs to make sandcastles with.

Earl and Emmett's caravans were right at the front of the park, looking over the cliff to the sea and the waves.

They liked to hang out there, looking out across the sea. The sea was one of the reasons why Luna wanted to move here when she was older. Plus Earl and Emmett, of course. Mae said she was in for any plan that put half the country between her and Mum.

Earl was sitting outside his caravan, wearing a faded suit and a top hat.

Mae took off at a run. 'Earl!' she called, launching herself at him.

'Ah Mae, you're looking all grown up. And you, Luna.' He smiled, still with a hint of his French accent. He was missing a tooth, just at the side of his smile.

'I know, right,' Mae told him. 'I got my period and everything.'

Earl laughed. 'We've missed you both a lot, haven't we Emmett?'

Emmett went red, but Luna was beaming. 'We missed you too.'

Just as they were talking, the door to Emmett's caravan

opened. Emmett's caravan was probably the worst-looking one in the whole park. There were no plant pots, and instead of the little curtains that the other caravans had, they just had some flattened cardboard boxes that Emmett's mum never took down because the light hurt her eyes.

His mum was coming out, and Luna was sure she was way thinner than last year; her clothes sort of hung off her as if she were a coat hanger rather than a person.

Emmett froze as soon as he saw her. They all did except for Mae, who said, 'Hiya Tanya, you're looking well.'

Tanya ignored her. Instead, she fixed her eyes on Emmett. 'Tell me what you've done with them.'

Emmett's cheeks were red but he was frowning at her. He stuffed his hands in his jeans pockets and shrugged his shoulders. 'I haven't done anything with anything.'

'You're a lying little shit and you know it.'

Tanya launched at Emmett but tripped and landed in the scuffed-up grass between Earl's caravan and her own.

'Hey now.' Earl knelt down next to her and started rubbing her back. 'It's alright.'

Luna felt helpless. She hated feeling helpless.

'Makes Jennie look like mum of the year really,' Mae said and Luna hissed at her to be quiet. Emmett's mum was sitting up now, sobbing big sobs with her head between her knees.

'Why don't you and Luna go for a walk, Emmett? Mae and I can handle this, can't we, Mae?'

'That all depends on what you've got in that caravan of yours, Earl?'

'Triple chocolate fudge cake?' Earl raised an eyebrow. 'Then lead the way. Come on, Tanya, let's go eat. You look like you need it, to be honest.'

Emmett and Luna watched while Mae and Earl half walked, half carried his mum into Earl's caravan.

Finally, they were on their own.

Chapter Six

Luna wished she didn't feel so much.

It would be much easier to watch things unfold with Tanya and Emmett if she didn't feel so much. She wanted to wrestle her feelings into order and tuck them neatly into a box.

Luna nudged her hand against Emmett's. 'Best summer ever?' she said. It was a promise that they made every year. Luna wanted it for Emmett more than herself.

He smiled back, but Luna could see that it was a weak smile, one that he didn't really feel. 'Best summer ever.' He linked his little finger around hers as they walked and there was no wrestling with the feeling which overtook her then, like being dunked under water, fully submerged in it. It was so intense; hot, powerful too, like a volcano about to erupt. Luna didn't have to grapple around to figure out what this feeling was, not like she normally did.

Oh no.

'I did, er . . . I did have something to tell you, Luna,' Emmett said, but Luna was distracted with trying to process what this feeling meant, what it could possibly mean. She already knew that it had the potential to change everything, forever.

In the distance, she could see the playground, and a couple of people hanging around it.

'Luna?'

'You do? I mean, you have something to tell me?'

Maybe Emmett had realised it too. How perfect it would be if they'd realised at the same time.

'Yeah.' He smiled a new smile, one that Luna hadn't seen before. A bit sly, almost.

And if the other feeling, the one she'd just discovered, was red-hot and powerful; this feeling, hope, was light and bright. The sort of feeling that swept you up and carried you forward.

Luna couldn't bear to wait anymore.

Up ahead, she could see the others coming closer now, coming to meet them on the path. Zadie and Ahmed, Emmett's other best friends, and someone else too.

'See, the thing is Luna, I didn't want to tell you in a letter.'

'Tell me what?' she asked. Why was that girl running towards them? Luna recognised her. She was called Cadence and she sometimes, but not very often, hung out with Zadie.

'It's just that, well . . . '

But Emmett didn't need to explain anymore. Not when it was clear as day what was happening. Cadence finished her run towards them and launched herself at Emmett. They were kissing. Like proper kissing, with tongues and everything. Luna had seen people kiss before, she wasn't a total loser, but it looked to her like Cadence was trying to swallow Emmett whole like a snake.

Luna couldn't help the stupid little giggle that escaped her, but her brain was struggling to compute. Emmett and Cadence. Cadence and Emmett.

But Emmett is mine. The thought hit her so hard, like a truck barrelling into her. Or that massive dog her neighbours had back home that charged at you and knocked you off your feet.

She watched as Emmett and Cadence devoured each other in a shockingly graphic manner.

Luna just stood there with her mouth gaping open. Catching flies, as her mum would say. She knew that she needed to say something, anything. Cadence was beautiful. So, of course, Cadence and Emmett were in love as Emmett was also beautiful. That was the way the world worked.

Oh no, Luna was going to cry.

She wiped her forearm over her face. 'Sorry, wind,' she said to no one even though it was as still as a mill pond.

'Are you okay, Luna?' Cadence asked, all sweet pastel colours with her bouncy blonde hair.

Luna sniffed. Already, she had a sense that she was being left behind somehow, as if Emmett and Cadence were sailing out to sea, leaving Luna on the edge of the cliff all alone. But she couldn't admit that, could she? She was sure that she was the only person alive who thought like that. 'I'm fine, totally fine. I just have a bit of a cold. But that's great, so you guys are together, right?'

'What gave them away?' Zadie asked, as she and Ahmed

made their way towards them. Luna loved Zadie. She wasn't all bouncy like Cadence. She was cool, without even trying to be cool. Like Mae, and unlike Luna.

'Yeah, they're really subtle about their relationship normally,' Ahmed said. 'Hi Luna.'

'Hi Ahmed.'

Emmett just laughed and put his arm around Cadence. It was meant to be Luna, wasn't it? She was the one who was meant to make him all happy. What would she do? Without that purpose, she was adrift.

Luna watched Emmett kiss the top of Cadence's nose. She really did not feel fine about this. That hope, that lovely light and bright hope, had gone.

Why was that? Why did she feel so sad and heavy?

And why was Luna imagining, like shoving Cadence? Pulling her hair?

All she knew was this. Seeing Cadence and Emmett together made Luna feel broken. So broken that she wondered if she'd ever feel whole again.

'And they just kept kissing, over and over. It was . . . I couldn't stop looking, Mae. Am I a pervert now? Does that make me a pervert?'

Mae and Luna were lying in bed in the dark. With only a little thin white curtain across the window, everything was silver from the moon.

'No, it doesn't make you a pervert. Cadence is hot. Emmett is hot, in a sort of brooding bad boy type of way.'

'He's not a bad boy.' Luna jumped to his defence. They were having to whisper since the wall behind them led right to their mum and dad's room. Mae said it's a really good job that they didn't have sex anymore, since they'd undoubtedly hear them if they did.

'I mean, I saw him smoking earlier but whatever. I just meant that objectively, if I didn't feel all, like, brotherly towards him, I'd find him hot. But more importantly, Luna, how do you feel about Emmett?'

Mae turned onto her side to look right at Luna.

Emmett's my best friend. That's what Luna thought. As Mae had said, he was like a brother to them. But Luna hadn't felt very brotherly towards him earlier. Earlier she'd realised that she desperately, more than anything else in the whole world, wanted Emmett to be kissing her.

'Do you think I fancy Emmett?' she asked her sister.

Mae let out a too-loud laugh at the same time a loud cough came from their parent's bedroom.

'Thank fuck we got there eventually.'

Mae had only just started swearing. But now, whenever she wasn't around Mum, she swore as much as she could.

'What do you mean?' Luna's heart was beating really fast, and she was warm and stuffy. Was this what liking someone entailed? Being all hot and sweaty and weirded out the whole time?

'You've liked Emmett for ages. It's good you've finally realised it.'

'I have not!' Now it was Luna's turn to be too loud.

Another cough. 'I haven't. I think I'd know if I fancied someone.'

'No, you're completely immature on that front, unfortunately. A late bloomer. Plus, you spend all your time studying.'

'That's because school is really hard for me. But that doesn't mean . . . Do you think I really do fancy him?'

'Head over heels, I reckon.'

Luna had twisted round to face Mae but now flopped back down on her pillow.

'But what do I do? He's with Cadence.' A picture of Cadence, all cherub-like, popped into her head. She was so perfect. If Luna were to draw her, she'd add wings and little chubby cherub cheeks to her face. She'd put her in a loin cloth.

'Cadence looks like her and I look like me,' she finished miserably.

'You and Emmett have a connection that goes beyond looks,' Mae said, pretending to be an expert on romantic connections, when Luna had never even heard her talking about connections before. 'Not that there is anything at all wrong with how you look, Luna. You let Mum get into your head too much. You need to block her out, with like, mental shields.'

'She's right though, I am horrible to look at. Why did I have to get Dad's genes?'

'You are not horrible. Stop that right now. You're iridescent. That's mainly the eyeshadow, mind.' Luna threw a pillow at her. 'You're perfect, Luna. Don't worry about Cadence and Emmett, they're what, fourteen? No relationship lasts longer than a few weeks at this age. I give it two weeks tops, and then they'll be sick of each other. You wait and see.'

But as the summer passed, Emmett and Cadence didn't seem to get sick of each other; if anything, they grew more attached. Literally.

Luna hardly ever saw Emmett's face, aside from when it was glued to Cadence's. And when Emmett got into a fight again, with one of the men who came to his caravan to see his mum, it was Cadence who used a tea towel to clean his eyebrow cut, not Luna. Luna was over here, getting taller and taller. Broader too.

She'd started doing this thing where she left a bar of chocolate out in the sun and then when it melted, she drank it down.

She couldn't stop drawing either, even though the lead so stained her fingers that no amount of washing could clean them, and even though some nights, her hand cramped so bad that she had to rub it with her other hand to ease the throbbing there. It was almost fevered in her, this need to create. To get some of the feeling out of her head and onto the paper. Even when she wasn't drawing, she sketched in her head. Over and over, she imagined the lines taking shape.

But no matter how hard she tried, the feelings wouldn't leave her alone. And rather than escaping them, drawing seemed to amplify them. But still, she kept going. She honestly didn't know what else she could do.

She'd been doing a self-portrait, inspired by *Ophelia* since Earl said that she was really good at drawing people. Luna loved *Ophelia*, how she seemed to be hovering between two worlds. But *Ophelia* was beautiful, and Luna had made her portrait horrid. She'd drawn her heart on the outside of her body, all black and dripping with dark blood that ran off it in rivulets, pooling on the floor.

'You're really taking this Cadence and Emmett thing badly, then, huh?' Mae appeared out of the front door, looking down at Luna's sketch where she was resting her book on her knee.

'What makes you say that?' She dug the pencil into where she was shading the edges of the heart. She wanted it to be dark. She'd never say this out loud, but really, she wanted it dead. As dead as possible. So dead and drained that it was nothing more than a black void, a place of zero feeling.

'It's not exactly sunshine and rainbows, is it?' Mae nudged Luna's sketch book with her big toe.

Luna made a sound to say that she neither agreed nor disagreed. She wished that she was drawn to drawing sunshine and rainbows. She was sure that she'd be the sort of person Emmett wanted to kiss if she were. To stop herself thinking these miserable thoughts, she unwrapped a melted chocolate bar and drank down the silky warmth.

Emmett appeared at the end of the driveway. Cadence wasn't with him, for once.

'Emmett, hi!' Luna was awkward, scrambling to her feet, dropping her sketchbook so that it landed open on her disfigured self-portrait. It had been a warm summer, and the backs of her legs were hot and gritty where she'd been sitting on the front step. There was likely melted chocolate all over her teeth. 'Hi,' she said again as he got closer. She was so lame around Emmett now.

Mae coughed and said 'tragic' at the same time.

'Hi.' Emmett smiled. The cut on his eyebrows was healing now, and the bridge of his nose was a bit pink. He had a few freckles, though you had to look pretty close to spot them. 'The others are down the beach – want to come?' he asked.

'Er.' The others meant Cadence. One hundred per cent. This was the way things were now. Luna felt like a total baby compared to everyone else. She didn't want to go to the beach. Not with Cadence and Emmett. She didn't want to watch them snog as the sun went down when all she had was melted chocolate.

'Come on, I've hardly seen you this summer.'

'Mate, you haven't seen anything other than Cadence's tonsils.' That was Mae; she made Emmett go red and now they had to go to the beach because Luna didn't want Emmett to think that they weren't going because she didn't want to see him and Cadence kissing some more. Even though that was the reason, he couldn't know.

Luna was sure that if Emmett ever found out how much it hurt watching him and Cadence kiss, she'd have to just walk right on out to the sea and let her desperate crush drag her under.

'Just one second. We'll grab some stuff and be right out.'

Luna and Mae bickered quietly and quickly in their bedroom. Luna didn't want Mae to mention Emmett and Cadence because then Emmett might realise that Luna cared. And that would be terrible. Mae wanted Luna to chill out and lend her a bikini.

When they got back outside, Emmett was looking at Luna's drawing.

'Luna, this is amazing.' It was like looking at the sun, watching him run a finger along the edge of her self-portrait. 'You're really good.'

Deep inside, her stomach fizzed like a cola-bottle sweet as she grabbed her sketch book back. She didn't want Emmett to look at it for too long and figure out that she'd just sketched herself half dead and heartless.

'Ready?' he asked, and they set off towards the beach. It was a lot easier to talk to Emmett when he wasn't kissing Cadence, and for the whole walk, it felt like it did all the other summers, with Mae and Emmett teasing each other and Luna laughing the whole time.

But then soon enough they were at the beach. Ahmed and Zadie were there, Cadence too. Luna took a breath and made herself smile and wave.

Cadence began to run towards Emmett. She was always doing that. If she saw him with Luna, she literally ran over to him. None of her body, not even her tummy, wobbled when she ran in a bikini. She'd pinned the front of her hair back with butterfly clips.

'There you are!' She reached us. 'What took you so long?'

'Just took a moment to partake in a séance together. How's your day going, Cadence?'

Luna snorted a laugh and so did Emmett, but Cadence didn't get it. She never got Mae's jokes. 'Never mind,' Mae said. 'Does Zadie have some more of them sherbet dipsticks?'

Mae made off towards Zadie and her sweets, leaving Luna with Emmett and Cadence. Luna was taller than both of them. She felt like a giant.

'I like your top,' Cadence said to her. This was the worst thing of all. Cadence was always nice to Luna. It just seemed really unfair that someone nice like that could look like she did.

'Thanks, it's from Tammy Girl.'

'Aw, I used to love shopping there.'

Cadence put her arm around Emmett's waist, where his trousers were being held up with a piece of rope. She rested her head on his shoulder. They were so perfect together. Out of the corner of her eye, she saw Cadence and Emmett start to kiss again.

'Please let it end,' Zadie said, sucking on the dib-dab she was sharing with Mae. Emmett stuck a finger up at her without breaking the kiss.

'I don't know, it doesn't look too bad to me.' Ahmed had the worst crush on Zadie but, unlike Luna, he wasn't exactly keeping quiet about it. If anything, he seemed proud of the fact that he was in love with someone who didn't love him back. He loved to read and was always carrying books around. The one he had now was called *The Female Eunuch* and he said it would help him to understand the female mind and convince Zadie to go out with him.

It was easier not to be around Emmett and Cadence when they were in a kissing mood (which was always), so Luna went to find Earl in his caravan. She wanted to show him her drawing.

'Very interesting, Luna.' He took the page from her and turned it around, looking at the sketch upside down. He'd been making a cup of tea, so he got Luna one too and they took it and sat on the little floral couch where the light was better. Even though it was warm, Earl was still wearing his blazer and the hat with feathers in the side. Luna asked him once, when she was younger, why his hat was like that, and he just told her that he liked feathers.

'You're very talented, Luna,' said Earl.

It made Luna smile. Earl was the best artist in the world in her book. His muse was a man called Sebastian. He and Earl were madly in love for one summer in Paris decades ago. It was the most romantic story Luna had ever heard. Sebastian and their summer in Paris inspired loads of the stuff that Earl painted.

So if Earl liked her work, it was a massive compliment.

'Thanks, Earl.' She smiled. 'I'm so glad that Mum let me take Art next year. It's the only subject I'm looking forward to.'

'Your teacher is lucky to have you.'

'Tell me about your time at art school again?' Luna settled back against the couch's cushions. She didn't glance out of the window. Or think of Emmett and Cadence in love and kissing on the beach below.

She didn't want to think about that. She wanted to hear one of her favourite stories from Earl.

Earl had a sip of his tea. 'Well, as you know, I was born in a village in Normandy. We were very poor.'

When he talked, you could tell that he had a French accent. 'But I went to study art in Paris.'

'Why did you pick Paris?' Luna asked him.

'Because there's no more beautiful city in all the world than Paris, Luna. I was young and an artist and I wanted to fall hopelessly in love.'

'So you moved to Paris and fell in love.'

'I did, little Luna, with the city, with art, with Sebastian. The 1950s was a strange time. No more war, but things weren't the same as they had been before, either. I think some of us felt invincible, that we'd made it through the worst thing to have ever happened to the world. We felt like nothing could touch us. I know I did. Of course, not everyone felt the same.'

Luna knew that it wasn't okay for two men to go out back then, so Earl and Sebastian had to keep it a secret.

'It's so romantic,' she told him, and he chuckled.

'Yes, but in a tragic way.'

'Very tragic.'

Sebastian disappeared after a single summer.

'I'd like to go to Paris one day.' Luna imagined Paris as full of life and colour, she wanted to see it for herself.

'Then you will, Luna.'

Luna hummed an agreement and tried to picture herself in Paris. Emmett would be with her, of course.

'Does it make you feel sad, the fact that you never really met anyone else?' she asked.

'A little, sometimes. But my life is very full. It makes me a better artist now. You don't have to suffer to make beautiful art.' Earl waved his hand around the caravan, which was full of art. Canvases, big and small, were piled up on the table, or else stacked against the kitchen cabinets.

Luna thought of her own art. How dark and gross it was this summer.

'But a lot of famous artists had hard lives. And what if you want to draw like, awful stuff? Weirdly dark and gloomy stuff. Would you say that there's anything wrong with someone who was drawn to that side of things?'

Earl chuckled and then had another sip of his tea.

'Not at all. You notice what you notice; you are who you are.'

Luna thought that this was just great. Clearly, what she noticed were dark, slimy hearts. Or people who were neither dead nor alive.

'I just wish that I noticed nice things.'

Earl took a drink of his tea. He was looking at Luna now; his eyes were very blue. 'Beauty cannot exist without decay;

the light is all the lighter set against the dark. Just because you feel drawn to the moon does not mean that you shun the sun.'

Luna thought that this was a very optimistic way of looking at things. A part of her still wanted to be drawn to the sun. She didn't want to embrace darkness, not yet.

'No, I suppose not.'

Luna looked out of the caravan's window, down to the beach beyond. She imagined Emmett and Cadence down there, tangled up together like they always were.

'Plus,' Earl said, smirking at Luna from under his hat, 'teenage boys are stupid. But we all become less stupid in time. That is all you need, little Luna. Time.'

Chapter Seven

NOW

> **The Weight of Light**: Oil on canvas. Bold, raw and charged, this is Spencer's most Expressionist piece and demonstrates the influence of the post-war movement on his work. Spencer focuses on distorting the waves of the Seine using frenetic, swirling brushstrokes to create an atmospheric piece which is as intense and passionate as it is beautiful. c. 2005.

'What the hell are you doing here?' I say, my voice less sharp than I'd like it to be.

The colours of Earl's painting go blurry behind my watery eyes. So much time has passed, how can it be that Emmett is here, in the gallery? And he is. He's really here. What is he doing? I look at him, and already the anger that I felt moments ago is disappearing. Replaced by what, I don't know. I have no words, none at all.

He looks better, that's what I think. He's wearing a light

grey shirt and trousers, proper trousers. I don't think I ever saw teenage Emmett in anything other than scratty jeans. Now, he looks polished as if time has taken teenage Emmett and scrubbed the past and all its problems from him.

I've now been frowning and weeping for some time. 'What are you doing here?' I ask him again, and I'd love to say that my voice isn't shaky, but that would be a lie.

'I came to see the painting,' he answers.

'Well, it's there.' I gesture to the wall.

Someone shushes us.

I go back to looking at the painting and reading the information on the little card at the side of it.

The Edge of Always . . . date unknown.

I'm aware of Emmett out of the corner of my eye. He's twisting his hands together where they're resting on his knee.

'Luna, we need to talk.'

'Do we?'

The desire to be cool and calm in this situation is overwhelming. I've played this out so many times in my head already, what it would be like if I ever saw Emmett again, how I would act. There were versions where I ran into his arms, jumped up, and kissed him passionately, versions where I just walked away because it hurt too much, and versions where I told him everything about what's happened since we broke up, about how no love has ever compared to him, how I'm sure that loving him back then broke me in a way that I've never been able to recover from. In no version was I silently weeping.

'You're in the painting, Luna.'

Another shush.

'Yes, I know.'

I have nothing else. I'm in the painting. I'm in the painting and I don't understand why. I don't understand why I'm there, and here. I don't understand how it can be that past me and present me, two people that are so wholly different that I thought they could never be reconciled, are here, in the same space. I'm not the person from The Time Before, I'm not the person in the painting. And yet she's me, and I am her. And how can that be?

The gallery fills up around us, blocking our view of the painting. Someone claps their hands, and when I look up, there's a woman in a suit with many gold buttons talking in rapid French. I've little hope of understanding her until she says, 'And welcome to this, the opening of our new exhibit showcasing the works of Earl Josef Spencer. I'm Mari Marigold, curator of this space.'

This is the woman who was quoted in the Rise Art article, the one who said that Earl is her favourite artist.

Mari's off in French again. I listen intently, trying to follow along, to do anything which might quiet the unease that's rolling off me, making my limbs stiff and straight.

'Meet me tonight,' Emmett mutters.

I don't reply.

'Luna, meet me later.'

Nothing.

Emmett belongs in the past.

I think I glean from Mari's speech that they believe this must have been Earl's last painting, since the composition is new. It sparks some long-forgotten memory . . . one that's been crowded out by everything else that happened that summer . . .

'Luna.'

'I can't.' I sound like I'm choking, or else in pain. The words sound like the sort of words you'd force out on your deathbed, right before you cease to exist in the world.

Someone coughs and looks down at where we're sitting on the bench. They do a double-take when they see me and start whispering to the person next to them. There are now so many people standing in front of us that I can't even see Mari or the painting anymore.

'At this restaurant.' Emmett slides a piece of paper towards me. 'I'll be there at seven.'

I just shake my head and leave the paper on the bench next to me.

More and more people are now looking at me from the assembled crowd. I've been so absorbed in myself that I'm only just realising that my literal worst nightmare is coming true right now. I'm in public, with lots of people, and they're all staring at me. I feel myself grow hot. My mouth is open. Someone takes a picture. No, no, no.

Emmett goes to get up.

'I'll be there. I think we should talk. I can tell you more about the painting.'

There it is.

I go to say that he should tell me now, that I've waited long enough for answers. But Mari is talking at us. At me. I don't know what, but it's probably along the lines of, who the fuck are you and why are you in our painting?

Emmett apologises, in French, of course he does, and then leaves.

When we were younger, it was me. I was the one who was always leaving, but twice now, it's been him. Maybe I never appreciated, when we were young, just how hard it is to be the one who's left behind.

I'd have more time to ponder this beautiful, if slightly tragic sentiment, were it not for the fact that the stuff of my literal nightmares is being played out in real time. Everyone, including Mari, is looking at me and firing questions in French. And no, the French specifically didn't feature in my fever dreams where I'm the centre of attention (I'm naked in those), but this is somehow worse.

Why didn't I think of this?

Why didn't I expect that turning up at the opening might cause a stir? This is what I get for not realising how popular Earl's work has become. This horrifying situation where people are actually pointing at me.

Mari, who seems to have realised that I'm English, and who is also probably working on the assumption that I'm some sort of an imbecile, since I've been frozen with my mouth hanging open this whole time, starts to talk in slow, steady, English.

'You are the girl in the painting, yes?' she asks. A man is still taking photos, and I really wish he'd stop.

'Yes,' I answer, dry-mouthed and focusing solely on Mari. She looks so well put together, as if she's the sort of woman who gets shit done. 'At least, I think I am.'

Mari looks between me and the painting.

'Yes, it is you. Older now, of course. More, how do you say, wrinkles, here.' She gestures to the side of her decidedly wrinkle-free eyes. 'And more sadness now, there is that too.'

Well, isn't this lovely?

'But it is your hair. It is very unique, yes?' Mae and I have always had red hair. It's quite distinctive, I suppose. I hated it growing up. I don't mind it so much now. 'You are still very beautiful, I think,' Mari finishes.

A public compliment, as if this situation wasn't despairing enough. I need to get out of here. Like, I cannot stay in this gallery a second longer. I need to be on my own. I knew it was a mistake coming to Paris. This, Emmett, it's all too much.

I stand up. The crowd have formed a semi-circle around me.

'I have to . . .' I indicate behind me with my thumb.

Mari is talking but I have no idea what she's saying. It turns out, in situations of high stress, I don't even understand English anymore.

At the last second, and possibly owing to the adrenaline coursing through me, making me act in stupid, insensible ways, I grab the piece of paper Emmett left with the restaurant details on. And then, with a whole chorus of French behind me, I turn and run.

Outside the MAM, I crack open the water that's in my bag and take two pills.

I'm half frantic as I set my sunglasses and headphones in place, my eyes darting around like a trapped deer. It's as if I expect Emmett to appear out of nowhere, as if that's just a thing he does in Paris. Or else some more French people will come and shout questions and take pictures of me at terrible angles. This is why it's just better to stay at home. Neither of those things have ever happened to me in Bamburgh.

I feel weak; I hate feeling weak. I try to do my breathing, four, four, four. It's meant to calm me down. It's not working. I'm too stressed. I've stuffed Emmett's little note in my bag and left it at that.

The urge to be alone is strong. It tussles with the knowledge that this is likely the first and last time I'll get to come to Paris. So, instead of going into hiding, I stumble back towards my hotel and sit in the quiet gardens again.

At least here, alone, I feel more myself.

I check my phone. The people on here understand, and this morning's video blog has gone down unexpectedly well. There are fifty-six comments already and a couple of hundred likes. I have a quick scan of what they're saying. Some of my regulars are complaining that it's not death art, but more people are commenting that they're looking forward to the mini-series.

There are messages from Mum and Mae, too.

Mum: Call me immediately Luna or I'm going to Dr Dave.

Mae: How was it? Message as soon as you've seen it.

I reluctantly reply to Mum.

Me: I'm fine, Mum. Honestly, Dr Dave knows and says it's okay. I'll be back on Wednesday.

It'll be a while till she replies. She has Ashanti yoga on Monday mornings.

Me: The piece is beautiful. I can't believe he managed to do it in secret. I wish you could see it.

Mae: It's online you know. Gorgeous. Go Earl! How are you feeling?

Me: I'm alright. Taken my meds. But some stuff happened and I'm kind of freaking out.

Immediately, my phone rings.

'Mae, you're meant to be at work.'

'Gemma says it's fine.' Gemma is Mae's boss and a part-time friend of ours. She gives Mae a huge amount of leeway on account of me and how I am.

I start to cry as soon as I hear Mae's voice. I hate this. I hate feeling so confused and feeble and like I need Mae to take care of me. It's not the way that it's meant to be. Plus, there's just so much more crying than I expected there to be in Paris. I'm breaking all of my rules.

'So, what happened?'

I tell Mae about the painting, how people in the gallery had realised that it was me and started asking me questions and taking pictures.

'Wow, that must have been so stressful. Especially since you're such a hermit.'

'It was awful. I escaped and I'm in a park now, which is better, but that's not all of it.'

I explain how Emmett had come to sit next to me on the bench and then asked me to meet him later.

'Oh my god, Emmett's in Paris. This is brand new information. Brand new.'

My chest tightens. I can read Mae like a book.

'Mae,' I say.

'What are the chances of that? I mean Emmett, in Paris, on the exact same day as you?'

'You didn't,' I say.

'Didn't what?'

'Don't play that with me. You told Emmett I was coming.'

My heart rate is up again. I haven't felt well all morning, and I can't help but assume that all this stress isn't exactly great for me. Dr Dave probably thought I was coming on a nice chilled mini-break; that's likely why he agreed. Instead,

I'm so high on adrenaline that even my fingers are stiff and tense. I didn't think that was possible.

'No,' she answers. 'I didn't tell him.'

'Mae, you're no good at semantics. You never have been. Just tell me the truth, I won't even be mad.' This is a total lie. I'm livid.

'Fine, Fine. Emmett just dropped into my DMs to ask if you were going to the new exhibit, which obviously neither of us knew about. I told him that you might be there today. I gave him a piece of my mind, though, too, don't worry about that. There were paragraphs in my rant, that's how long it was. I made it very clear that I didn't forgive or condone what he did back then.'

'Mae, I can't believe you've done this to me. It's so . . . so . . . ' I can't even find the words to explain how betrayed I feel right now. Mae is the last person I expected to lie to me like this.

'You said you wouldn't get mad!'

'I lied. Just like you did. This is already a lot for me, how can't you see that? Throw Emmett into the mix and it's . . . it's . . . too much.'

'I called him pond scum, if that helps?'

'What? No, of course it doesn't. Why would you . . . ? Never mind.'

I'm so angry at Mae that I start pacing up and down a little patch of path in the park.

'It wasn't your call to make. I've told you already: stop trying to turn my life into a bucket list.'

'It was one sky dive! One. And you didn't even go, even though it cost me a fucking fortune. I'm trying to help you.'

'I don't need your help.'

'Fine. Come home then and be miserable here. Never speak to Emmett again. Never find out why Earl painted you in his last-ever painting. Never see any bit of the world outside Bamburgh. Just come and hide here for the rest of your life.'

I gnaw on my lip as my anger subsides. Replaced instead by regret – or what might become regret. I'm well acquainted with regret. Regret for me has always felt like an absence of colour. It's not even dark, it's not dull, it's just nothing. An empty space even, less than nothing.

'I don't know what to do,' I tell Mae honestly.

I hear, rather than see, her breathe out.

'Think of it this way: if you don't listen to what he has to say tonight, how will you feel?'

Regretful, empty.

I don't answer.

'All I'd say is this,' Mae carries on, and I think, really, she's said an awful lot in the last five minutes. I'm exhausted, though, drained by everything that's happened. 'When it comes to Emmett, it's always been about him. I know you stalk his socials and think about him more often than you should be doing. You need to remember that you're not as good a liar as you think you are.'

'I don't think I'm a good liar.'

'Oh, I don't know, you're doing a good job of pretending

to wonder whether to go to that restaurant tonight when we both know you're already there.'

'It just . . . maybe this is my last chance.'

'Don't talk like that.' Mae's tone is sharp all of a sudden.

I roll my eyes. 'I just mean because it's not like we live in the same country.'

I can hear shouting in the background.

'I'd better go – a hen party has just ordered fifteen scones. But what I was going to say is that it's always been about him, what he needs. I typed a whole paragraph to him about it. It wasn't your fault, what happened. He made you feel guilty, but it was not your fault. So this is your chance to get some closure for *you*. Because it's what *you* need. I think it'll be good for you. I wouldn't have agreed to tell you about the exhibition if I didn't think that.'

I'm wound so tight I'm starting to ache all over. I make an effort to relax my shoulders.

'Go back to work, Mae.'

'You'll let me know how it goes with Emmett?'

'Course.'

More shouting in the background.

'Go, I'll call you later.'

'Bye, love you, sorry for being a lying bitch, bye.'

I sit on my park bench, shell-shocked and dazed, thinking about what Mae said, about not letting it be on Emmett's terms. When we were young, I was always the lucky one. Like it seemed as if my life was so much easier than Emmett's. Objectively, it's true. And youth doesn't understand the nuance that things can be true and not true at the same time. I didn't have the same issues as Emmett had with Tanya, but I had problems even if I wanted to pretend that I didn't.

So maybe Mae is right. When things ended, it was on his terms. It was him who never returned my calls, to the point where I stopped trying. Because of him, I cried myself to sleep every night for a year. Mum blamed him when I dropped out of law school. That wasn't Emmett, though; I hated law and law hated me.

Emmett didn't give me a chance to explain why I acted like I did back then, so I never got any closure from the past.

But the painting . . . Emmett . . . Paris. Maybe everything that happened in the Time Before can finally be put to rest.

I spend the afternoon wandering around Paris, thinking about how I promised Earl that I'd come here one day. I keep my headphones in place as I take in the sculptures of *La Danse Triomphale de Pallas Athénée*, the wide avenues of Voie Georges Pompidou.

I pay for a tour of the catacombs and amidst the thousands of skulls I learn that, in the eighteenth century, undertakers would display unidentified dead bodies in shop windows, hoping that someone would claim them. Earl once told me that beauty can't exist without decay, but it's even more than that for me. Beauty is decay, because without decay, beauty is stagnant, frozen.

Decay is life, if you think about it. I smile to myself in the catacombs, and for the first time in a long time, my fingers twitch with the urge to sketch. Paris is a wonderful place to be a Deather. Paris is a wonderful place full stop.

Outside, the pavements are dusty after a warm summer, and there's only the most gentle autumn breeze. Compared to the still death of the catacombs, out here in the world of the living, every café is fit to bursting, every boulevard is full. People hustle past me, and I step over a man sprawled out on the pavement, snoring loudly. I leave him a couple of euros just for good measure. I stop for coffee, which comes in a tiny little cup that I drink in one gulp. When he clears my table, a cute waiter tells me that I'm very pretty.

'Do you have a boyfriend?' he asks.

'Non . . . merci,' I say in stilted French. *'L'addition, s'il vous plaît?'*

'Oui, très bien.' He smiles and leaves.

As I head back to my hotel to get ready for the evening, I think that I was always going to go and meet Emmett tonight. I've never had any sense of self-preservation around him. None at all. Hopefully, this is my chance to explain why I did what I did. To put the past firmly behind me, once and for all.

That's it.

But as I wearily climb the stairs to my hotel room, I think that Mae was right. I really am a poor liar. And the person I'm lying to here is myself.

Chapter Eight

If this were a movie, I'd spend an inordinate amount of time transforming into my best and most beautiful self before I met the man who left me broken-hearted on the edge of a cliff twenty years ago.

I'd do my hair. I'd have a smoky eye. There'd be a cocktail dress involved, possibly an off-the-shoulder one. I'd be Julia Roberts in *Pretty Woman,* Belle in that gold ball gown. I'd burst out of my room to a catchy and uplifting soundtrack, ready to take on the world.

Unfortunately, it's been some decades since I had any sort of sense that I could take on the world. And I haven't brought a cocktail dress with me. I'm also late.

I'd felt drained this afternoon when I arrived back at my hotel – exhausted by so much feeling. I'd taken my pills and lay down for a short second, except the short second became several hours, and now I have no time. Not having enough time is a founding principle of my being. When I die, they'll cut me open and it'll be there, I'm sure, etched on my heart, 'She didn't have enough time.'

I quickly change into a crumpled black dress with little embroidered strawberries all over it. It's cute, one of my favourites, and I'm wearing it for Paris, not Emmett, an essential point of clarity. I tie my hair up, brush my teeth, throw on my boots, and I'm good to go.

I'm panicked. My hands are shaking a little, as I fiddle with the key to the room. It's a heavy metal thing, which I appreciate, but it makes a loud clang when I drop it on the floor. I *hate* feeling like this. I've spent a great deal of time cultivating zero feeling, zero emotion, and I've become very good at it, thank you very much. Paris, with its paintings and catacombs and Emmett, has robbed me of all my chill.

'Bon soir!' the receptionist calls.

'Bon soir,' I say back. 'Have a nice evening.'

'And you!' She waves.

I'm hustling out of the hotel doors, ready to rock and roll with my headphones and Google Maps. It says that it's a twenty-minute walk, and I am not a woman known for beating Google Maps. Still, I set off at a pace, missing almost all of Paris on an evening to stare at the little blue dot of myself as it moves slowly along the street. I have a sense that, around me, the streets are swarming. In Bamburgh, it's quiet on an evening, like the village sleeps at night. In Paris, the opposite seems to be true. There are even more people outside, I'm sure of it. I'd stop and take it in if I could. But I'm already late, and I don't want to think about how I'll feel if Emmett has already left by the time I get there.

I scuttle onwards, ignoring the tightening feeling in my

chest. I stop and wheeze for a moment, gasping for breath on a street corner, embodying the antithesis of Paris chic.

'I'm fine!' I call to a worried passerby. It must be bad.

I'm thirty minutes late by the time I get to the restaurant, defeated again by Google Maps.

It looks . . . fancy. One of those restaurants that just has a name. *Maison*, as opposed to any sort of indication as to what they might serve. I start trying to rub off the mascara that's migrated under my eyes. There is literal heat coming off my face, but the restaurant looks dim. Hopefully, some darkness will serve to neutralise all the red.

I don't give myself time to back out before pushing the doors open. But even with zero thinking time, I'm struck by just how weird it is to be here, meeting Emmett. Emmett and I never existed in any place other than Northumberland at any time other than summer. How can it be that we're here, in Paris, in autumn? It's like the axis of the world has tilted ever so slightly.

And we are here, in this place, at this time. Because Emmett is sitting at the bar. A waiter takes my shacket, but I hardly notice him. I'm drawn to Emmett, I barely see anything but him, and for a fraction of a second, he doesn't see me. I've always been drawn to him, I think, as I make my way towards the bar, music from a pianist tinkling away in the background. It's dangerous and powerful all at once, knowing how drawn to him I've always been.

But while in the past my love for Emmett excited me, thrilled me and lit me up with purpose, now the thought of all that emotion terrifies me. He might have had good reason, but still, he took my love and marred it, and oh fuck, what am I doing here? I should leave, right, right now.

'Luna.' Emmett spots me and smiles the smallest of smiles.

I'm frozen, two feet away from him. He looks delicious. It's a messed-up, toxic thought to be having, but objectively, it's the truth. He's expensive and delicious, and I want to run my hands up his chest and over his shoulders. Wind them up into his hair. It's shorter than it used to be, but still curly. Even my fingers are moving, twitching to get to him.

'You came,' he says.

'I came.' I slide onto the stool next to him.

'I didn't think you would.'

'Neither did I,' I admit. 'But Mae . . . Plus, I want to hear about the painting.' Emmett said he knew more about *The Edge of Always* and I'm greedy for that knowledge.

Something like the shadow of disappointment passes across his face as he tilts his head to the side, just a fraction, before he schools his features into something neutral.

'Wine?' he asks.

'Yes please, just a small red.'

'Our table should be ready soon.'

I can't help but laugh.

'What's so funny?' he asks, having a sip of his own wine.

'It's just that you're so . . . different, from before.'

He smiles at that. I've always loved his smile, the way that two of his teeth at the side are slightly twisted. I'm glad he didn't Invisalign away his special smile. 'And what about you, aren't you different from when we were teenagers?'

I laugh again. 'That it was a long time ago.' The truth is, I know that I'm different. The me that lived for those summers doesn't exist anymore, and for so many reasons.

'Not so long.' I don't know if he's making me feel so off-balance on purpose or if it's just an accident, but I feel like the whole restaurant is tilting. I'll be furious if I end up on the floor. Surely then he'd know.

Except a waiter comes to let us know our table is ready, and Emmett is gesturing for me to move. I grab my wine off the bar's edge and make my way to our table in the corner. I was right; it's so dark here, but there are candles everywhere. A literal fire hazard.

I sit and try to clear my head. To ground myself.

Except I can't think of anything to say to Emmett, which is insane. I've practised this meeting, many iterations of this meeting, a tragic number of times.

But it's like my brain is made of candyfloss. It can't seem to recall any of the things that I wanted, no needed, to say. Oh, but Emmett's teeth, we have them committed to memory just fine.

It's strangely intimate sitting here at a little two-person table in the corner with a candle.

I should apologise. For what I did then. That's what I should do. Except, to bring it up would take us straight back there, to that cliff edge and I'm just not sure that I can.

For want of something to do, I study the menu. No prices

are never a good sign. It's code for 'this will cost you a fortune' and I do my best to decipher the French. I skip straight over the '*escargots*' and towards '*poulet*' with something I think might be mushrooms. It strikes me as the sort of place that would escort me off the premises if I loaded up Google Translate.

'So, do you come here often?' I ask Emmett because I can't think of anything to say, and the silence is thick and stifling.

'Whenever I'm in Paris. The headquarters of the organisation I work for are based here.'

'Oh,' I say, thinking that this meal will be a real test of my mental agility. Now is not the time for candyfloss brain since I refuse to let on that I've been stalking his social media for twenty years. That's insanity of the highest order. So I can't let on that I know he works for Médecins Sans Frontières. 'How interesting,' I say instead, still reading the menu.

I have my phone on the table in front of us. It's really annoying that I can't turn it off; it lights up constantly.

'One second,' I tell him. 'It's Mae.'

I send a quick message to her to tell her that I'm fine and I'll call her after dinner. I feel the eyes of everyone in the restaurant on me as I type, pushing my thumbs to move quicker even though my hands are stupidly stiff.

'Mae,' Emmett laughs. 'Her message was . . .' He pauses, possibly sensing that taking the piss out of my sister would not be the best move right now. 'Long,' he finishes.

'I'd never have agreed to come, if she'd told me.'

'And why is that?'

I shrug. Have a drink. 'I think the past is just better left in the past.'

'You say that like it's an easy thing to do.'

'Ahem.'

We're forced to pause while we give our order to a waiter wearing a tuxedo. The process is painful, since I have to point and jab at the menu to order, while Emmett speaks perfect French. The waiter bows to him and leaves.

We don't go back to talking about why I came, which is good, since it's difficult to put into words. Instead, Emmett seems determined to be polite. He's pouring me water from a carafe, and telling me that he likes my rings (I'm wearing several). He's asking about Mae's work and the cottage. He wonders if we're still in touch with Zadie and Ahmed.

'Yes, Mae is a baker. She loves it.' I say. And then, 'Yes, we see Zadie a lot, Ahmed less so since he moved down South. But I've read his books, they're brilliant.'

'Yes, me and Mae still have the cottage. We live there the whole time, actually,' I answer in response to a question of whether we still visit in the summer.

It's the first time I've looked Emmett properly in the eyes, and wow, big mistake. Fucking eyelashes.

'Not much has changed since you left. Well, aside from the fact that they got rid of The Edge. Coastal erosion risk.'

'I heard about that.'

'Of course, your mum. How is Tanya?'

'Better,' he nods. 'She's living with her sister,' he tells me. 'Down in Exeter. She's clean.'

'That's good. I'm pleased for her.'

Emmett nods. 'Things were hard back then,' he says delicately. 'For both of us.'

I refold my napkin and avoid eye contact.

'What are you doing up there?' he asks.

'Oh, this and that.' I'm absolutely not divulging that my main income is disability benefit; that would lead to way too many questions. 'I have a blog on the art of dying. Death art basically, my followers are called Deathers. I'm just super into decay now. I have a dead squirrel in my room at home.'

Emmett coughs to hide his surprise. The last time we spoke, I was headed off to law school.

'I always hoped that you'd do something with your art. What about law?'

'I lasted less than a year,' I shrug, thinking that hopefully this whole thing sounds cooler as a recollection than it was as a reality. My year at law school had been, by any definition of the term, a disaster. I hadn't made any friends because, apparently, crying the whole time doesn't make people like you. And then, Dad.

'You're doing art – Earl would love that.'

'No,' I answer, smoothing the already smooth tablecloth. 'I'm not *doing* art. I just talk about it. I haven't so much as picked up a pencil for years.' Drawing, another thing that's consigned to the Time Before.

Emmett doesn't ask any more questions, so I guess he realises that it's a touchy subject.

'And what about you?' I ask like a person who couldn't recite his LinkedIn profile by heart.

'Doctor,' he tells me.

'Congratulations,' I say, surprised to find that I mean it, that I'm proud of him. 'You did it.'

'Yeah, it's weird. I don't know if I ever really believed that I'd get out of Bamburgh.'

'See, I always knew that you'd go.'

Memory is nothing if not an unreliable narrator, so I don't know how true this is. Back then I certainly hoped that he'd stay, that he'd see that part of the world the same way that I did. As an adult, I can see that with everything he endured, his leaving was an inevitability, something as sure as the tides.

He catches my eye. 'There's something different about you, Luna. You're the same person, but different too. I can't put my finger on it.'

'Yes well, people grow up. They change. None of us are who we were then. Tell me about the painting. Please.'

Emmett takes a deep breath in and out. I watch his chest expand with rapt attention.

'I don't know a huge amount. But I do know it was the last thing he painted. I know for sure because he told me about it.'

I lean forward, just a touch. That half a memory I'd had at the gallery, it's right there again, just a hair's breadth out of reach.

'Really, he told you he was working on it?'

Emmett nods and I won't lie – I'm a little hurt that Earl

told him, not me. Art was always *our* thing. It was Earl who taught me about art and artists, and Earl who encouraged me to try new things in my own art. Really, it was Earl who opened my eyes to a different way of looking at the world – he made me feel like it was okay to want to make the sort of art I wanted to make; I've always been grateful to him for that.

But Emmett lived next door to Earl his whole childhood. It was Emmett whom Earl wanted to protect, when he had the choice.

Our food arrives, and while I'm desperate to know more, I wait while our dishes are presented with a flourish.

'So, he told you about it?' I ask again, once we're alone. '*The Edge of Always*.'

'He told me he was working on a new piece, one that he thought was his best work, and that he hoped I'd like it. It was, you know, before what happened, happened.'

I flush with shame. Guilt, for lying like I did back then. I try to swallow around it, but it's as if my jaw won't work properly.

'That's what the woman at MAM thought.' I talk slowly. 'She said that they assumed it was one of his later pieces.'

'His last. I know it.'

'But where's it been since? All his other work came to light years ago.'

Emmett shrugs. 'Private collector, apparently. I wish we knew who.'

'Me too. But I suppose it's not that uncommon. There's

no way Gregor would be around to ask either. I just wish I could meet the person who had a picture of me hanging on their wall for two decades. It's a bit weird when you think of it like that.'

'Very weird.' He smiles. Those teeth. 'What did you make of it? The painting?'

'I love it,' I rush out. It's the truth. I can't remember the last time I felt so moved as I did in front of Earl's art this morning. 'Just, there was so much movement in it; he caught the wind in my hair perfectly. I can see why people say it's a divergence from his other stuff. It was more whimsical, I think, the colours, the shadowy figure in the corner. I loved it.'

'Earl would be happy that you like it.'

'Mm hm.' My throat feels thick all of a sudden. Earl. I hope he'd be happy.

Emmett leans across the table, as if he's about to touch my arm, but thinks better of it.

'I never said . . . ' He's looking at me so intently as he speaks. 'How sorry I am for what happened back then.'

In the background, the pianist continues to play as finally, something is freed within me and the words I've been desperate to say come pouring out.

'No, you shouldn't be sorry. It's me, I'm the one who . . . ruined everything. It was my fault. If it helps, I've hated myself ever since.' It's the truth.

I mock cheers and have a drink. Emmett looks tense, there's a stiffness about him, but you'd have to know him well to notice it. It's in the set of his shoulders, his jaw.

'It doesn't help. Luna, we both know that what happened then, it couldn't have happened any other way. I don't want . . . fuck, I didn't want you to feel like this. I should have reached out, before. I'm an idiot.'

There are a few moments of uncomfortable silence. I'm already tiring, on the food front. I wish I could go back to my body from The Time Before and apologise to all the horrible things I said about myself. Now, I'd give anything to feel properly hungry and strong.

'Please don't feel guilty, Luna. You were young, we both were . . . I can't bear it,' he finishes.

He's right. I felt so old when I was eighteen, but I know now that it's all relative. Maybe we always feel old because in that moment, we're always the oldest we've ever been. But time marches on, regardless. And what was once the frontier of our experience melts into the past.

So, I thought I was old at eighteen. I thought I was worldly-wise and in love. But now I know that this, now, *this* is what feeling old is like. Ground down and exhausted. At least I'm not naive anymore. I'm not sure there's anything worse than ignorant naivety. At least for me.

'How long are you in Paris for?' he asks, and I'm jolted out of my trance.

'Only another day. I'm going back to MAM tomorrow to try and speak to the curator, see if she can tell me anything more about the painting. Then it's home on Wednesday morning. I run an art therapy session at the hospice on Thursdays.'

I mean, in reality, no one is going to die if I don't run the class. Well, they might die, but not because of that.

'So you didn't give up art entirely.'

'It's not quite the same thing. And I haven't given it up – I'm just on a hiatus.' A hiatus spanning several years.

'And why was that?'

'No real reason. How long are you here for?' I ask, changing the subject.

'Until Friday,' he answers after a drink. Emmett looks like he's going to say something, but stops himself.

'That's a good thing that you do, at the hospice.'

'I enjoy it,' I answer honestly.

He goes to talk again, but has a drink instead.

'What?' I ask him.

He has another drink.

'It's just . . . Well, I wondered what you made of the message in the corner of the painting?'

'The answer is always in the art?' I ask, remembering the sentence in the corner above Earl's signature. I push my plate away.

'That's the one.'

I shrug. 'You know Earl believed that everyone should be creative somehow. I guess he's telling people that you should look to art to answer . . . I don't know, life's big questions.'

'So you don't think it was a message for you?'

'For me? Why would it be for me?'

Emmett neatly puts his knife and fork across his plate.

'Because you're in the painting. What if it's a message for both of us?'

I laugh, too loudly in this fancy restaurant.

'Why on earth would Earl send us a message from beyond the grave?' For a smart person, Emmett has always had the capacity to be really fucking stupid.

'Not from beyond the grave. He painted it that last summer, and we had more going on than what happened. I think he knew that we'd find it hard to stay together. Neither of us knew what love was meant to look like.'

His words sting. 'I wouldn't have found it hard, Emmett. That was all you.' My voice is sharp. But even as I say it, I know it's not exactly true. He's right: we had other obstacles, so many obstacles.

'You knew Earl – he saw things.'

Some of the fire goes out of me as Emmett reaches into his pocket and unfolds a neat piece of paper. It has a list on it.

'What's that?' I ask.

Emmett slides it across the table to me.

The Weight of Light
Longing for Human Connection
Montmartre in Motion
The Juxtaposition of Life and Death
The Rubicon
The Edge of Always

'Why do you have a list of Earl's final paintings?'

'These are the ones that are included in the exhibit.'

'I know that, but why are you showing it to me?'

'What if Earl wanted us to go to them, the places he painted? What if he saw it as a way to bring us back together?'

'In Paris? Why would Earl want us to come to Paris? It makes zero sense, Emmett.'

'Luna, *he* had a great love story in Paris. You know he did. I don't know, it's just an Earl thing to do. He loved helping people.'

I think of all the painstaking hours that Earl spent with me as I learned to draw, of all the support he gave Tanya and Emmett. Emmett's right: it *would* be just like Earl to try and help us from beyond the grave.

'What are you suggesting here, Emmett?'

'Come with me. Let's go and see the places he painted. It could be like, in his honour. We never did say goodbye to him properly.'

I mean, *I* did. I did say goodbye to Earl. But thinking about his funeral makes it very hard to remain neutral about almost anything at all.

'I don't know about you,' he says with an air of finality, 'but I could do with some answers right now.'

I mean, fuck yes. I would love answers. And if life were a question that could be solved, I'd be all over it.

'So we what? Spend tomorrow traipsing around all the places that Earl painted hoping that some magical answer to a question we don't even know appears before us. That's insane behaviour.' I try to ignore the fact that I'd had that exact thought, the moment I'd walked into the exhibit.

Emmett shakes his head. 'I'm not saying we do it in a day. It'll take the rest of the week. Luna, say you'll do it. Spend the week in Paris with me?'

There was a time when I'd have done anything that Emmett asked of me. I've come to see it as a weakness, the way I was back then, giving him the power to make me miserable, just handing my happiness over on a plate. I don't do that anymore. No one gets that power.

I'm no longer the person that I was in The Time Before.

Chapter Nine

THEN

Luna was 14
Emmett was 15

For the first time in ten years, Luna didn't want to go to the cottage that summer. Well, maybe that wasn't entirely true. Part of her was desperate to get there. To see Earl and the others. She remembered what Earl had said last year, about beauty and decay coexisting and she tried to see it, she really did. She was just struggling to see the beauty. Instead, the world felt marred in a way she'd never noticed before. In her fourteenth year, Luna had become strangely angry at the world. At everything, in fact.

'If you keep frowning like that, you'll give yourself wrinkles, Luna,' her mum said, catching her eye in the rear-view mirror.

Luna tried to relax her face; it would be easier if she didn't feel so tense all the time.

'What'll we do this visit, girls? We could go and see the puffins?'

'Yeah, Dad, let's hit up the puffins,' Mae answered after a long silence.

Luna was too lost in her thoughts to even think about an itinerary, too preoccupied with how she'd react when she saw Cadence and Emmett this summer. On balance, she thought that she'd done a pretty good job of hiding how she really felt last year, depressing self-portraits aside. But now, she feared that her newfound anger would make it impossible to contain. It was as if her emotions were right there, simmering away just under the surface where she had no hope of concealing them. There was an Andrex puppy advert on TV just last night that had made her weep. A toilet roll advert. Her mum had threatened her with counselling.

'I'm looking forward to some well-needed R&R,' their mum chimed.

'Well, your life sure is exhausting.'

If anything, Mae had become more Mae than ever this year. Annoying their mum was like a full-time job for her. Luna felt halfway to jealous about it. At least Mae had a purpose. Luna didn't feel like she had any purpose; instead she felt adrift, apart. Even now, she felt like she wasn't quite fully present in this scene. It felt as if she was hovering above it. Distant. It made her feel like she wasn't in charge of her own life.

'I wonder what Clive has been up to,' Mum asked, oblivious to Mae's sarcasm. Luna felt that there was something deeply troubling about people who didn't understand sarcasm.

'Hopefully he didn't like die or anything. But then at his age, anything is possible.'

Even their mum couldn't ignore the fact that Mae was trying to get a rise out of her. Luna suspected that Mae was just bored. But now they all had to suffer through Mum telling them how Clive couldn't possibly die because he's super virile for his age. Just the word virile grossed Luna out and made her irrationally angry at Clive. And her mum. And the whole world, come to think of it. She wanted to turn up the volume on her iPod, but it had run out of battery. Life was just so cruel.

The chat about Clive's virility ended when they pulled up to the cottage.

Emmett wasn't there. He wasn't waiting on the step like he did every year. It's not that Luna expected him to be there, since she hadn't told him they were coming, but still, his absence stung.

'You are like emitting hatred. Will you chill out?' Mae muttered as they carried their bags into the bedroom. It felt smaller than before.

Luna was just so big. Broad, her mum called her, in a tone that made it patently clear that being broad was the worst possible thing a girl could be at fourteen. Her dad said that she took after him, that she was just strong. And it was true, she was strong. She could throw the javelin further than anyone else in her year. It didn't exactly feel like a win.

'Those puberty hormones really are playing you today, huh?' Mae asked.

Luna didn't know what Mae meant. So what if she was sat on the edge of her bed, clutching *New Moon* to her chest and crying silently because Emmett wouldn't ever love her like Edward loved Bella.

Luna sniffed. 'It's not hormones.'

'I don't know, I don't think jealousy is normally quite so stabby.'

Luna flopped back on the bed.

'Will you please just trust in the plan?'

Like she did every summer, Mae had come up with a plan. Why she persisted in coming up with plans, since she was otherwise completely chaotic, Luna didn't know. What she did know was that this year's plan was called The Man Plan. And it involved no small amount of lying.

'I just can't see how—'

'That's because you have zero experience, which is a whole other level of tragic. If I've said it before, I'll say it again: you could have been using this year to get some practice in. Look at me – I let Liam in Year Nine touch my boob. And I felt his dick through his trousers. It was amazing.' Mae paused for a second. 'Well, it would have been if he wasn't crying about England getting knocked out of the World Cup the whole time.'

Mae sighed as if she were recalling some great love story as opposed to being groped by a weeping Liam round the back of the swimming pool.

While Luna's teenage hormones were making her angry, Mae's were making her horny.

'Now let's get changed and get out of here before Dad drags us off to look at the freaking puffins again. I can't wait to see Earl.'

Luna unzipped her duffle bag. There was a lot of black in there. She picked out some jeans and a black vest top and added another several layers of eyeliner, just to be on the safe side.

'You're spiralling again.' Mae was busy backcombing her hair. She was wearing the mesh top that you could see her bra through, the one that their mum said made her look like a whore. She'd added a set of decorative rosary beads. Luna was certain that they either looked really cool or absolutely terrible. She couldn't decide which.

'I'm not spiralling.'

'Good, come on. There better be some cute boys here this summer. Or girls. I'm not fussy you know. I wonder if Zadie and Ahmed got together.'

Luna rolled her eyes as Mae pulled her through the cottage. In some awfully selfish way, she hoped that Ahmed and Zadie hadn't got together, since she couldn't bear the thought of everyone being happy aside from her. Her misery wanted company.

She didn't feel good about hoping that other people were miserable too, and she hoped that that counted for something. And anyway, she didn't feel quite so miserable herself once she was out in the sea air.

They ran all the way to The Edge.

Luna was breathing in big gulps of fresh air, wondering if it was possible to feel drunk off the stuff when she saw them. Emmett, Earl and Emmett's mum, Tanya. Zadie and Ahmed were there too, the group sat in a little circle on the edge of the cliff between the caravans.

Suddenly, it felt like the most stupid thing in the world to have avoided talking to Emmett this year. Why didn't Luna call him? Why didn't she reply when he wrote her letters? It felt like control at the time, but now she thought what a stupid thing to have done, to deprive herself of Emmett just because he didn't love her like she loved him.

Cadence was there. Still beautiful, still bouncy. Luna just took a deep breath as Mae whistled loudly and shouted, 'Surprise!'

They were surprised. Earl hugged them both, so did Tanya, her frail arms making it feel like a hug from a baby bird. Ahmed quoted something that sounded like Shakespeare and Zadie said, 'Alright,' tipping her head back to get a good look at the pair of them. Even Cadence bounced over and gave them a hug. It was only Emmett who didn't say a thing.

More chairs were fetched.

'Looking good, Tanya,' Mae said, as everyone shuffled back to widen the circle. Emmett's mum smiled, cradling a mug of tea in her hands. She looked worn out and paper-thin, but she was here.

'And you, Mae. You've grown, you both have.' Luna knew this, since she was basically a giant now, but it made her feel uncomfortable. She went about squishing her legs together and sitting on her hands. She was trying, and failing, to make herself as small as possible.

It was a cloudy day. Big white clouds dominated the horizon, taking up an impossibly vast amount of the blue sky. Luna wondered how it was possible for her to feel so much darkness in a world that was filled with something as beautiful and light as those clouds. Maybe it was only here, maybe here was the place where she could recognise the dark and the light.

'We've grown up, Tanya. In more ways than one if you get me.' Mae winked and Luna felt unease welling up from somewhere deep inside her. The wink had felt like some sort of an activation code for The Man Plan. Luna shifted on her white picnic seat.

Earl laughed and went to get some cake from his caravan.

'So, how's things?' Luna asked Emmett, her voice a tiny bit thin. She tried her best to ignore the fact that Cadence was sitting on his knee, fully draped around him. Like, why? When there was perfectly good grass right there.

'Yeah, not bad.' He wouldn't look Luna in the eye.

'Emmy got top of the year in his mocks.' Cadence stroked his hair off his forehead. *Emmy.*

Mae slapped her thigh and Luna's sense of unease increased a notch.

'No. Way. So did Luna. Well, only in Art. But still, top of the year. She flunked Maths and Mum had a nervous breakdown. So now we *both* have to get a maths tutor. How shit it that? Mum thinks failure is catching.'

Luna couldn't be sure, it seemed like there were hints of The Man Plan in there. But also, it was very much just Mae.

'I didn't know you were struggling with maths.' Emmett looked ... well, Luna thought he looked hurt. He was frowning.

'Emmy's going to be a doctor,' Cadence told them all proudly.

Emmett shrugged and went somewhat red. Luna couldn't help but notice that he seemed taller this year. She wondered if she'd still be bigger than him. 'I just said I might. I thought it would be cool to like help people. And you can be a doctor anywhere, once you're trained.' He looked out at the sea, his voice quiet. 'I could have helped you with maths,' he told Luna.

'Oh, she hasn't had the time to be studying, that's all,' Mae announced. Tanya's eyes bounced between Emmett and Mae. The Man Plan didn't feel like a good idea at all.

'She's been busy with boys all year. Taking virginities left, right and centre.' Mae finished proudly as Tanya spat her drink on the floor and Cadence shrieked with laughter.

'I think I'll go and help Earl.' Tanya stood up, her legs so thin, so small. Like a little deer.

'Good job, Luna. Never realised you had it in you,' Zadie said. Luna wondered as to the logistics of swan diving off the edge of the cliff. It wasn't exactly high, and there was a sandy beach below, but at least she wouldn't be here anymore. With a bit of luck, an unexpected wave would come in and sweep her out to sea.

'You know we could also . . . ' Ahmed waggled his eyebrows at Zadie. They were pretty substantial eyebrows, not as massive as Eyebrow Clive's obviously, but still.

Zadie ignored him.

Everyone was laughing. Aside from Emmett, that is. Emmett looked furious. There were red patches high on his cheeks and he was looking away from them all.

Earl reappeared with a tray of cherry muffins. 'How's work going, Earl?' Luna asked loudly over all the sniggering.

'Sold a piece last week.'

'That's amazing! Which one?'

He settled down into his chair again as everyone made grabby hands for the cakes.

'The Weight of Light.'

Luna knew exactly which painting it was that Earl had sold.

'River one,' Mae shouted, making a snapping sound with her fingers.

'I think you'll find it's the Seine, Mae,' Ahmed said.

'That's one of my favourites. Where's it gone?'

'Gregor came and took it for the same buyer who bought *Longing for Human Connection* last year.'

Longing was one of Luna's favourites. It was a carousel horse, just one. Sebastian was riding it and it was beautiful, super colourful and happy, but just a tiny bit sad. It was the sort of thing Luna wished that she wanted to draw. Earl's paintings always seemed to her like proper art, the sort that people would hang in a gallery one day. Luna had spent a whole week in January drawing a rotten apple she'd pulled out of the bin. Each day, as it decomposed, she'd sketched it again. No one was ever going to hang decomposing fruit on their wall.

'Do you have anything to show us, Luna? We missed you sending us your work, didn't we, Emmett?'

Emmett shrugged. 'Suppose so.' Cadence kept stroking his head, which made Mae roll her eyes.

To Luna though, watching them felt like physical pain. For a horrifying second, she worried that she was about to start crying, right here in front of everyone. Then she really would have to swan dive off the cliff.

'She's been super busy, you know what with all the . . . ' Mae did an exaggerated wink. That's it, thought Luna. The Man Plan stopped tonight.

Luna coughed to clear her throat and hoped that no one noticed that her eyes were glossy.

'I made a sculpture for Art. We used clay and recycled materials. It was on the theme of environmentalism, so I made a carp because they're going extinct, and we'd learned about them in Geography. I have it eating a plastic bag.'

Luna had been able to tell, at the time, that other people in the class thought her sculpture was strange. She'd purposely made it as ugly as possible, since global warming wasn't exactly something nice. Everyone said it was 'interesting' but they said it in a way that made her think that interesting was code for awful. People always said her stuff was interesting.

She was trying to think about her sculpture some more,

but it was hard to think clearly when Cadence was busy walking her fingers up Emmett's arm.

'What did you think about them as materials?' Earl tried to bring her around. He always asked her opinion, and talked to her like a real adult.

Her mum had started to suggest it was strange that Earl wanted to hang out with Luna and the others. But Luna didn't feel like that at all. Earl was like family.

'They were steadier, I think, than paint. It felt more like they'd do as I asked them to.'

'How interesting. Perhaps I like the element of surprise.'

'You like the element of colour.' Luna smiled because Earl's art was always so colourful.

'What are your plans for the rest of the summer?' Tanya asked. She never talked much, and when she did her voice was always quiet, like she'd worn it out somehow. Emmett was looking at Luna, even as Cadence stroked his hair. It made her want to squirm in her seat.

'Well, aside from all the kissing we hope to be doing, Tanya,' Mae answered before Luna could stop her. 'Not with each other, obviously, though if I wasn't her sister, I'd be all over that.'

Not for the first time that night, Luna wondered if she could simply disown Mae as her sister.

'I mean kissing other people.' Everyone laughed – everyone except Emmett. Luna really wished they'd stop; they only encouraged her.

'But, yes, aside from that we'll just be tagging along with

whatever you're doing. Plus, Dad wants to see the birds again, he freaking loves those puffins.'

'We were going to go to the dunes tomorrow,' Zadie told them. 'If you're up for a walk?'

The dunes were a couple of miles away. Big sandy hills that led down to a great beach.

'Sounds good. Are you coming, Mae?'

'Sure,' Mae said, taking another cake. Luna thought that she could probably relax now, since Mae's mouth was full of cake. But she should have realised that Mae was not averse to talking with her mouth full. Normally she did it to annoy their mum, but it meant that she got a lot of practice in. 'And hopefully Emmett will be in a better mood tomorrow. Because you know, Emmett, if I had someone as hot as Cadence sat on my knee, I don't think I'd be looking quite so pissed off about it.'

Chapter Ten

The first thing Luna heard the next morning was her mum laughing in the garden. Her shriek was followed by the chortle of Eyebrow Clive.

Mae's bed was next to the window. She pushed the curtain aside a little to get a look at the garden. 'Jesus, she still has her rollers in.'

'Poor Dad.'

'Does he care, though? He'd rather spend time with his models than her. Not that I blame him for that.'

'Maybe.' Luna thought of Dad laughing when her mum had described Eyebrow Clive as virile.

She sighed and flopped back on the bed. 'It's 9am – we'd better get dressed if we're setting off for the dunes in an hour.' Luna started and tried to force herself to move. She was so sleepy. All the time. Every morning she didn't want to get out of bed. She hated getting up. It just felt so unfair.

'Remember,' she told Mae, from where she was still lying in bed, 'no more Man Plan.'

Mae, also still in bed, rolled her eyes. 'You've already said. Personally, I thought it was going great.'

'Emmett has barely spoken to me.'

'That's the beauty of the plan!' Mae launched herself out of bed as their mum laughed again. 'First, you make him angry, then that anger jolts him into realising that the reason he's angry is because he's madly in love with you. It's a classic. It's working perfectly.'

'You are literally evil. It's terrifying. But I mean it, no more plan.'

'Okay, fine.'

There was an especially loud shriek from the garden. Luna had never heard their Mum laugh like that with them or their dad. Mae must have been thinking the same thing because she said, 'Must have been shit, being born in a time when it was expected that you had a family and kids, even if you didn't really want them.'

Mae rarely said anything sympathetic about their mum, so Luna was taken aback.

'I know.'

As quickly as the sympathy came though, it began to retreat. Replaced instead with one of the dark negative emotions that came so easily to her these days. The darkness clouded her vision and made Luna feel like she didn't quite have a handle on her own brain.

'Let's go have breakfast with Dad,' she said on impulse, finally extracting her bikini and black denim shorts from the mess of her holdall. She tugged out a grey Nirvana T-shirt that someone had given away for free. Really, it was all just quite dark at the moment.

They were just about to leave for the dunes, having promised their dad that they'd go on the puffin trip tomorrow when their mum came in the back door through to the tiny cottage kitchen.

'Where are you off to, girls?' she asked. Luna felt guilty. She didn't even know why she felt guilty.

'We're just going to the dunes with Emmett, and the others,' Mae answered.

Their mum's lips turned down. 'Well, make sure you're back for three.'

Luna was confused.

'Why, what's happening at three?'

'We're interviewing some potential maths tutors.'

Everyone started to talk at once – the general theme: outrage. Aside from their dad, who said, 'I didn't know you'd found some local chaps.'

'It's sexist, Michael, to assume that they're all men.'

'Are they men?' Mae asked.

'Yes, but that's not the point. We can't take a summer off, Luna, not passing Maths is not an option.'

'Mum, will you chill out,' Mae said and then laughed. It was a ridiculous concept. 'She didn't flunk it really bad. Getting a D is not the worst thing that can happen to a person. There are loads of grades after a D . . . E, F, G, U.'

At this, their mum looked set to pass out. Luna wasn't

exactly sure that Mae was helping her cause. Once again, she had this weird sense that she wasn't directing her own life. As if it were a ship and there was someone else at the helm.

'Plus, Emmett said he'd help her. He's like a maths genius or something.'

Emmett hadn't said he'd help Luna; he'd barely spoken to her or looked her way yesterday, except to frown. Luna wondered if this was some deviation from the Man Plan that Mae was plotting.

Their mum's lips pressed into a thin line, evidently torn between her obvious dislike of Emmett and the fact that he might help Luna to avoid the dreaded U in Maths.

'Well, that's very kind.'

'Yeah, he was really upset that Luna didn't tell him she was struggling. He said unequivocally that if she'd called him, she would have passed her mock. You should get Emmett to mentor her – he could do with the money.'

Mae was unhinged. There, Luna had thought it.

'Well, I'm not – I've found some nice men. All retired.'

'They probably won't know what the syllabus is now, then. Emmett scored top of his year – he got full marks.'

It wasn't the best feeling, Luna thought. Standing there watching Mum and Mae argue over who should make her less bad at maths.

'Well, I—'

'We'll ask him today and circle back to this later.' Mae made a circling motion with her finger. 'See you guys later, have fun.'

Luna had barely said a word, but Mae was pulling her out the door.

It was a bright, dry day. It hardly ever rained in Northumberland. It wasn't just some warped or wishful thinking on Luna's part either – it was the truth. Northumberland was part of the country that got the most hours of sunshine. It was another thing she'd picked up in Geography, a subject she wasn't exactly excelling in, but at least she wasn't flunking it either.

Free from the cottage, the girls laughed and ran towards The Edge. They always ran, though neither of them could properly say why – it's just what they did. Mae had a carrier bag with their towels and a bottle of water, and Luna had some pencils and her notebook in her rucksack. The darkness of the morning was long gone by the time they saw Emmett, Zadie and Ahmed waiting between the caravans. It looked to Luna as if they were having a serious discussion, with their heads bent close together. But as Mae shouted, 'We're here!' Zadie turned towards them and waved while Emmett refused to look their way.

'We brought no food, though. There's nothing edible in the whole cottage. Mum made us have courgetti for dinner last night. It's like spaghetti but made out of courgette.' Mae made a show of pretending to stick two fingers down her throat and failed to mention the Monster Munch they'd eaten in her bed later on. The whole room had still smelled of pickled onions when they left it this morning.

'It's a good job that we have plenty then, isn't it?' Zadie

tapped her rucksack. Zadie always had sweets. Her mum and dad ran a corner shop.

'Let's go, people,' Ahmed said loudly. Emmett shushed him.

'Sorry. Mum's not feeling well,' he said, looking over his shoulder towards his caravan. The cardboard boxes they used as curtains were pushed tight against the window. There were dark shadows under Emmett's eyes. The skin there looked like tissue paper, so fragile. And not quite black, not quite purple, but somewhere in between.

'I'm sorry, Emmett,' Luna said, her voice small. She meant that she was sorry for everything this year, though she didn't say that. It sometimes felt impossible to say the things that she meant.

Emmett just shrugged. 'Cadence can't make it either. It's just us.'

'Well.' Mae slapped her thigh. 'What a beautiful day this is turning out to be. Emmett, good man, we have a proposition for you. But for now, shall we get going?'

Ahmed held out his arm for Zadie to link, but she held hands with Mae instead, and they set off. There was a coastal path, the dunes about three miles north.

Luna and Emmett were left to bring up the rear. They walked in silence at first, and the only thing for Luna to focus on was how awful and sticky things were between them.

It was the first time she'd dared to get a good look at him, since she hadn't wanted Cadence to notice that she was obsessed with him. She just really wanted to do something to relieve the ache that lived permanently in the pit of her stomach. And the person she wanted to relieve it with was Emmett.

This year, she had a much better idea of what that might entail. A couple of months ago, she and Mae had been at a sleepover when their friend had produced her dad's entire collection of porn. Mae had taken notes with a Bic pen and sheet of A4 paper. Luna had been horrified. There was a lot of grunting. But she'd been sort of intrigued, too. Mae was right. They really were disgusting little critters.

None of these were helpful things to be thinking about as she walked alongside her friend. Especially not since Emmett was finally taller than her this year. His hair was slightly longer, the curls more defined. He was pale too, and hairier. If nothing else, it was good to realise that the hairiness wasn't just affecting Luna.

Luna should say something. But what? Something sparky.

'It's a nice day,' she tried eventually, feeling about as sparky as a sliver of seaweed.

He didn't answer. Emmett got like this sometimes. Dark and sullen. This time, though, Luna knew it was directed at her. 'What's this about a proposition?' he asked finally. He sounded exhausted, Luna thought.

'Oh right, yeah, well it's just you know Mae mentioned that I failed Maths.' Luna started talking really quickly.

'How bad did you fail?'

'Got a D on my mock. Mum treated the news like I'd announced that I was dying of syphilis.'

'That's not so bad.'

'Syphilis or the D?'

'The D. Syphilis is an awful death. Your brain melts.'

'It does not!'

'Yep, happened to King George.'

The smallest of smiles ghosted across Emmett's face and Luna felt delighted that she'd helped to bring him out of his dark mood. But then he seemed to remember that he was annoyed at Luna and quickly went back to frowning again. Luna wanted to reach up and smooth out his frown lines. Possibly her crush was so deeply depressing that it was driving her insane.

She cleared her throat.

'But Mum is dramatic, remember.'

Emmett nodded.

The depressed grass path they were walking along was only really wide enough for one person. It meant that Emmett's arm kept brushing against Luna's in the most alarming way. It was like being zapped with a live wire every time it happened. Luna decided to walk in the grass.

'So this morning . . . ' she breathed and started lifting her knees with each step to cope with the grass. Emmett noticed and moved further to the side of the depressed grass. 'She was talking about needing a maths tutor and Mae suggested you.'

'Me?'

She went immediately red.

'Just because you're so good at maths.'

Emmett mumbled something under his breath.

'Sorry, what was that?'

'I said, I'm surprised you'd want me to, seeing as you've ignored me all year.'

Luna stopped walking.

'I haven't ignored you. Emmett, I . . . I've been busy.'

Luna didn't have an excuse. Or not one that she could admit to. It had felt like such a power move, not replying to Emmett's letters, but now, she just felt crappy.

'Too busy to write a couple of letters, that's bullshit, Luna.'

Mae and the others, walking ahead, turned to frown at the pair of them.

'Whatever you're arguing about, I side with Luna,' Mae called before they set off again.

'We aren't arguing.' Emmett looked out at the sea.

Luna had secretly hoped that like her, Emmett was just miserable about the state of the world. Now she knew for sure it was her though. 'Look, I'm sorry Emmett. I didn't mean anything by it. I was, I don't know . . . ' Once again, the things that Luna wanted to say were floating around, just out of reach.

Emmett smacked his hands down to his side in a move of sheer exasperation.

'You're meant to be my best friend, Luna, and I haven't heard from you all year. I missed you. I didn't even know that you were coming yesterday. I've never not met you at the cottage, not since we were like seven or something.'

Something that felt a lot like guilt started to wrap itself around Luna, starting at her ankles and squeezing her as it went, like an anaconda might. It made her feel hot and sticky and a bit sick. And also, she was crying. Which was humiliating.

'I didn't think . . . Cadence maybe . . . '

Emmett realised that Luna was crying. Why was she like this?

His voice softened. 'What's Cadence got to do with it?'

Oh God, Luna couldn't . . . she couldn't admit that she'd spent the year obsessing over the fact that Emmett had been up here doing god knows what with Cadence. She'd never recover from the humiliation.

Not since Emmett was reaching up to wipe her tears away. Swiping them off with his thumbs. Luna found that she couldn't breathe.

'I just thought . . . it doesn't matter,' she finished weakly through sobs.

He was so close to her now. She could see his eyelashes, all of them. The slight line between his eyebrows, where he was still frowning. Luna thought it was now a frown of concern rather than anger.

He wiped another tear.

'You're my best friend, Luna. Cadence has nothing to do with me and you.'

Luna sniffed.

'I needed you this year. Things with Mum . . . it's been hard.'

The guilt made her cry all the harder. Luna was forced to admit that she was the villain in this here tale. It was one thing being disappointed with the state of the world. It was quite another being disappointed with yourself.

'I'm sorry, Emmett.' She turned to face away from him.

She couldn't bear it anymore. But then Emmett's hands were on the tops of her arms. Her skin felt hot under his touch. 'I wasn't thinking properly. All year,' she finished.

'I always want to talk to you, Luna.'

Luna was actually amazed that her heart didn't just swell straight out of her chest. She always wanted to talk to Emmett too.

'Friends?' Emmett tacked on as her swollen heart deflated like a comedy balloon. But really, being friends with Emmett was better than nothing. 'Friends,' she agreed, trying out a smile.

They kept walking. 'So about this maths tutoring?' he asked.

'You don't have to do it. Who wants to spend their summer doing maths?'

'Someone who loves maths?'

'Oh yeah, I forgot how strange you are. Mum said she'd pay you.'

'She doesn't have to. I'd do anything for you, Luna, you have to know that.'

Luna didn't know how to answer that. She suspected that she should say something back, like how she would do anything for Emmett too, but she didn't know how. It was so hard, wanting the things that she wanted.

Emmett too seemed to retreat into his own head. As if he'd said too much and now there was no way forward.

'I'd rather have you than some dusty old man,' Luna tried, making light of things as she often did to help Emmett.

'Why is your hypothetical maths tutor dusty?'

'It's just a saying.'

Emmett nodded. It looked like Luna had a maths tutor. At least she'd stopped crying.

He took a breath and looked at Luna. 'Best summer ever?' He held up his little finger.

Luna smiled, lighter already. 'Best summer ever.'

Chapter Eleven

Everyone was in the sea. Everyone apart from Luna. She sat on the dunes, sketching. It was a beautiful scene, the way the sun light reflected on the water like that. It was a beautiful scene and yet Luna wasn't drawing it. No, she was drawing a discarded can of coke half poking out of the sand.

Still, she felt happier since she'd made up with Emmett. Happy, but still drained.

Along the beach, she saw a figure walking towards them, wearing a top hat with feathers.

'Earl!' Luna shouted. 'Earl!'

Earl spotted her and began to make his way up the beach. He had a dog with him. A scraggy-looking Labrador.

'Luna, hello!'

'Hi Earl, what are you doing here?' The dog had charged at Luna and almost knocked her over. It started to run in excited circles around her.

'Walking Fred's dog. He can't get out so much since he had his hip operation. He's quite excited, aren't you, Scout?'

In reply, Scout began to wag his tail so forcefully that Luna was at risk of getting a mouthful of sand. Fred was a man with a horse who lived at The Edge.

Earl lowered himself next to Luna on the sand dune. He threw a ball for Scout, who charged off for it.

'He has a lot of energy. We've been walking all morning.'

They sat for a while, as Luna sketched and Earl continued to throw the ball for Scout. Whatever the weather, Earl had a little grey beard and long hair that he wore in a ponytail.

'You'd be drawing the waves,' she said, not looking up. She couldn't get the dimensions right on her can.

'I don't know for sure. The waves can be really challenging. Movement. Water. I was friends with David Hockney when he went through his water phase, trying to capture the uncapturable.'

'Still, it would look better than a drawing of trash.'

Whatever Earl had said last year, it still bugged Luna that she wanted to draw rubbish more than she wanted to draw the beautiful scene in front of her. She wanted to be like Earl.

'I disagree. Try adding more shading along the line where the can meets the sand. The contrast is not quite right, I think.' Luna nodded and start shading with a vengeance.

Earl watched her as she shaded. His eyes were somewhere between green and yellow, but they were bright. Mae said that it made him look like a wise old owl.

'There, much better, I think.' Earl went to stand up. Luna looked at her can of coke – it was better. 'I'll go and say hello to the others before I get back.'

Luna nodded. She squinted at her drawing some more.

'It is very beautiful, Luna. I hope you can see that.'

'What topics in maths are you struggling with?'

They were in her room, sitting next to each other on her bed, maths textbooks spread between them.

Luna loved how close together they were. The only downside was Mae, sprawled out on her own bed.

'Pretend I'm not here,' she'd said, plugging her headphones into the iPod to play music loudly. She had one leg crossed over the other. They could hear the beat of *When the Sun Goes Down* coming through them.

'Er, all of them,' Luna admitted, trying not to recall the trauma of her school maths lessons. 'I don't know how I managed to get a D, honestly.'

'Right, well, let's start with trigonometry. It's really tricky, loads of people find it hard.'

'But not you, right?'

She nudged his shoulder with her own. 'No, but I find other things more difficult.'

Emmett was taking his teaching role very seriously, and Luna was trying so very hard not to find it hot.

'Oh really, like what?'

'You're not going to distract me from this, Luna.' He started thumbing through a textbook.

'I wasn't trying to. I was just asking what part of school you find hard, looks to me like you're acing it all.'

He found the trigonometry page, filled with little triangles, and set it across his lap.

'I find school easy. But not everything else.'

Luna reasoned that Emmett probably meant something to do with his home situation which, when you thought about it, was so much worse than bad maths lessons five times a week.

Mae's music was still blasting out.

'I know,' she told him, hoping that he did know. She was barely managing full sentences; everything was scrambled from such close proximity to Emmett. Unrequited love really was the most torturous thing ever. She thought of the *Fisherman and the Syren*, a painting she'd seen in a big book of art she'd taken out of the library. How desperate the syren is to get the fisherman's attention. That's what it was like. Desperation. She needed to draw it. Get it down on paper. 'How about then, for every question I get right, you tell me one thing that you find hard. And I'll see if I can help you. Payback for helping me with the strange triangles.'

'It's an isosceles, and I'm already getting paid for this. But if you need an incentive beyond passing your Maths test and not watching your mum have a nervous breakdown about it,' he knew Luna's mum well, 'then for every *five* questions you get right, I'll tell you something that I find hard.'

This was possibly the most motivated that Luna had ever been in a maths-based context. Still, it was an incredibly painful process for all concerned as she struggled through trigonometry for the next twenty minutes.

'When will we ever use SOC A TOAH again?' she huffed. 'It's pointless.'

'If you want to build a bridge or something, you'd use it then.'

'Because that's likely. You know I'm going to law school.'

Emmett sniggered. He'd been perfectly patient this whole time.

The thought of law school and not quite so much time spent drawing made Luna feel queasy. And guilty, since she was so lucky to have parents who encouraged her, wasn't she? Her mum called law a noble profession. It was more noble than drawing blades of grass.

'That's five questions. Fess up, one thing you find hard.'

Emmett wasn't often in a playful mood and Luna intended to take full advantage of it.

'One question was technically the example that we did together but alright.' He drummed his fingers on the edge of his chin. Emmett had a couple of strange straggly hairs there.

'I could have come up with ten things already,' Luna said.

'Mum,' he answered simply and Luna thought that the game wasn't particularly fun anymore.

'Oh.' Luna feared that she might cry again.

Emmett shrugged. 'One of her friends died earlier this year, of an overdose. It's not the first time, you know that. It's just shit. I always think it'll make her stop. But it never does.'

Luna couldn't imagine living a life where these things happened. 'What can I do to help?' she asked. 'I want to help.'

'Nothing . . . There's nothing anyone can do to help. Fuck knows Earl has tried. I don't want to always be so angry at her, but it's hard when she picks . . . *that* over me. Like every day.'

Luna fiddled with a loose thread on the bed. She hated feeling hopeless when it came to Emmett and Tanya. She wished there was more that she could do.

'I don't know that she has much of a choice in the matter,' she said, after way too long. 'Parents get caught up in their own stuff too, I guess.'

She meant her own parents, and the fact that their constant arguing was incredibly hard to live with.

'I guess so. Still shit, though.'

'Super shit,' Luna agreed. 'It's fine to be angry about things that are hard.' Luna meant this for Emmett. Her own anger always came laced with a side of guilt.

Emmett nodded. 'Right, more maths.'

Somehow, Luna seemed to be getting worse at the triangles. Emmett was very patient though, and never laughed at her, even when she couldn't manage to add three to four successfully. Luna reckoned that her brain just didn't work in that way. (She also reckoned that she'd have been better off with one of the dusty old teachers. Maths was hard anyway, but maths with Emmett next to her was pure torture).

'Five more, done.' At this point, Luna would normally reward herself with a biscuit, a chocolate hobnob for something as soul-destroying as maths. But settling for one of Emmett's sad secrets would have to do.

Emmett coughed and shuffled on the bed some more. Mae had moved onto Celine Dion, 'My Heart Will Go On' – she had her eyes shut and was conducting an imaginary orchestra.

'Another thing that I find hard is with Cadence, right?' Emmett shuffled again, immediately uncomfortable while every cell in Luna's body felt like it was standing to attention. 'Er, I'm not sure I want to hear about your love life,' she said, even though she did, she absolutely did. Tell me, tell me it all, Emmett, she thought.

He laughed. 'No, it's not that. It's just the fact that sometimes, she like wants me to be happy all the time. But I don't think I'm built for that. And she wants to stay here, after school and stuff. I can't wait to leave.'

Luna had mixed feelings about this revelation. Emmett wanted to leave. She knew this and that hurt, since Luna couldn't imagine Emmett in any place other than this. But also, with a bit of luck, bouncy Cadence would be the architect of her own downfall. Emmett twisted his fingers together. Luna felt that the air of the room had become thick.

'Well, I mean, I don't really know about this sort of thing.'

'Sounds like you have plenty of experience to me.' Emmett frowned. Luna wondered if she'd ever recover from the Man Plan.

'Yes, about that,' she said, wondering why she sounded so breathless all of a sudden. His leg was practically touching Luna's on the bed. His bare leg (he was in shorts) and her bare leg (also in shorts). Bigger than his but still, naked skin, it was basically pornographic at this point. Luna couldn't think of a way to confess at this exact moment that Mae made the whole thing up with regards to The Man Plan. She would have to scrape her self-esteem off the floor. 'Well in my experience, I think you should be able to be yourself, in a relationship. Like, you don't have to be happy if you're not feeling it.'

Emmett looked, for a fraction of a second, as if he was studying her face, looking at her so intently. He was closer than he was a few minutes ago, she was sure.

They heard Luna's mum laughing with Eyebrow Clive and while Luna knew logically that she could hear them because Mum was in the back garden, to Luna it felt like they were in a different galaxy, a different universe perhaps. She was almost certain that the way Emmett was looking at her meant something. And Emmett looking at her like that made her feel like they were the only two people alive.

'I don't know how to do it. Act happy if I feel depressed.'

'Are you depressed?' Luna asked. 'It's okay if you are.'

'Sometimes I think I am. I feel angry all the time. Do you think that's okay?'

Luna shrugged. She really didn't know. 'I don't know. Honestly. My mum and dad are angry with each other a lot.'

Emmett laughed a soft laugh. 'My mum doesn't know who my dad is.'

'I wish we'd known Earl and Sebastian when they were together.'

Emmett was closer still, so close that Luna could see the few freckles on the bridge of his nose that he said go away when it wasn't summer.

Was he, was he leaning forward? Like as if he might kiss Luna?

Luna tilted her head forward, heady with anticipation. They didn't kiss, but he rested his forehead against hers. This was the closest they'd ever been. Luna had a slightly strange, vaguely dark thought that if she could, she would fuse their brains together like this. Then all of his thoughts would be hers too.

Teenage love is an unwieldy creature, but she could feel his breath, and she loved it, so who cared?

'It's just so much easier with you.'

So love me instead! Love me most of all! Luna thought. End it with Cadence, and let's live happily ever after already. The thought made her pull back from Emmett. They were still close, though, so close that she could see the light flecks in his eyes.

It was obvious that Emmett just didn't like Luna in that way. Otherwise, he'd be with her. She was sure it was because she was so big. Who wanted to kiss someone who could pass for a teenage wrestler if they were all oiled up.

She gazed with longing into his face.

'Don't mind me.' Mae cut through Luna's frantic, desperate thoughts, talking in an exaggerated whisper and rolling off her bed. Emmett whipped his head away from Luna's so fast, she jolted forward from the lack of support. 'You two look to be having a moment, so I'm just going to . . . ' She pointed at the door.

Whatever moment they were having was ruined. Chances were that what Luna thought (hoped?) might be a moment was actually just Emmett confirming that even though it would be easier to go out with her, he still didn't want to do that.

'Sorry,' Emmett said, looking at the newly vacated space on Mae's bed. 'I don't know what I was thinking. I forgot she was there.'

'That doesn't often happen with Mae.' Luna wasn't sure where to look or what to say. 'Anyway, should we get on with some more maths?' It was the best she could come up with, and possibly the only time in her life when she'd realised that more maths might be a solution as opposed to a problem.

Emmett agreed. They slowly and painstakingly worked their way through the rest of the little triangles. Both careful not to say anything untoward, both careful to stay focused on the problem at hand.

'Hopefully, there'll be no cause for maths when I'm a lawyer,' she told him.

'Nah, you'll need it to work out all the money people owe you.' He closed the textbooks and got up to put them on the dresser. Luna could sense his mood shifting, like the rolling of dark thunder clouds across the sea.

'They have calculators for that.'

He laughed, a sad laugh, and Luna thought, for the hundredth time, how it would be so much easier *not* to feel like she did.

'Are you coming to The Edge later? Earl said something about a fire,' he said.

'Definitely. Mum and Dad are having Eyebrow Clive over for dinner so we might be a bit late, but we'll be there.'

'Cool, see you later, Luna.'

It could be so much easier than it was.

'Yeah, see you, Emmett.'

Chapter Twelve

The rest of the summer was a stupidly warm one. Hot and close (though not quite in the way that Luna might like it to be) like an ice lolly that melted in the sun, leaving a sticky, sweet residue all over your fingers.

Luna had a strange sense all summer that she was neither here nor there. Like she was standing on the border of two countries, a foot in each one. She saw the friction between Emmett and Cadence now, like dark fissures in an otherwise beautiful landscape. It should have helped her. It should have made her feel better about everything. Except it didn't. Because Emmett wanted to leave, Luna now knew for sure.

And when Emmett got into another fight, one of his worst, Cadence wasn't there holding a wet tea towel to his cuts; she was asking him why he couldn't control his anger, for her sake if nothing else.

Emmett's mood worsened. Becoming stormy and sullen.

Luna felt in some way responsible for this, though she wasn't sure why. She painted and drew and listened to David Bowie on repeat. Anything to get the feeling out of her. She read grown-up books like *Brave New World* and *The Grapes of Wrath,* both loaned to her by Earl, and then she drew some more. When she wasn't drawing, or trying to coax a smile from Emmett, she sketched in her head.

'Another super cheerful piece, I see.'

Mae had appeared at the edge of the garage that Earl used as his studio. The door had to be kept open. There was a good chance the paint fumes would knock them unconscious if it wasn't.

Luna stepped back from the canvas. She'd painted an eye. Not as part of a face, just on its own. It was dark and bloodshot, and she'd got the inspiration from *1984.* The flecks of green, so similar to Emmett's, were pure coincidence.

It was quite dark.

'Eyes are really interesting,' she said defensively.

'And technically very challenging,' Earl added over his shoulder. 'Watch your lines there, Luna.'

'I get that. But painting dismembered body parts over the course of summer wasn't quite what The Man Plan was meant to achieve.'

Earl laughed; it was unspoken between them that Luna felt the way she did about Emmett.

'Are we having a fire tonight?'

It was their last night. A fact Luna was trying not to think about. It only added to the sense that she was floating, hovering somewhere between two opposite worlds. One here, and one at home, which didn't feel like home.

'Yeah, let me just finish up. Earl, are you coming?'

'Perhaps, if I finish here.'

Earl's piece was decidedly brighter than Luna's. She wandered over to look at it, tilting her head at the way the shapes were all blurred. There was a face in the middle, the clearest thing on the canvas, but there was something not quite right about it. In the background, there was a white building on a hill, its borders also blurred.

'Is that?'

'Paris,' Earl nods. All his pieces lately were set in Paris. 'It's Montmartre. Sebastian and I were very happy there. Lots of artists you see. It was always so busy. Buzzing, as you say.'

'It's just like, really interesting.' That was the best way that Luna could describe it. It didn't feel adequate, but it wouldn't be right to describe it as beautiful. Deep and interesting, maybe. 'What will you call it?'

'I'm thinking *Montmartre in Motion*.'

Luna looked some more at the blurred lines.

'How did you do that? Make it so that the people in the background look like they're moving?'

'It's easier when you have a subject that gives itself over to movement. But I used brighter colours at the front and kept the desaturated tones for the shadow. That helped.'

'It's perfect.'

'Thank you. Here, you try.'

Earl handed her the pallet knife and she very carefully added a small sliver of shadow to the edge of one of the people in the background of the painting.

'That's all I dare do,' she said.

'You artists are so dramatic,' Mae said. 'Couldn't paint the sunset, could you? I'm joking, I'm joking,' she tacked on quickly. She knew that Luna worried about the fact that she didn't want to draw or paint nice things. That she worried that there was something dark inside her.

'We don't paint things Mae, we paint—'

'Feelings,' she cut Earl off. 'I know, I know. Always the drama.' They were both smiling, though.

'We'll meet you at the beach, Earl.'

Luna dumped her brushes in the bucket they kept for cleaning.

'Can we go home first, Mae? I need to change.'

'I wouldn't go home,' Mae warned her, still waiting in the sun by the entrance. 'Mum is in the garden with Eyebrow Clive. She's wearing a bikini. It has frills.'

'Jesus.'

'I know, what a time to have eyes.'

Luna felt like there was a rock in the bottom of her stomach, as if she was weighed down by guilt. It was impossible to ignore the fact that their mother had been spending an awful lot of time with Eyebrow Clive.

Mae told them how Eyebrow Clive had asked her mum to apply some bronzing oil as she'd gone into the kitchen.

'The door was open – I heard it all. Who wears bronzing oil any rate? It's like dousing yourself in butter and getting cooked. No wonder his skin's so leathery. So that's when I decided to make a run for it. It's four o'clock anyway.'

Four. Wow, the whole day had passed Luna by, though

time always seemed to speed up the less they had of it. Luna had been surviving off a family-sized bag of cheese crisps; the tips of her fingers were stained orange. Dorito dust and sand were not a good combination, experience had taught her this, but she'd no desire to see her mum with Eyebrow Clive either.

'Okay,' she agreed. 'I'll take your word for it. We can go straight to the beach.'

Luna looked a mess. She was sure of it. The heat of the garage had made her frazzled and her clothes were paint splattered. She thought of Ariel, the mermaid, and how great she looked on the beach in that sparkly dress. Unfortunately, Luna was not Ariel. She felt like the love child of King Titan and Ursula.

'Excellent,' Mae says.

Earl's garage was just on the edge of the village, alongside three others; an old couple let him rent it because they didn't have a car. They called goodbye to Earl and headed towards the beach, cutting across the bowling green and behind the castle to get there.

Luna kicked her flip flops off; the sand hot under her toes. She loved this beach. No beach that she'd ever seen was as nice as this one.

She and Mae trekked along it as Luna tried to commit every detail of the scene to memory. They wouldn't be back for another year. Even with all the darkness swirling around inside her, she still loved it here more than anywhere else in the world.

Mae snaked an arm over Luna's shoulders and Luna realised that she was crying again.

'Is it because The Man Plan failed?' Mae asked, hanging back and looping an arm around Luna's shoulders.

'No, it's not the Man Plan. That was a terrible idea. You made me sound like a sex addict.'

'When in reality, you're more like a nun.'

'I just don't want to go home.'

Mae linked their hands together. 'Don't blame you, it's a hellscape there. But the end of summer means we're another year closer to getting out.'

'Yeah, that's true.' Luna didn't exactly feel great about getting out either. It was just hard to envision a future that involved quite so much writing, quite so little drawing.

'And maybe this year you really will get a boyfriend, since Emmett and Cadence have lasted way longer than I'd predicted. I'd wonder what he sees in her, since they always fight.' Mae thought about it for a second. 'Her tits are great, so it's probably that.'

It was impossible not to laugh.

'Speak of the devil,' Mae said, nodding ahead. Emmett sat alone on the beach, just down from The Edge.

'Couldn't fall for someone a bit more cheerful, could you?'

He was looking out to sea. His knees were up and his arms were resting on top of them. Luna thought that the vast expanse of sand before him made the sea feel a million miles away.

'Emmett, hi!' Mae went running towards him. Luna

didn't run. Running wouldn't resolve the unending pressure she felt, so what was the point and – oh no.

'What happened to your eye?' Luna asked Emmett, sitting next to him on the warm sand, Mae sat on his other side as he held a bag of frozen peas to his eye. They were used to seeing Emmett with cuts and bruises, though it was always still shocking to Luna to see his face all marred. And this was much worse than normal. Luna was sure he needed stitches.

'Mum,' is all he said. Luna knew that he was trying to hide how much the bruises made his face throb.

This couldn't keep happening. Could it? Why wasn't anyone doing anything about it? Whenever Luna looked at the cut on the side of Emmett's eyebrow, it was like white noise in her head. There was already a bruise there, and now this.

Luna saw Zadie and Ahmed, sitting together a little way off, looking their way. She moved over to talk to them.

'I can't believe his mum actually did that.'

'It's been bad this summer.' Zadie was cool and Luna felt this like the slight it was. She'd barely seen Tanya this year, too busy stewing in her own dark thoughts. 'Emmett threw out her supplies,' Zadie finished.

'Crap, that's bad. But why is Emmett on his own? Where's Cadence?'

'He said he wanted some peace,' Ahmed answered. 'We're just giving him space.'

'It's different for you and Mae,' Zadie finished.

Luna looked back; Mae still had her head on Emmett's shoulder. He'd shrugged an arm around her. Maybe Luna was wrong, all this time thinking that Emmett only wanted to be friends. Maybe Emmett had always thought of them as family.

Luna was making her way back towards him, totally at war with the soft sand.

She thought about how they skimmed over the worst parts of the way that Emmett lived – flattening the edges like a rough stone made smooth by water. But sometimes there was no getting away from it, like how he always ate really quickly, and how he let Mae cut his hair because he couldn't afford a barber. This was far from the first time he'd had a black eye.

Luna didn't even talk, she just plonked herself on the sand, graceful as a hippo, and took hold of his hand, lacing his fingers between her own. Earl arrived with a tea towel wrapped around some ice, and Luna pressed it gingerly to the side of Emmett's eye, watching as he winced.

'Me and Cadence broke up,' he said eventually.

Luna found that she didn't feel any sort of a way about this news, actually. It was hard to feel anything but worry with Emmett like this.

'Never mind,' Mae patted his knee, still sat on his other side. 'She was a bit annoying, to be honest.'

That at least made them laugh. 'She just didn't get it, about Mum. She doesn't understand. It wasn't right for ages before, though. I'm not even sad. Or not about that anyway.'

Luna hated any insinuation that Emmett could be sad about anything. Hated it.

They didn't talk any more about Cadence or Emmett's mum for a while. They were all strangely polite, in fact, while they built a fire. They kept it up, the politeness, as the sun began to set and the temperature dropped. Emmett gave Luna his jumper. It had holes in the cuffs.

Zadie sat close to Ahmed around the fire, and Luna wondered if maybe, finally, his persistence was wearing her down. Or perhaps it was just that on the other side of Emmett getting hurt, they all felt soft and malleable.

It was late, almost fully dark now, and Luna knew that they couldn't stay much longer. Her mum would realise they weren't back at the cottage at some point.

'Fancy a walk to the water's edge?' Emmett asked, stretching out a hand to pull her up from the sand. She went willingly, all thoughts of mum and Eyebrow Clive forgotten.

'I can't believe that it's our last night,' she told him as the moon appeared hazy in the sky.

'Every summer goes too quickly.'

'It does.'

Luna had a sense that they were on the edge of something. She didn't know what. There was a tension in the air, like Emmett was holding back. His black eye looked darker still in the dark.

'Do you think your mum will be okay?' she asked and he smiled, finally. Luna felt something loosen within her. Like a tight screw that had finally given. 'What?'

'I like that you care about her, that's all.'

'Course I do, she's your mum.'

'Not everyone is like you, Luna.'

She didn't know how to respond.

'I've missed you this summer,' Emmett said suddenly. They were at the edge of the sea now, dipping their toes in the freezing water. 'I don't think I realised . . . ' He paused and Luna was sure the world held its breath. 'How much I would until you weren't there.'

'I've been right here,' she told him, half laughing, half worried that she might cry.

'I know, it's just, I don't know. It felt different.'

Oh god, she thought. He knows, he knows it all.

'Not bad different.' Something in her face must have given away. 'Just different.'

'I suppose we're both growing up,' Luna tried.

'Yeah, it's probably that.'

They kept walking, skirting the edge of the water.

'But promise me,' he said, stopping to turn to her, 'promise you'll never leave me, Luna.'

'I'm leaving tomorrow.' Luna felt urgent, for what she wasn't exactly sure.

'Not in that way. Promise me I'll never lose you.' She saw his desperation in the white of his eyes.

'You won't,' she told him, meaning it but not asking for the same from him.

They walked some more. Emmett was calmer, now that he'd extracted the promise from Luna.

'Earl said your drawings this summer have been amazing,' he said. 'You're so talented. He said you could be a prodigy.'

A red flush hidden by the darkness appeared over Luna's face. 'I'm definitely not. I've been frustrated all summer, trying to capture the uncapturable.'

'And what's that then?'

Obviously, she wasn't going to tell him about drawing dismembered body parts and what that may or may not have to do with unrequited love so instead she said, 'I've just got really interested in anatomy. It started last year, with hearts, I suppose. Thinking about how intricate they are but also how we give them so much power, on lots of different levels. Like emotional, biological. I don't know, I'm not making much sense. But yeah, hearts, I think I like drawing them. I even painted some. And eyes. Ears even. I drew a single finger last week. It's a bit weird. I liked the hearts the best.'

'Not weird,' he said. 'Awesome.'

Growing up where she did and with whom she did, Luna wasn't quite sure what to do with such a persistent stream of compliments.

'Thank you.' She was stiff and awkward as she stopped walking. They were facing each other now. Emmett's eye looks so sore, it made Luna want to weep, or else break something.

There was a pause.

'I'm worried that my brain is broken,' Emmett admitted. 'Sometimes I just think what's the point, things will never be good.'

'You can't think like that,' Luna rushed out. 'It's just a bad patch now but you'll get away, like you want to. You'll have a good life, Emmett.' Emmett having a good life, Luna realised, was what she wished for more than anything else in the world.

'Do you think I should feel broken-hearted about Cadence?' he asked.

And still, they were on the edge of . . . something?

'Only you can know that, Emmett.'

He shook his head. 'I don't. I don't even care. I don't like the thought that someone could ever break my heart in that way.'

'That's sad.' The moonlight was making Luna truthful. More truthful than she should be.

'Luna, look,' he started and she wondered for the briefest flicker of a second whether he felt it too. That growing bundle of feelings, like the rise of dawn ready to break. Emmett reached for her hand, taking the edge of her fingers in his. 'You know you're my best friend, right?'

'Right.' She dragged the word out. She wanted more, she knew she did. But she always wanted to be his best friend.

'And I couldn't ever lose you.'

This was it. Surely this was it. The sea, the sand, the freaking mood. This. Was. It.

'Yes.'

'Emmett, Luna. LUNA!'

Mae.

Luna thought, not even apologetically, that she could kill her sister right now. She was running down the beach towards them, panting. 'Mum called the police because we weren't home! She's gone batshit. Properly batshit! Earl is talking to them now.'

'Fuck.' Luna looked back at the fire and beyond, the flashing lights of the police car parked right on the edge of the cliff by the caravan park. She couldn't help it – she started to laugh.

'Why are you laughing, you lunatic? She's going to ground us for a year.'

They were so close. So close.

'I'd better go,' Luna told Emmett, moving to take his jumper off.

'Keep it,' he told her.

'See you next summer, Emmett dude. If any of us survive that long.' Mae hugged him hard.

'Yeah, see you next year. I'll write,' Luna promised. She hugged him too, trying to squeeze every last drop of this evening out of him.

They started to run up the beach.

'See you next year!' he called after them. 'I'll be waiting.'

'I'll wait too!' It was a pointless thing to say. After all, Luna was never not waiting for Emmett. She might always be the one who leaves, but when she looked back to see him smiling, his black eye half swollen shut, she knew that she would wait for him always.

Chapter Thirteen

NOW

Longing for Human Connection: Oil on canvas. Psychologically intense, this piece features more detailed brushstrokes to create a haunting yet romantic depiction. While there is some perception of depth, other features, such as the horse's eye, are distorted. Despite this, the work contains elements of levity, the colours are jovial. c.2006.

'You want me to stay in Paris. With you. For a week. Visiting the places that Earl painted,' I state as the piano hammers out a crescendo in the background.

It's not how it's meant to be, Emmett and I in a place like this. A place that's quaint, refined, distinctly unwindswept. It's not how we've ever been.

We're messy and ill-defined. We don't just come out and say what we want from the other. We tiptoe around it for years instead.

'Give me until Friday. Look . . . ' He pauses and pushes his hair back, and I think that this, this is more familiar ground, with neither of us exactly able to say what it is that we want. 'I've been working on this.'

'What is this? Working with who?'

'Communicating. I've been having therapy.'

'That's good, Emmett. I'm pleased for you.' I say the words and will them to be true. I am pleased for him. I just wish that things were different.

'I miss you, Luna,' he tells me, and I'm taken aback. He catches my eye and I shake my head, trapped somewhere between awe and fear and confusion. Sometimes I think I hate him, but not for the fact that he left me. I deserved that, since I lied to him. What I hate is the fact that I was the happiest I'd ever been in my life until he left. I hate that I've never been as happy since, that the world has never again felt so colourful. But then at other times, I think that loving Emmett was so intense and lonely that I half prefer the duller tones that I live with now. Hate is exhausting.

'Emmett. I—'

He cuts me off. 'I should have reached out before now but I needed, I don't know, time. So much has changed but you've always been my best friend, Luna. Always.'

He doesn't look away.

I'm rendered mute by the directness of his words. Honesty always came at a cost with Emmett in the past. But not now, it seems.

'Let's visit these places, the ones Earl painted. It just feels, I don't know . . . right.'

I should say no. There's no point in getting close to Emmett again; there's no point in getting close to anyone. It only makes it worse when it has to end.

But I've never had any control when it came to Emmett. I've disliked myself more than him for it. How I just waited for him back then, how I'd have done absolutely anything for him. It makes me feel so weak. So I should gain some of the upper ground here, tell him that I have my own plans for tomorrow and then I'm going home. That I'm worried that getting close to him and then losing him again would destroy me.

But then maybe humans have never been very good at doing the things that are good for them. Because despite how on edge I feel, how much I'll suffer for this later, how much of the truth I'm hiding from him right at this second, I do want to spend more time together. I'm a glutton and time with Emmett is my punishment.

'How would it work, logistically?' I ask.

Emmett smiles. 'Well, I do know the city pretty well.'

'Course you do.'

'We'd visit the places from his final collection in Paris. There must be a reason that the last painting he ever painted, the one of you, is the only painting he ever wrote a message in. I think it was for you. All these places meant something to him and Sebastian. Maybe it'll answer some questions and I don't know, settle some things. For us.'

I drum my fingernails on the table. The truth is, the thought of trekking around Paris, visiting the places that

Earl painted, well, it terrifies me. Knowing that he loved Sebastian so much that he painted him decades later is a frightening thought. I don't want to believe in a love like that. It's devastating, knowing that a love so potent it endured and endured exists in the world. Imagine knowing that and yet never having it.

'I just don't know if I can, Emmett. I'm meant to be focusing on my blog. I'm mid mini-series I can't let my followers down. We're a very close community.'

'What's the mini-series on?'

'Earl's paintings,' I answer guiltily, knowing exactly how Emmett will respond to the news.

'Well, that's perfect then,' he promises. 'We can go back to MAM and film there and then see the places in real life.'

I pretend to take some more thinking time. It's a small win, infinitesimal really, but when you lose as often as I do, you have to take what you can get.

'If you give me until Friday, I'll make sure that you have the best mini-break in Paris that ever there was. In Earl's honour. We can do it together,' he finishes.

It's a slightly painful reminder of what we'd promised each other every summer, when we were a 'we' and not a 'he and I'. I've always been good at hiding my heartache from Emmett. I'm torn. On the one hand, I want to tell Emmett to please leave. That no one gets to steamroll straight back into my life and send me on some art-inspired quest. But I also want to honour Earl's memory, I want to see these places. I, too, have so many unanswered questions.

'Okay fine,' I say, already feeling like something is unravelling – I just don't know what. 'One mini-break slash quest in Paris. For Earl.'

'One *perfect* mini-break, quest in Paris, for Earl,' he agrees, holding out his hand. I reach over to shake it and I'm struck by how warm and firm his grip is. It's like everything about modern Emmett. Assured. 'Now,' he says, after quite a substantial shake, 'are you having dessert?'

Scrolling through the comments underneath my Art of Dying post from earlier, I'm not surprised to see that a ton of my regulars have figured out that I'm in the new Earl Spencer painting. I should have told them right away, since not much gets past the Deathers (well, in the very niche world of death art), but I'd planned to blog live from the MAM until I got accosted there. I do have twenty-five new followers though.

> **DarthPainter:** Deathers! Does it look like our leader might have been keeping something from us ...

Darth is my favourite follower. He joined a couple of months ago and he's always just so supportive. He has a link to the MAM exhibit under his comment and there are seventeen more comments discussing it underneath his. An argument has broken out between followers who think I shouldn't have kept them in the dark and those who think I have a right to privacy. Darth is defending me, as usual.

VincentVanGetOutOfHere: I knew Luna was famous!

ColourMeIntrigued: Do we think it's really her though?

DarthPainter: Why are you always so quick with the conspiracy theories? It's obviously Luna. The face, the hair. Course it's her.

TheRealPicasso: I've been researching and Earl Spencer lived in Bamburgh, Northumberland. I cross-referenced some stills from Luna's earlier video blogs, and I think she might live there too.

Under this comment, there are some screenshots from the background of earlier vlogs, taken out of my front-room window. Behind me, they've cross-referenced the picture with a shot of the centre of Bamburgh. You can see the corner of the castle in the background.

There's nothing an internet sleuth can't find out. Once, they figured out that I'm left-handed because I had an ink stain on my left thumb. It's like the Wild West out there.

I settle on my balcony. It's dark, but the light from the hotel room lights me up enough. Normally, I do a mixture of written and video blogs, but my hands feel weirdly stiff, so I'll be videoing all the way in Paris. I hit record.

'Good evening, Deathers! And welcome, new followers to the Art of Dying, the channel that connects you, the slightly morbid public, with works of art concerned with death and dying. I can see already that some of you have figured me out. You're right, yours truly does feature in the newly discovered painting by Earl Josef Spencer. Course it's a much younger version of me.'

I hit pause while I have a coughing fit, trying to ignore how decidedly not well I feel.

'It's a bit freaky to think that someone's had a painting of you hanging in their living room for two decades. Mona Lisa has my sympathies. But now you know why I want to do a deep dive into Spencer's work.'

Another pause, another coughing fit.

'So I'm planning to visit the sites that feature in Earl's final works and seeing if I can uncover some death art along the way. But for now, Deathers, I'll say goodnight. Tomorrow, my quest begins.'

I listen to the clips and edit them together. My voice is raspy from so much talking today, but it's good enough, so I add a link and hit post.

There are a million messages from Mae, and I'm still feeling tight-chested and tanked up on adrenaline, so once I'm done, I call her.

'I've agreed to spend the rest of the week with Emmett.'

'And a very good evening to you too, dear sister. It's nice to hear from you, but a message at some point in the last four hours would have been appreciated, you know.'

I hear someone calling out to her in the background.

'Have you literally broken off mid-fling to come to answer the phone and lecture me?'

'No, and anyway, it's not a fling. It's less fling, more regular hook-up now.' I hear mumbling in the background. 'You're welcome, babe.'

'I presume that wasn't for me?' I ask.

'No, that was for . . . the person staying here.'

It's not like Mae to be cagey about her love life. There's too much going on to worry about that, though.

'You know, we don't need to talk right now.'

'I think we should since this is big news indeed. You're off gallivanting around Paris! Proud of you, sis.'

'I couldn't gallivant even if I wanted to.' I'm trying to be funny, but I just sound sad.

We're both quiet for a minute then. Just listening to each other breathe down the phone. It's probably a bit weird.

'You haven't told him, then?' Mae asks.

'He doesn't need to know.'

'It's just like last time.'

'It isn't,' I say, trying to convince myself as much as Mae because, really, so many things feel exactly the same.

Chapter Fourteen

When it comes to Emmett, it's hard to feel in any way neutral. In fact, there are so many emotions when it comes to him, all jumbled and confused. But one thing has remained true this whole entire time: I've missed him.

And today we get to spend the day together.

He'd told me not to have breakfast and to meet him at some café, which isn't far from my hotel, at 10am. So that's what I'm doing. I round the corner and spot the café. It's on the edge of a tree-lined street, and it's proper Paris. A red and white striped canopy reaches out from above the windows, giving some shade from the early September sun.

I've even forgone the headphones.

Emmett is there already, at a little round table just outside. Again, I'm struck by how far away from Northumberland Emmett this Paris Emmett is. It looks like he was born to be here, not some decrepit caravan with cardboard boxes for curtains. He's wearing a soft grey T-shirt and dark jeans, and it's not a combination that I am spiritually prepared for.

He stands up as I get nearer and puts down the newspaper

he's been reading. It's in French and I'm thinking it's going to take every ounce of my determination not to fall back in love with him by the end of breakfast.

'Luna.' Another smile. Those blasted teeth. 'You look great.'

I mean, I'm happy with what I'm wearing. I have my denim cutoffs on and a white shirt with a big collar with red and pink flowers all over it. I love this shirt. But I don't look neat and polished like Emmett. I'm crumpled and messy, every inch a woman who has a small cauldron in her bedroom and is allergic to ironing. I'm wearing so much statement jewellery that I'm weighed down by it. It's a good job that I'm determined that I won't fall in love with him in Paris, because chances are that I wouldn't be new Emmett's type at any rate.

'Here, sit down.' He pulls a chair away from the table for me and I sit. Last night felt weighty and heavy, and there's still some of that between us this morning. But mostly, the new day has brought a freshness too, and I'm excited. Plus, when I checked this morning, The Art of Dying had over a hundred new followers.

I catch Emmett looking at me and tuck some hair behind my ear. Young Emmett was never still, he never stopped moving, like a ball of pent-up electricity, always ready to spark. Whereas older Emmett, he's still all of the time. He's assured in a way that seems so grown up.

'There's only a couple of things on the menu,' he tells me. 'But I think you'll like what they're offering.'

'Okay, but remember, I'm paying.'

'Fine.' He smiles.

This had been agreed last night since he'd covered the cost of dinner. I hadn't even seen how much it was, but the bill had come in a little velvet pouch, and the dramatic waiter had bowed when he presented it, so I know it was bad.

A waiter wearing skintight black jeans and a black tank top with sleeves of tattoos on his arms comes to take our order and I ask for the same as Emmett ordered. I heard croissant and chocolate so I figure I can't go far wrong with that.

'Where's your hotel?' I ask as the waiter leaves.

'Just around the corner. It has a great pool.'

'Wow, a pool. You've changed, Emmett,' I say, looking at him over the top of my sunglasses.

'I don't have the things most people have to pay for. No house, no car. I help Mum and that's about it.'

'It's good that she has you.'

He shrugs. 'It's just what you do.'

It isn't what my family do, or did, not anyone except me and Mae, but still, I get it. It's what you're meant to do.

The waiter returns with a tray. It has two croissants on it and cups of what appears to be liquid chocolate. There's another little dish too, this one with whipped cream. I watch, suddenly starving as he decants the cream on top of the hot chocolate. I am here for this entire process. Excellent Paris. Best city in the world.

'*Merci beaucoup*,' I say, diving straight in. 'Oh my god,' I say after a sip. 'It's like drinking chocolate.' It reminds me of the Dairy Milk bars I used to hide in the sun to melt and then drink.

'It is.' Emmett rips off a bit of croissant and dips it under the cream.

'Yes, I'll do that too.' I follow suit. 'Wow, excellent, no notes.'

I continue to proclaim just how excellent my breakfast is while Emmett watches on with a kind of bemused smirk.

'So you come here when you aren't being a doctor? Or are you a doctor here?'

He shakes his head.

'I'm mostly posted abroad.'

'To, like dangerous places?'

'It's not so dangerous, honestly.'

I roll my eyes.

'What?'

'Just stop being humble about it. You always were too humble about your brain. You should be proud of it – it's a solid brain.'

A smile. 'Well, when you put it like that.'

More eating. 'No, but seriously, it's pretty safe.'

'What made you do it? Over like just getting a job in a hospital like normal doctors?'

He shakes his head. Okay, so he hates that idea. 'I always wanted to travel, to get away . . . '

I think of young Emmett and all of his *National Geographic* magazines.

'Yeah, but I thought you meant backpacking around Laos, not dodging land mines in – where did you just get back from?'

'Somalia.'

'Yeah, Somalia.'

'No land mines though.'

'Right, well, that's good then.'

'It is. I don't think I'd be able to focus on work so much if I was dodging land mines the whole time.'

'Land mines are no laughing matter, Emmett.'

'No, I suppose they aren't.' He smiles. 'I don't know, initially, I think I just wanted to get as far away from home as I could, after uni. I feel comfortable moving around a lot and I can relate to people living difficult lives. Not that I grew up in a war zone, or anything like that. Though The Edge felt like it came with proverbial landmines.'

'Come on, it wasn't that bad.'

'It really was, Luna.'

It's strange how my memories of The Edge are those of a child. When I was younger, I was sure that The Edge was such a cool place to grow up, a fun little community. Of course, as an adult, I can see it for what it was: a pocket of poverty, tucked away on a cliff edge. Mostly, I can see that.

'Hey, remember when that couple from plot forty-three held a swingers party in their caravan and someone called the police?'

'The police were always at The Edge. Mae was at the party, wasn't she?'

'Yeah. She said she never realised that dicks could go wrinkly.' I laugh at the memory.

A lady at the table next to ours in a perfect pink two-piece gives me a dirty look.

Emmett sees, and then he's laughing even harder.

'Stop it,' I tell him. 'You're going to get me thrown out of Paris. And I can't believe you just compared a war zone to Northumberland – which is lovely.'

He stills a little, more serious all of a sudden. 'That was part of the problem, though. You always wanted to stay, and I always wanted to leave.'

Ah. It had been nice, to have a break from being sad for a while, even for a few minutes. At least I got to enjoy the hot chocolate of my dreams before it came back. Because Emmett certainly did leave. He left me, on the side of a cliff, weighed down with so much guilt it threatened to flatten me.

'I really am sorry,' he tells me. 'I was young and stupid and fuck I know they're not good excuses but it's the truth.'

'It's okay, Emmett, it was a long time ago. Please stop saying sorry.' I don't think I can stand it.

I want to tell him that so much has happened since then – some things just as bad – no, worse – than him leaving me on that cliff's edge. But I don't want to go there, not on our perfect mini-break in Paris.

'Here, let me pay, and then we can head off. We need to go to MAM remember?'

'It's our first stop.'

We've decided to go back to MAM to look at the exhibit properly.

'Do you think Mari will tell me where the painting came from?' I wonder out loud to Emmett.

He pauses for a second and then shrugs. 'You could ask her. She might not even know though, if the seller used a broker.'

'True.' It's probably hopeless.

I pay for our breakfast, assuming that it was a fraction of the cost of our meal last night. 'Actually, maybe I should pay for lunch too.'

Emmett stands and fixes his sunglasses in place. He looks like he should be on a billboard some place.

When we emerge from a short subway ride, my hair is running static, and my pulse is erratic. The steps of MAM are right in front of us, and I'm doing my level best to forget about the fact that yesterday, a whole crowd of people tried to talk to me in there. I've been resisting offers of therapy for some time but do you know what, perhaps I could hypnotherapy that particular memory away.

'Ready?' Emmett asks. It's quite possible that my newly formed trauma is written all over my face. Oh, and my hands are shaking. So that's excellent.

I nod.

We take the wide white steps slowly. Emmett leans forward and says something in French to the woman with the pixie haircut behind the counter. He flashes her a smile, and she repays his efforts with a look that screams, 'Impregnate me!' and scuttles off.

'She's gone to check whether Mari, the curator, is in the office today.'

I make a hmph sound, attempting a sort of moral superiority. As if I too didn't fall head over heels for Emmett's smile that very first time. Well, not the first time, we were five and that would have been strange. But as soon as it was age-appropriate to be lusting after his canines, I was there.

'What?' he asks. But he's smirking.

All around us, people pay and get tickets to the special exhibit on Earl in MAM; the museum is free otherwise. I still have my sunglasses in place. It's hardly the disguise of the century but needs must.

Assured Emmett is unsettling. He doesn't appear to need fixing anymore, that's for sure. He's all fixed and it's like someone set off a myriad of tiny fireworks just under my skin. It's reassuring, too. This is the man he was always meant to be.

It just leaves me feeling out of sorts.

Our little French pixie is back and my French might be crap by any standards but I get that saying '*Désolée*' over and over and shaking her head isn't good.

Emmett gestures to me and I reluctantly lift my sunglasses up. I do it by pressing on the bit behind my ear so it's like they're on a hinge.

I see Pixie's eyes go impossibly wider, and she begins tapping on a computer, before writing something on a scrap of paper and handing it to Emmett. I swear, if it's a phone number I'll . . . I'll do what exactly? Nothing, I'd do nothing.

But I'd be fine with Emmett hooking up with the French pixie while I trudge around Paris in disguise and try not to die. That would be fine.

'So, good news and bad news,' Emmett cuts in as I'm mid-spiral. Wow, I can't wait to get home. In Paris there's just so much spiralling. It's dizzying.

'Hit me with the bad.'

'Dark – I like it.'

I roll my eyes.

'Chloe was just telling me that Mari isn't here today.'

Okay. That isn't even in the same ballpark as Emmett running off with Chloe to have wild, passionate sex by a set of open windows while tulle curtains flutter in an autumn breeze – and wow, that image came to me way too easily.

'Does Chloe know where the painting came from?' I ask, hopeful.

'No.' He shakes his head. 'But when she saw you, she said that Mari had mentioned the girl who was in the painting. She said you fled yesterday.'

Now would be a good time for it all to end.

'Fled is a strong word. More like I made a regular exit from the exhibition space. I don't like being around lots of people.'

'I thought you ran a blog with loads of followers?'

I don't think I told Emmett how many followers I have.

'It's just a regular amount. But it's different when the people aren't like, right there.'

I cannot tell Emmett that things got so bad that I

developed an unhealthy obsession with death art or that I got so lonely that I started looking online for friends.

'Okay, well, Chloe said that Mari mentioned you yesterday and said that she'd love to talk to you again.'

'Right.'

I draw the word out.

'Apparently they all have access to each other's diaries here and so Chloe has booked you in for eight tomorrow morning. If that's okay?'

'That's fine,' I say, only slightly disappointed that I won't get to ask about it today.

'I'll come with you, if you like, in the morning.'

It's a reminder that we have three whole days together after this one. Time with Emmett has always been like this, snatched and short, but never feeling like that at the outset.

'Okay, that would be nice, thank you.'

The space around us is full, and I'm starting to feel claustrophobic in the entrance.

Emmett smiles. 'I'll go tell Chloe.'

Chloe is waiting by the counter, looking over at us both. As Emmett walks towards her again, her face lights up, and I have to turn around and stare at the floor – you know, a totally normal reaction.

There's a hand on my shoulder. Emmett.

'Would you still like to go in today? We could see the exhibit properly? And plot out a route of all the places Earl painted in Paris?'

Emmett has his list already and I dare say we could both

recall all of the paintings in our sleep. But seeing Earl's art was always guaranteed to cheer me up, so I readily agree.

Chloe has apparently given us a free pass, a perk of being the subject of their star painting in their star exhibit. It's not much, but I'm a woman living a wholly perk-free existence, so it brings me momentarily out of my funk.

We walk past some of the main exhibits, catching *La Danse* by Matisse, and I spot a collection of Gromaire's. He'd be a good one to feature on the blog, another artist whose life and work were shaped by the First World War.

Earl's exhibition space is quieter today, but small clusters of people are still milling around. Unlike yesterday (how was it only yesterday?), I don't make a beeline for *The Edge of Always*. Instead, I walk to the closest painting to the entrance. I realise that they've ordered them chronologically, covering the last five years of his life, from the first painting he sold, down to his last. Earl didn't always work as an artist, though none of us know exactly what he did the whole time. There were rumours that he'd been everything from a circus performer to an undertaker. He always painted, of course he did, but so much of Earl's truly early work has gone, disappeared forever.

I recognise everything here; all of it was painted in the garage in Northumberland, a county he was apparently drawn to because he heard it had good mint cake. A part of me just wonders if he wanted to escape after years of looking for Sebastian.

'His paintings were so bright, weren't they?' Emmett asks,

standing next to me. It's true, we're looking at *The Weight of Light,* the river one as Mae called it, since it's the Seine. It's more expressionist, bright colours and heavy strokes; we wouldn't even know that it was a painting of the Seine if Earl hadn't talked about it. He'd told me that though he didn't like boats particularly, the views from the Seine were some of the most beautiful he'd ever seen. And this is a beautiful painting. It's reds and oranges and pinks, which give way to blues and purples. It's romantic and lovely, and it's impossible not to smile when you look at it.

'I always wanted to paint things like this,' I say to Emmett. 'Pretty colours, you know.'

'But you rarely did,' he answers.

I shrug. 'It wasn't what I noticed.'

The little card at the side says, *The Weight of Light*, to reflect the fact that the river looks to be holding up the sky. '2005.'

'Are you going to record, for the blog?'

Emmett had suggested this yesterday, but I hadn't taken it seriously. I'd never normally record somewhere like this, with so little preparation.

'Do you think I should?' I ask.

'Definitely. The Deathers demand it.' Emmett laughs.

It would be a nice touch, to record next to Earl's first painting. 'Could you, maybe, record me?' I ask Emmett.

'My pleasure,' he says, taking my phone and pointing it at me. I take a deep breath, I'll only get one shot at this, since I'd rather die than ask him to film me over and over.

'Okay, I'm ready. Go.'

Emmett holds up a thumb.

'Hi Deathers, and welcome back to the Art of Dying, the blog where we connect you, the slightly morbid public, with works of art related to death and dying. That is, until today. As you all know, this week I'm in Paris at the new exhibition of Earl Josef Spencer, since Spencer, very mysteriously, painted yours truly into his last piece. I didn't know about *The Edge of Always*, but I did know Spencer, or Earl, as I think about him. So here I am in MAM, standing in front of the first painting that Earl ever sold. *The Weight of Light*.

'I was there while Earl painted this. I watched him use an old kitchen towel on the waves. He told me once that water was hard to paint, but I think we can all agree that he did a brilliant job of it. When I asked him why he painted this particular river, he said that it was just a really beautiful place. He was good at that. At seeing the beauty all around us. It's something I've struggled with, over the years.'

I keep talking, whispering since we're in the exhibition space still. Although I didn't plan to film in here, it feels right. It feels so right to talk about Earl, too. I thought it would be hard, talking about things from The Time Before but that's not the case. It's easy. Emmett had said that this mini-break was for Earl, and I don't think I realised what that meant, but perhaps he's right: perhaps neither of us got the closure that we needed . . . after.

So it comes easy, talking about this painting, about why it's so full of love and life, because that's what Earl was. It doesn't even feel strange talking about a painting like this on a channel devoted to death and dying. The Deathers know about me. Mae thinks that they're all just there to watch my slow decline like a load of weird grief tourists. But there are others in my followers, too, and I like that it feels like I'm not alone in this. Honestly, it often feels like they're the only people who get it.

I finish what has only been a couple of minutes by saying how proud I am that Earl's work is getting the recognition it deserves, and Emmett turns to pan my camera down the length of the exhibition so that the Deathers can see the scope of it.

He comes back to me.

'And that's everything. Have a great day, Deathers.'

I've already decided that I won't tell them about Earl and Sebastian, that's private, but for an off-the-cuff video, it couldn't have gone much better. I don't even edit it.

Emmett is still pointing the camera at me.

'It's fine now, you can stop filming.' I tell him.

He's still staring at me.

'That was brilliant, Luna.'

I laugh. 'Hardly, it was a three-minute video blog.'

'It was brilliant. Earl would love that you're doing this.'

I can only hope that Emmett is right. I'm self-conscious now, though. Speaking into a void is so much easier than speaking to people.

'I don't know.'

Emmett is on his phone. 'How do I sign up, to the blog?'

'No, don't.' I'm louder than I plan to be. I even reach for

Emmett's phone before I quickly drop my hands. 'I have a no friends or family policy,' I tell him. 'It's private, that's all.'

He frowns, and I silently urge him to drop it. To not push me on this.

'Am I a friend again?' he asks.

Of course, the answer is that I don't know if I could ever be just friends with Emmett; we're playing with fire even spending this time in Paris together.

'I've recently amended the policy to include ex-boyfriends.'

He laughs at that, and the tension passes.

'So will we take a trip on the Seine, since Earl painted it?' I ask.

'I think we should.'

Emmett slides his phone away and instead pulls out a notebook and pencil out of the back pocket of his jeans. The whole carrying-a-notebook thing is seriously hot. He checks his list of paintings as we walk.

The Weight of Light – The Seine

Longing for Human Connection LG.

That's the one of Sebastian on the carousel horse. I don't know where it might be, but LG must mean something to Emmett.

Montmartre in Motion.

That's easy, we know where that is.

The Juxtaposition of Life and Death – PL cemetery.

And finally, the enigmatic blue door.

The Rubicon ????

My heart sinks. It's clear that Emmett doesn't have any clue where the blue door in Earl's second from last painting might be. There are other smaller paintings between the main exhibition pieces, sketches too, some half finished. I recognise Tanya in one or two, or else parts of Northumberland, like Holy Island, the dunes we often went to. But the main ones, they're all Sebastian. Sebastian was undoubtedly Earl's muse, until he wasn't.

Frankly it seems ridiculous that Emmett thinks we can get any sort of answer from visiting these places – we don't even know where all of these places are. How do you discover an answer when you don't even know what the question is? And yet it still feels right to be embarking on our Earl-based pilgrimage of grief and longing. The exact sort of thing I should be doing right now, in the final furlong.

My legs are starting to ache from all the standing up. I'll need to go and rest soon. We don't look at *The Edge of Always*, since the closer I get to it, the more I notice people starting to look at me. I tell Emmett I need to sit down, and he doesn't question why. Instead, he takes me to the café here at MAM where I sip on a coffee, feeling quite unwell.

'Is it okay?' Emmett asks.

I nod my head and force myself to take a drink.

He doesn't say anything, and when we're done, we make our way back outside. I already feel better from the warmth of the autumn sun.

'What do we do now?' I ask Emmett.

He's put his sunglasses back on, and would it be strange if I asked him to warn me before he did that? It's inhumane, looking at him in those sunglasses. He tilts them down, the way that Mae used to do, to look at me.

'It's river cruise time.'

We walk along the path on the banks of the Seine, a slow pace which, let's be honest here, is necessitated by me, and clamber aboard a vast boat with low sides and several vending machines.

I feel this isn't the same as the boat Earl and Sebastian probably went on, but needs must – a boat is a boat.

Emmett, of course, looks like he was born to live on a fucking river cruise. We're standing up top, by the front of the boat as it skims the water – the Eiffel Tower on one side, Notre Dame in the distance on the other. The wind from the cruise is making me all ruffled, but I love it. It's familiar and comforting, the wind. Emmett points out parts of Paris as we glide past them, and I find it incredibly sexy, how much he knows, how erotic it feels to have him stand behind me like this. I allow myself to think, just for a millisecond, how it might be if things were different. If everything were different. It hurts too much to think about a future where Emmett, in some indefinable capacity, is back in my life. Or it would hurt, if it weren't for the fact that I'm not going there.

My phone rings, and I take it as a welcome reprieve until I see that it's Mum.

Mum rarely calls unexpectedly. We normally talk at 7pm on a Sunday night, a ritual that we endure for reasons that I can't quite recall.

'Sorry, it's Mum,' I tell Emmett, half relieved to have a reason to move away.

'Mum,' I have to half shout into my phone to drown out the water smashing against the sides of the boat, even at this sedate pace.

'Luna, it's your mother.'

'Yes, I saw that. What's up, has something happened?' I come from a generation genetically programmed to believe that if someone calls you, it's because there's been a death. Unless it's Mae, who knows no boundaries, personal, digital, or otherwise. It'll be Clive. The guy's ancient. He still has the most impressive eyebrows, though.

'Is Clive okay?' I ask. The signal is patchy and I can hardly hear what Mum is saying. It doesn't sound like she's saying that Eyebrow Clive has died. I think she'd be happier if he did. She once said that it'll be nice not to have to argue over the TV remote when he goes.

'Clive is fine, Luna. But listen, you need to come home right now.'

I lose her a little at the end. But I got the 'come home'.

'Friday, I'm home Friday,' I tell her as we pass under an ornate bridge.

'No, Luna. You must come back.'

'Why?' I ask her. 'Has something happened?' I'm a little confused.

'Think of your health, Luna.' For one short minute, I'd like to not think of my health, actually. But never mind.

'Dr Dave okayed the trip. I could get back quickly if I

needed to. Don't worry. And I messaged about Art Therapy. They were happy for me.' It's the truth. Hospices are much more about living than dying, after all. If anyone would know that, it's me.

'Except I do worry, Luna. Because I'm your mother.'

Her worry has always felt like an obligation, a millstone around her neck forcing her to act in a certain way. It's not dissimilar to how mothering was to her – it just doesn't come naturally. And we're long past the time where I did as she asked.

'Well don't. I'm having a nice time in Paris and I'll be home on Friday.'

She goes to talk some more but we pass under another bridge and so I call down my phone, 'Sorry, signal's bad. Got to go, bye!'

As I hang up, I feel rattled by the call. Anyone who lives with illness knows that you can't ever fully escape it. If you're not thinking about it, then you *know* that you're not thinking about it, which is still thinking about it, in a roundabout way. I know I can't escape my illness in Paris, just like I couldn't escape it if I went to the ends of the earth, but it was still nice to try for a moment.

I walk back to join Emmett. He has two hands on the railings and is studying the impressive façade of Notre Dame as we pass it on our left.

'How is your mum?' he asks as I slide my phone back in my bum bag, slotting it in between my meds and hoping that Emmett doesn't see.

'She's okay. You know that she always was a lot, but she's become an even more extreme version of herself as she's got older.' The boat comes to a stop and starts to turn around.

'I didn't think that was possible.'

'Yep. And the age difference between her and Clive. He's a really old man now – I don't think she enjoys looking after him. But then she never was super maternal. Last Christmas she told Mae that having us was a mistake. Blamed Dad for making her have kids. She had been hitting the port hard, though.'

'Still, that's . . . not good.'

'Nope.'

'I don't think I realised, back then, how tricky things were for you at home. I was so fucking selfish.'

'You weren't. And anyway, even if you were, that's the teenage brain, isn't it. Designed for self-involvement. I know mine was. It's no one's fault, how Mum and Dad were.'

Emmett looks at the water for a second and then nods.

'How is your dad?' Last time Emmett saw Dad was the summer we broke up, so of course, Emmett doesn't know.

'Oh, he died.'

Over the years I've trained myself not to sugarcoat delivering this news. I just don't believe that it's my responsibility to make the person I'm talking to feel more comfortable about the fact that my dad died.

Mae says that it's my 'heinous bitch' move.

It happens before I even realise that it's happening. Emmett wraps his arms around me, and at first, I'm struck by how much bigger his arms feel. I thought that at eighteen, Emmett was a man, but I see now that he wasn't, not properly. Neither of us was an adult then. I think that, really, I should be pushing him away. It's not conducive to living a nice, neutral life, being on the receiving end of hugs like this, where the colour is becoming dialled up. Hugs that are warm, tender and firm all at the same time. But it's like my body refuses to stage any sort of resistance. Instead, I'm practically dissolving into the hug, letting Emmett take all of my weight. I'm a rag doll in his arms, and my bones are melting. I'm hanging on for dear life here.

'I'm fine, honestly, it was ten years ago.' I pull back from Emmett as a tear escapes from behind my sunglasses. My dad wasn't really any sort of great man. He's not in any of the history books. But I worry that no one thinks about him, that one day, there'll be no one to remember that he ever existed.

'He got the cottage in the divorce. Everyone wondered why he wanted it so bad, seeing as it meant living next door to Clive and Mum initially. But he fought for it. He knew he was dying, you see. Before anyone else understood what was happening. He left the cottage to Mae and me.'

'Shit, Luna. He was way too young. That summer . . . I didn't know.'

'I know. It's okay. Death doesn't know to wait for old age.'

'No, it doesn't.' We're still standing really close together. 'I'm glad he had you and Mae at the end. People who are dying are even more in need of love than those who aren't.'

He must mean that this is something he's seen in his work

as a doctor. It's impossible that he'd be talking to me, though that's how it feels. Anyway, I'm not sure that I agree. Part of me thinks it's a waste, loving someone when there's no hope of a future. It just makes everything worse.

'Anyway, it was a volatile situation – Mae and me living next door to Mum and Eyebrow Clive. They cruised a lot and then moved away. We hardly see them now.'

'She called just now though.'

'Because I never go on random trips. I hardly ever leave home.'

We aren't far from the dock now.

'Why is that?'

I shrug. 'I just like it there. I'm happy, or content at least. I don't need loads of excitement in my life.'

'I don't know if that's sad or admirable.'

I laugh. 'Being out in the world was always your dream, not mine. Earl got that, I think.'

Emmett nods. 'I just wanted to get away,' he says.

'I know,' I answer. 'Maybe I just didn't realise how badly you wanted to go.'

This cruise, inspired by Earl, has thrown up more questions than answers. Emmett and I don't talk for a while, both lost in memories of the past. It was true what I said to Emmett. I am content. You don't have to be over-the-top happy every day. It's fine. A perfectly serviceable life is fine. And so what if it's a little greyer than I would have liked? That's just the way it goes. A degree of cynicism gets everyone in the end.

Except, I'm looking out at the most beautiful of sights.

Emmett, against the backdrop of the Seine, the sun catching every place where the water ripples. So when I say that everyone becomes a cynic one day, it feels like I'm trying to convince myself of it. And when I picture Earl, out here on the water with Sebastian, I think that cynicism didn't come for him. Not ever.

'What do you think Earl was trying to say, painting this?' Emmett asks after a while, looking back out at the river. A beautiful woman with huge gold earrings is leaning against the railings while her boyfriend snaps pictures.

'Maybe he wanted to remind us that whatever happens, the world can be beautiful,' I suggest.

He follows my line of vision across the water, and then he's looking at me.

'He wasn't wrong.'

I hold his gaze until I'm uncomfortable again. Hot and flustered from too much feeling.

'Or maybe he just wanted us to enjoy a nice river cruise.'

Emmett laughs and offers me his hand as we get off the boat. The Eiffel Tower is right there.

'Can we go up it?' I ask, thinking that I'm ready to move on now.

'If you like?' Emmett phrases it like a question.

'I can't come to Paris and not go up the Eiffel Tower.'

'In which case, follow me.'

When I said I'd like to go up the Eiffel Tower, I'd assumed we'd take the lift. But there were no tickets left for the lift, only the option to walk. It genuinely hadn't occurred to me that people would actually climb this giant metal tower. Like as in, up a set of never-ending stairs. And yet here we are. Mostly because I didn't want to admit to Emmett or the man in the ticket booth that my heart is not cut out for this. I consider bowing out, saying I'll do it next time. But I of all people know how precarious that kind of promise to yourself can be.

We've just passed a sign that says we have ten minutes to go until the first viewing deck. I presume first, as in, not the top. Emmett has barely broken a sweat. I admire the bravery of a man who attempts to climb a gazillion steps in grey.

'We should go back down.' He looks worried. It goes without saying that while Emmett, who is probably naturally fit from dodging land mines, sails up the steps, I am, quite literally, dying.

My face is red. I'm gasping for breath; I can feel my puffy ankles throbbing. Emmett looks concerned.

'We definitely should just go back down.' he says, frowning from a few steps above me.

I wave him off. 'Sorry, I'm just really unfit. I'll be fine. I just need to go slow.'

'Are you sure?'

'Just. Need. To. Go. Slow,' I pant, entirely winded.

He nods and mutters something that sounds exactly like 'stubborn'. 'We can rest on the first viewing platform.'

'Great,' I wheeze, giving him a thumbs up. My other hand is clinging to the handrail. I really am unfit.

And go slow I do. I lose track of how many people pass me, zipping up the steps. Emmett doesn't know it, but I've entered my own personal battle of the wills. I will climb these steps. It might kill me. But I'll climb them.

Someone passes me, carrying a small child on their shoulders. Well, they're just showing off.

A family, too, jostle past us, all joking. The grandma, an old lady with a grey perm and a cigarette hanging out of the side of her mouth, snaps something in a language I don't recognise and takes off ahead of me.

Dr Dave, Mum, Mae, so many people would be annoyed if they could see me now. I should tell Emmett the truth, I know I should, I just . . . don't want to. Mae was wrong – this isn't the same as before. This time, the decision to lie to him is mine and mine alone.

Still, there's a very good chance that all will be revealed when I die here on these steps and they autopsy my poor little wrecked heart.

Maybe I'll get a plaque at the point where I expire on the climb. Even though if I look down, we don't seem quite so far away from the bottom. There's more tower above than below us.

But finally, miraculously, I see the first floor ahead. I've made it. I'm a mess, but I'm here.

'I'm going to get back to the gym when I go home,' I tell a now very concerned-looking Emmett. I catch a bit of my own reflection in some glass and almost scream. I look like I crawled out of the catacombs.

'Okay, let's go and sit down.'

Emmett was right. There's a café on the first floor. I don't want to sit down, though. I want to look at the view, fat ankles be damned. 'Could you maybe just get me some water? I'll be fine. I want to look out for a bit.'

'Course, if you're sure?' Obviously, I look like I'm about to drop dead.

'Sure. Thanks.'

I move to look out at the view. It's expansive. I don't know if I ever realised that Paris was quite so vast. I guess that some people might have something of an existential crisis in the face of so much vastness, the realisation that they're just one of billions of people. But I like it. I like thinking that I don't matter, that I'm unimportant. It makes it all so much more bearable somehow. Pondering the meaninglessness of my existence while I die a third of the way up the Eiffel Tower is comforting if you think very hard about it.

'Here you go.'

Emmett, thankfully, has opened the water. I don't think I have the strength of bicep, and my arms are shaking. I drink, feeling like it's restoring some of what I sweated out on the walk. I'm all gross and sticky.

'You look deep in thought,' he says and I suppose I must be, since it takes me a moment to respond.

'Just thinking about how big it all is.' I look out some more.

He nods. 'It reminds me of Northumberland. The beaches and the sea. I never liked how big they were. I was worried that I'd get lost.'

It's not the same landscape, not by half, but I see what he means.

'Whereas I always liked that about it there, I think.' It's true. I just want to pass through, unnoticed. Causing as little turbulence as possible.

'You never did realise how important you are.'

Emmett, I'm sure, is standing closer than he was a few moments ago. And oh no, he can't say things like that to me. I'm not important, I'm not. I can't be. It's all so much worse if I'm important.

We aren't going there, so I change the subject. 'I might need to nip back to my hotel and change after this. It's not far away.'

The idea that I might nip anywhere after that performance is quite frankly laughable. A tortoise could do more nipping than me.

'Course, no problem.' It's disconcerting. Not just being in a giant metal tower in the sky, but the fact that Emmett is so easy here.

We're still looking out over Paris, where it stretches off in the distance, and I feel a little sad that there's no way I could possibly see it all. There's not enough time. There's never enough time.

Emmett is standing next to me, close but not too close. It amazes me, that after all these years of feeling guilty, or sad, or guilty and sad, and some periods of neutrality too, I suppose, it amazes me that we're here, brought together again by Earl.

Over his shoulder, there's movement, a shriek of delight, and a whoop of a cry.

'Look,' I tell him.

There's a man on one knee, holding out a ring, his partner standing in front of him, her hands over her mouth, sobbing.

For a second, I'm choked up myself as she shrieks, 'Yes, YES, of course yes!' and then there's a fair bit of kissing and some gentle applause from those of us standing watching them. Proposals are probably ten a penny up on the Eiffel Tower, but it's still nice to think that you've witnessed a life-changing moment for two people. It's a lovely moment. I don't quite know why I suddenly feel so melancholy.

'How do you think they know?' I ask Emmett.

'Probably, people just know. It's letting themselves believe it that's hard.'

Neither of us say anything for a moment and yet the air feels charged. Emmett and I have always been good at dancing around what needs to be said, and this is no different.

'Should we go down?' I say eventually, and Emmett nods. We obviously aren't going any further up. I'm not sure I can. I need to lie down.

We begin a slow descent. Going down is easier than going up, but I'm still winded from that. My legs feel stiff and wobbly. I have a sense at all times that I'm going to miss the next step. Emmett is two steps ahead of me and he keeps looking over his shoulder, I assume to check whether I'm going to collapse and crash down the steps.

Down, and mercifully on the ground again, we begin the slow walk back to my hotel.

'I just need to rest for a little while,' I tell him. 'I had glandular fever last year and it really knocked me. I didn't realise that I'd got so unfit. You don't have to stay with me, though; I can meet you later if you still want to have dinner?'

It's late afternoon now. My medication alarm beeped on the way down, but I didn't see how I could reasonably stop and explain taking a bunch of pills.

'I'll stay,' he says. 'But only if you don't mind. Just want to make sure you're okay.'

'No, I don't mind. There's a balcony; you can sit out there if you like. And when I get home, I'll get a personal trainer. A Russian one who makes me cry.'

Emmett nods, only mildly appeased. We keep walking in silence. Emmett looks to be thinking; there's a frown line between his eyebrows, which is a dead giveaway. I'm not talking because I'm concentrating on survival.

'You've never been married,' Emmett says eventually and I don't know if it's a question or not.

'I could be married now,' I answer.

He looks down at my slightly swollen hands; my rings are digging into my fingers. I'm wearing a giant owl ring on my ring finger.

'But you aren't.'

'No, I'm not.' I think about pretending to have a boyfriend, but I've been there before with Emmett, and it was a total farce. Mae said only yesterday that I'm a bad liar. And when you consider how much lying I do, you'd think that I'd have honed my skills a little.

I've never seen a partner on Emmett's sparse social media, but still, I ask the question.

'How about you? Anyone special in your life?'

He shakes his head. 'There have been people, over the years. It just never worked out.'

'Same.'

Because none of them were you, I think but don't say. It's normal, according to Mae, to compare all subsequent loves to your first love. It's less normal, I suspect, to break up with all of your subsequent boyfriends because they weren't your first love.

And now we're here, together in Paris. I try to ignore the little flicker of hope; snuff it out like a fading candle. I shouldn't even be thinking that way about Emmett. We have this one time – that's it. Brought together by Earl for three more days. It can't ever be anything more than that. His work, my life, the fact that I'm lying to him again. It's an impossible situation.

'It's here.' I'm so exhausted by the time we make it to the hotel – and so angry about the fact that I'm so exhausted – Emmett has to take my elbow to guide me up the stairs, a deeper than ever worry line between his pinched eyebrows.

'It's the glandular fever,' I babble as we climb the last steps, 'I have post-viral fatigue. I'll be fine soon. Just a quick nap and I'll be good to go.' I'm slurring my words. And Emmett looks seconds away from performing CPR.

I root around in my bag for my key, and then we're inside, and Emmett is guiding me towards the bed. He's pulling off my boots and socks, my shacket. He's right up in my personal space, and it's strangely comforting. I breathe him in deep. I'm acting weird, I understand that, but I might never get this again. In contrast, he is stony-faced and concerned.

He's tucking me into bed.

'Balcony . . . half an hour . . . ' I mutter.

'It's fine. Just rest.' He's still frowning, but I'm drunk on exhaustion, I've no energy to reassure him as I fall into a deep, dreamless sleep.

Chapter Fifteen

I wake up heavy and groggy because I didn't take my meds before I fell asleep. I reach over to get them – I always have them next to me – but it's not my medicine box that I feel, it's a solid mass – a man-shaped solid mass.

'Sorry,' Emmett says. 'There wasn't anywhere else to sit, and it was getting cold.'

Fuck, fuck. I've been asleep for hours. Outside the window the sky is the colour of burnt orange. The sun is setting, and the day has gone completely to shit.

Emmett is sat next to me, on the very edge of the bed, on top of the bedding. His long legs are stretched out before him, crossed at the ankles. He's wearing matching socks.

'I didn't want to leave without checking you were okay, and there wasn't anywhere else to sit.' He's still explaining the fact that he's on the bed, I think.

My room has always felt minuscule, but with Emmett here too, it's almost claustrophobic. Stretched out like this, he almost touches the wall opposite.

'It's fine, don't worry.' I scramble to sit upright, my head all woozy. I'm still in the clothes I wore to hike up the Eiffel Tower. I feel like I did when I was fifteen, gross and well . . . just gross mostly.

I look around for my bag. I need my meds. 'Are you looking for this?' Emmett holds up my pill organiser alongside a bottle of water. 'I saw some medicine in there when you were looking for the key. I thought you might need them for your post-viral fatigue.'

He's talking really slowly like my made-up illness has made me made-up stupid.

I reach for them. 'Yes, I definitely do. Thank you.'

I twist away from him and then throw down the afternoon pills like I won't survive without them, which I won't. When I turn around again, Emmett is smiling, but it's the smile of a porcelain doll. Slightly haunting and dead around the eyes.

'All sorted?'

'Absolutely,' I smile, making myself be genuine. 'Would you mind waiting while I take a quick shower? I feel all groggy. Then we can head back out. What's on the itinerary for the rest of the evening?' I try to peer out of the window to work out what time it might be. The sun is beginning to set behind the line of grey buildings by my windows.

'Course, take all the time you need. There's only one more place that I really wanted to show you today, anyway. It's not far from here.'

It has to be LG. The carousel horse.

'Okay, if you're sure.' I get the impression that Emmett has significantly scaled back his plans for the day after I moved like an injured sloth all afternoon.

'I am, don't worry.'

I pull out an outfit from my suitcase, doing my best to shield the chaos from Emmett. It's a long, swishy skirt and a bardo top that's super Paris.

I manage to shower and dress in the tiny bathroom, feeling slightly more human as a result. I give my body a pep talk in the small mirror, begging it to give me three more days. I'm Faustas, making a deal with the devil. But I don't want to know the whole world; I want this infinitesimal fraction of it.

Dr Dave says that if I accept the need to rest, I'll likely feel better for it in the long term. Dr Dave and I disagree on many points, and for just this day, that's one of them.

But still, I do feel better, and there's something bubbling deep in my stomach that feels like excitement as I emerge from the bathroom. I forgot how much I love this top. A good top can always save the day. I've pulled my hair into a low bun, and I have big hoop earrings in.

Still, I'm self-conscious, super aware that Emmett is in my personal space. Especially when he says, 'You're beautiful, Luna,' and smiles a genuine smile.

It's a reminder of how different this Emmett is, and I'm not mentally prepared for it. I just return his smile and say 'thanks' and try to pretend that I'm unmoved by the whole thing. Especially since I'm already dreading saying goodbye again. Our last goodbye nearly killed me.

Emmett obviously isn't getting changed, so we head down

the stairs. I need to check that I can extend my booking until Friday.

'Hang on a sec,' I tell Emmett and approach the front desk.

'I'm sorry, madame,' she tells me, 'but the hotel is fully booked.' She does look sorry, too. 'It's the views of the tower. They make it very popular.'

I mean, you can see the tip. But still, I tell her that it's no problem and walk away. For some reason, it hadn't occurred to me that I might not get the extra days. I could look for another hotel, I suppose . . .

'Bad news,' I tell Emmett. 'I can't stay the extra nights in my hotel. Do you know any other cheap ones?' I emphasise the cheap.

'Let me have a think,' he tells me as we begin to walk, slowly, towards where we're going.

'Where are we?' I ask Emmett as he leads me into a park.

'Jardin du Luxembourg,' he answers. 'The Luxembourg Gardens. It's one of my favourite parks in Paris.'

LG.

'It's lovely.'

The park has wide paths and colourful flower borders and bathed in the light of the early evening, it has an almost ethereal feel to it. There's a pond, a bundle of little wooden boats with tall sails gathered together at one side.

It's quieter in here than on the regular streets. Sleepy and peaceful.

'Come on, before it closes.'

I nod, overly emotional once again as Emmett leads me to the far corner of the park. Then, I see what he wants to show me.

It's a carousel. Old and wooden and . . . closed for the day.

Emmett goes to speak to an old man who is busy locking up the little green shutters on the ticket hut. I hear him and Emmett nattering in French as I wander round to look at the carousel. There are only two rows of horses, but they're beautiful. Delicately carved and painted, lifelike but also a little sad. It's so obvious now that this is what features in *The Longing for Human Connection.* I start taking pictures, thinking that it's impossible to feel neutral in Paris. It's just not the place for it. I send a picture to Mae.

> **Me:** Look where Emmett brought me.
>
> **Mae:** Omg he loves you still.

Behind me, the lights around the edge of the carousel flash on, sparkling in the early evening. It's magical.

'Giuseppe says we can ride it, if you like?'

'Guiseppe?'

'A friend of mine. His pa knew Earl.'

Guiseppe comes over, a wooden stick in each hand.

'You have to catch the wooden hoops he holds. Winner gets the most,' Emmett says.

'You're on.' I take a stick from Guiseppe, saying 'merci' over and over because it's clear as day he thought he was done with work until me and Emmett showed up.

'He's been here forty years,' Emmett tells me as I climb on a horse, running my hands along the smooth main.

'It's gorgeous.'

Guiseppe starts to push the carousel. He's obviously stronger than he looks because I think that's how it moves, manually.

I'm right; we gather some speed, the lights begin to blur and I'm taken back to another time that Emmett and I were on a carousel together. From the Time Before, when it felt like a whole lifetime was stretched out before me, a mass of colour. As I hook my first wooden ring and laugh when Emmett misses his, I sense it, hidden among a bunch of other emotions that are tricky to place, that same feeling of optimism for the future. It's not escape anymore – it's hope.

Optimism, I think, feels a lot like hope.

Longing too. I wonder if that's what Earl wanted us to take from this painting. Whether he knew somehow, that we'd need a reason to feel hopeful again.

I get another ring, and another. Guiseppe is making it extra hard for Emmett. I'm laughing, free, almost. Earl's painting brought to life.

At the end of the ride, I want to go again. But I also want Guiseppe to go home and rest since he looks as close to keeling over as I do.

'Merci,' I say again.

'You very good, Emmett very bad,' he tells me. 'Yes, yes, very bad indeed.' I smile. Emmett has one ring on his wooden pole, but his eyes are dark where he's looking at me laughing with Guiseppe.

He walks over with the air of a lion about to rip into a gazelle and I'm the gazelle, helpless to stop it. But instead, he hands Guiseppe twenty euros to much protest, and bids him '*bon soir*'.

It's almost fully dark by the time we make our way over to a patch of grass by the boat pond. The night is clear and the moon is bright, and I do my best to ground myself in the moment. To live for now, not some unpredictable future.

'Do you think that Earl wanted to remind us that life can be fun?' Emmett asked.

'I'm sure he did.'

'I don't have a lot of fun.'

'Me neither.'

We don't go into it any more than that.

I think about how it's just par for the course that Emmett looks impossibly even more attractive in the moonlight. Moonlight makes everything just a fraction more beautiful. Throw in the stars and it's practically obscene.

Emmett looks at me when he thinks I don't notice. I feel the same way, as if this can't quite be real, but I keep my peace until he finally breaks the silence.

'Would you consider staying with me?' he asks, not meeting my eye.

'What like, in your hotel?'

He nods. 'It's a suite. There's plenty of room for us both. It has a spare bed.'

This feels like a bad idea, the latest in a long stretch of bad ideas regarding Emmett.

'I don't know . . . '

'Think about it. You don't need to decide now.'

'Okay, thanks. And thank you for the offer.'

Emmett nods. Once.

After that, we just talk. I tell Emmett about how my blog started, an abridged version. 'I guess I just finally accepted that I'm drawn to the darkness.'

'Earl would have said you can't have one without the other.'

He means dark and light. And Earl did think that. That the light only shines so bright in contrast with the dark. But that's not what I feel. I'm not drawn to the dark to make the light ever more stark. Sometimes the dark isn't special, it isn't poetic. It's just dark.

Emmett disappears for fifteen minutes and reappears with a bottle of red wine. I take a sip straight from the bottle.

'I didn't really expect it to take off. The blog, I mean.'

'That's brilliant, Luna. I'd have a look, you know, if friends and family and ex-boyfriends weren't banned.'

He's smirking.

'It's important that we follow the rules, Emmett,' I say, even though I don't know what the rules are. I'm certain that Emmett and I are not following them at the moment though.

I messed up a couple of months ago and posted a link to The Art of Dying on my personal Instagram. I realised after half a day and deleted it straight away. It's easier to bare your soul to strangers.

The Deathers know I'm dying. Like I said, some of them are dying too (not in the way that we're all dying, which, by the way, is one of the worst things you can say to someone who is actually dying).

'Why did you stop drawing, Luna?'

'Lots of reasons, they aren't important.'

I think he's about to say more. To push me on this. I didn't want to answer him yesterday and I can't answer him now.

He doesn't though, so we drop it.

I have another sip of wine. 'How about you – how did you end up working for Médecins Sans Frontières?' I ask, trying for a French accent but sounding stupid.

He shifts a little. We've been sitting on the floor for some time.

'I specialised in emergency medicine and applied. It was pretty straightforward.'

Something tells me that the process is slightly more competitive than Emmett is making out. I'm rarely drawn to humble; I haven't found it so attractive in the past. But none of my rules seem to apply when it comes to Emmett.

'And that's when you learned to speak French?'

'Yep. It's not, like, a requirement. But lots of the countries we work in have French as their first language, so it helps. I'm not fully fluent.'

'You sound it.'

He shrugs. 'It comes back, the more time I spend in Paris.'

I assumed that he'd arrived at the same time as me, to see the opening at MAM. 'Haven't you just arrived?'

He shakes his head, looking off into the pond where the stars are reflected on the now-still water.

'I was here before. I'm between postings.'

'Do you know where you're going next?' I ask.

'There are a few options. I'm still weighing them up.'

I laugh, I don't mean to, it just comes out.

'What?' he asks.

'It's just that you're so calm here. So level-headed.'

'Ah, yes, well that would be the antidepressants.'

I put down my cup. Balance it precariously on the grass.

'Sorry, I didn't mean to pry.'

'You didn't. I offered the information. And you knew how I was, when we were younger. Therapy and antidepressants were an inevitability, I think.'

I don't feel ready for this yet, for a little heart-to-heart about his traumatic childhood. Back then, I tried not to think about it. Now, it hurts too much. I say something inane about how I'm glad the medication helps.

'It does, my head feels much clearer these days.'

'That's good. Really good, Emmett.'

And even though I wish things were different for me, for Emmett at least there's hope. It's everything I used to want for him.

I spend some time looking for other hotel rooms in the city but it's stupidly short notice and so I agree to stay with

Emmett. It a classic case of how things can feel so wrong yet so right at the same time.

There's a breeze in the air by the time Emmett walks me back to my hotel. I promise myself, that even if I never see Emmett again, after this time in Paris, at least we'll have had this evening. This evening has felt a lot like closure, and I've waited an awful long time for closure.

'So I'll see you outside MAM at eight tomorrow?' he asks, even though we've already agreed this.

'Yes, I'll be there.' I'll be setting alarms and then back-up alarms to make sure I'm there. We're standing on the street outside my hotel, spotlighted under a street light. He's close and I think how often we stood like this before, and how easy it would be to reach up and kiss him. He wets his lips, his eyes focused on mine, maybe having the same thought.

But no, I'm not going there again. It wouldn't be fair to me, or to him.

With hitherto untapped strength, when it comes to Emmett at least, I take a step back.

'I'll see you in the morning.'

He straightens too, shaking his head, just a touch.

'Yes, see you in the morning, Luna. Thank you, for a perfect day.'

And with that, Emmett walks away.

I'm desperate for some of my own space, some peace and quiet so that I can reground myself, but my phone has been blowing up constantly since I sent Mae the picture of the carousel. So, once I'm in my room, I skim through the gazillion messages she sent, focusing in on the last couple.

Mae: Are you shagging him now?

Mae: I can't believe you're having sex with Emmett.

Mae: Have I taught you nothing?

Mae: Is it good at least?

Mae: I bet he's really kinky. The mysterious ones always are :/

Me: I'm not having sex with Emmett. I'm in my hotel room, alone!

Mae: Okay, I don't know whether to be proud or not.

Me: He showed me around all day and looked after me when I took a funny turn this afternoon.

Mae: What do you mean, funny turn?

Me: I just got shattered walking up the Eiffel Tower. I'm fine now.

Mae: YOU WALKED UP THE EIFFEL TOWER?? I'LL KILL HIM. WHAT WERE YOU THINKING??

Me: That it might be nice to feel normal for once? I told him I had glandular fever.

Mae: Shit.

Me: I know.

Mae: You still didn't tell him then?
Me: Nope. I won't be telling him tomorrow either. Or the next day.
Mae: What are you doing tomorrow?
Me: Going to see The Edge of Always again. The curator wanted to talk to me. And other places from Earl's art. There was a cemetery, and a door, we don't know what that is though. I'm staying with Emmett until Friday. The hotel didn't have more space.
Mae: Wow. Lot to unpack there. Ask one of your internet sleuths to figure out the door. A whimsical art-inspired tour of Paris and staying in his bed. This is all sounding very romantic to me.

Mae might be onto something with the Deathers.

Me: Yeah, in a completely tragic way. Plus, there's a spare bed.
Mae: Course there is.
Mae: Aren't all the best love stories tragedies?

I shake my head at my phone. This isn't a love story. It's just a tragedy.

Mae: For the record, I still vote for telling him.

In a way, Mae is right. I should tell Emmett my secret.

I'm so weary of it all, but my being weary doesn't change the fact that I'm doing exactly what I did all those years ago – by not telling Emmett the truth. I barely admitted the truth to myself back then. But that one lie – it devastated Emmett so much that he left and never came back. I've thought so often about how I'd do things differently if I could have that time again.

So many secrets. Mistakes too. Earl, Emmett, *Ahmed.* Ahmed. That was not my finest moment.

But that's the thing: honesty this time around makes no difference. It makes no difference at all to how this ends.

Chapter Sixteen

THEN

Luna was 15
Emmett was 16

The older Luna got, the more it felt that time was moving faster and faster. When she was younger, the gap between summers seemed to drag on for an eternity. She had no sense of it; it was so big.

But this year had passed quickly. A blur of studying and exams and final days of being at school. Signing shirts and crying with her friends over their lost childhood even though they were all going to the same school for college. The feeling that things were ending and just beginning all at the same time.

'And I've double, no triple checked with school, Luna. We'll get your results first thing on results day,' her mum told her from the front of the car.

Luna was nervous. Her exams had been hard. Sometimes

she wished that her brain would just work better. It seemed odd that something which was so intrinsically a part of her wouldn't bend to her will and learn the equations she needed it to with more ease. She'd taken to drawing brains. Studying prints of them and wondering how it could be that that mass of slimy tissue could contain the essence of who someone was. It fascinated her. Mae had called the drawings her most detailed yet horrific to date.

'We'll be proud of you, however you do,' her dad said, smiling at her in the rear-view mirror.

'Yes, of course,' her mum agreed, her voice more clipped.

'I'll disown you if you fail Art,' Mae tacked on.

'No one will be failing anything, Mae,' their mum said. It sounded like a warning.

Mae rolled her eyes. Last year, Luna would have felt so angry at this exchange. She felt so angry at everything, it was all that she could see. She felt less angry now, but she wasn't the same either. Mostly, she felt like she'd been through something.

'You *have* been through something,' Mae had said when Luna tried to describe it to her. 'It's called puberty.' They'd had a lot of time to chat since they were grounded forever after their mum called the police when they disappeared to the beach last summer. She referred to it as the time they were missing persons, even if it was for a total of eighteen minutes. And even though Luna and Mae were the ones who were grounded, Luna's mum also blamed Emmett and Earl.

When they were finally set free, Luna tried to get on with

living her life. She'd gone out and tried to do normal stuff, like drinking and kissing. But even when she was kissing Jacob Grangemoor from the year above, a tiny part of her was still wondering what it would be like if it was Emmett who she was kissing instead.

At least she seemed to have stopped growing, though she was still as strong as ever.

Mae was trying to paint her toenails in the back of the car and their mum was complaining about the fumes.

The usual chaos, basically. This summer's plan was The Glam Plan. Mae had said (and Luna was quoting directly here); 'If you don't get with Emmett this summer, I swear I will lose the will to live and emancipate from the both of you.'

They'd spent the last couple of weeks trying to become glam. Their mother, who honestly seemed delighted that Mae was finally taking an interest in looking like she lived 'somewhere other than a bin' had given them her Beauty Bible book. It was a massive pink thing with all sorts of hints and tips for being demure, ladylike, beautiful.

Mae had said it explained a lot about Mum.

The Beauty Bible was the reason Luna was wearing shimmery gold eyeshadow; she wasn't allowed blue anymore because she had blue eyes and according to the BB, as they'd taken to calling it, 'you wouldn't display sapphires on a blue cloth.'

She'd also put some lightener on the ends of her hair and bought a set of hair straighteners. She was wearing a cute denim skirt, which is stretched just a bit too tight over her thighs, and a massive brown belt. She was now the proud owner of three really thin scarves which were definitely just for fashion.

She still wanted to be smaller, softer, but she felt that she was making a decent effort to become the type of person that someone like Emmett might want to kiss. She wasn't exactly sure whether this was the type of person that she was meant to be. Luna wanted to be truthful, she wanted to know who she was and be that person. But mostly she felt like an enigma, even to herself. So being glam was better than nothing.

Mae had adopted a more lax approach to the suggestions of the Beauty Bible. She'd read the inspirational quote 'When you want something with all your heart, the whole universe conspires to help you achieve it' on the last page, called it horse shit and went back to dressing how she liked.

'The Glam Plan only applies to you,' she'd explained when Luna asked why Mae didn't have to wear clothes to match her skin tone, or put on so much bronzer that she was unrecognisable as the same person. Mae was wearing neon yellow right now, which made her look like she was dying from liver disease. 'I don't need a Glam Plan to win anyone over. I'm perfectly happy with the state of my love life.'

It was no real surprise that Mae was happy with her love life. Mae was perfectly happy with all of her life. Sometimes it felt unfair to Luna that Mae had just grown so easily into the person she was meant to be as an adult. Luna often felt like she was at war with herself.

'That's because you're an artist,' Mae had told her when Luna had confided that she didn't feel like she knew who she was, or not fully at any rate. 'You guys spend way too much time thinking about everything.'

That was part of the problem though. The only time when Luna felt like she was close to becoming the person she should be was when she was drawing. But she wasn't an artist. Her A-level choices were designed to help her get into law school. She'd convinced her mum to let her take Art as an extra on the side, but it had come with a warning that her mum 'expected Luna to make the right choice, if it all became too much'.'

The right choice was dropping Art.

But more and more, Luna worried that without art, even her weird art, there was nothing. Less than nothing even. A void.

'Isn't it a bit unfair that we've got to fly high at school *and* look amazing the whole time,' Mae had complained to Mum.

'That's the cost of being a woman in the modern world, Mae,' her mum had replied without a hint of irony.

Now, her mum and dad had started their regular A1 argument about their dad driving too slow. Luna tried to tune them out. She'd sent Earl and Emmett a drawing a couple of weeks ago. A small canvas where she'd sketched Bamburgh Beach at night, even though landscapes weren't her thing. She hoped Emmett got it. On the back she'd written their arrival date.

'Chill out,' Mae muttered. Luna was sitting on her hands

by the time they pulled up to the cottage. He was there. Emmett was living with Earl this year, since Tanya had gone to prison.

Luna was out of the car, Mae too. 'Emmett!' she called. He was taller again, and his hair was longer than ever, curling over the tops of his ears. He looked better than he had for years. Clean and bruise-free.

He wrapped Luna up in a big hug. He was thin, but Luna couldn't feel his ribs for a change.

Mae barged into them, and he let out a small 'oof'.

'You're here,' he said, looking at both of them and smiling.

Yes, Luna thought. And even though she was an enigma to herself, one thing she knew to be true was that here was exactly where she was supposed to be.

After they'd unpacked (read – dumped their bags at the foot of their beds), they decided to walk to see Earl in the workshop.

Luna couldn't stop looking at Emmett. It was always like this. The first few days, he didn't quite seem real.

He caught her looking and smiled.

'You look so different, Luna.'

Mae butted in and coughed something that sounded like, 'Glam Plan.'

'I know,' she carried on, 'she's ditched the black. Makes her look a lot cleaner, I think.'

They all laughed.

'Everyone's entitled to an Emo phase. I was always clean,

aside from paint. And Monster Munch dust,' she added as an afterthought. She used the conversation as an excuse to ogle Emmett. 'You're taller.'

'Er, that tends to happen when people get older.'

His face had more angles to it too, though Luna didn't say so. Instead, she went to punch him in the arm, except Mae got there first. 'Sarcasm is the lowest form of wit, Emmett.'

'And how are you doing, little Mae?' he asked her, which was plainly ridiculous. Mae was taller than Luna now.

They rounded the corner past the walled gardens, a few minutes from Earl's studio.

'Smashing life as per,' she answered.

It was true. Mae moved through life as if running through a slipstream.

They could see the garage door open ahead. Mae took off at a run, shouting 'Earl, Earl!' as she jogged.

'How were your exams?' Emmett asked as they walked towards the garage.

'Awful,' Luna answered truthfully. 'I'm so worried that I'll fail Maths. Mum will have a fit.' Luna worried, moments after the fact, that she was being insensitive. 'Sorry,' she tacked on. Tanya was in prison, after all. Emmett's problems had always been so much worse than her own.

'Don't be. Honestly, it's easier living with Earl. And my exams went pretty great, thanks for asking.' He was smiling and Luna thought that Emmett too, had lost some of his anger too. He seemed lighter, brighter. Hopefully, with Tanya gone, there'd be less fighting, or maybe it was just that fourteen and fifteen are dark years for everyone. As he walked, Emmett's hands waved about, his head constantly twisting. But his movements seemed more restrained than before. Less frenetic.

'No need to be so smug about it,' Luna said, but she was smiling. Seeing Emmett happy made her happy. It was as simple as that really.

They were at the garage now and Earl was right there, same as always in his shirt and trousers. His hat propped just next to his painting. 'Is that a . . . ' She asked.

'Graveyard.' Earl answered right away. 'The Pere Lachaise in Paris, though I admit, my memory of its paths is becoming hazier now – I'm not completely happy with it. Hello to you, Luna and Mae.'

Earl turned round and smiled and Luna thought that it was so so good to be back.

'Isn't it a bit jolly for a graveyard?' Mae asked. The headstones and statues were all painted bright colours – shades of purple, reds and pinks.

'How Victorian, Mae,' but Earl was smiling. 'Death can be colourful, I believe.'

'Well, let's hope none of us test that theory too soon. This summer better be a good one because we've had a year. Haven't we, Luna?'

'It hasn't been that bad,' Luna answered diplomatically, when really, Mum and Dad had been arguing more than ever. From their vantage point, eavesdropping at the top of the stairs, Luna and Mae had heard the word *divorce.*

'I wish they'd just get on with it,' Mae had said. But Luna found the thought of such a big change unsettling. They hadn't heard their parents speak of it since. So Luna tried to put it out of her mind.

'Well, you're here now.' Earl was wiping his hands on a dirty tea towel. 'Are you coming to The Edge? I took some brownies out of the oven this morning.' Luna would never be small while Earl was around.

'I thought you'd never ask, Earl. Lead the way,' Mae told him, linking arms and then launching into a blow-by-blow account of her year without coming up for breath. 'Ups and downs mostly. You know how it is.' she said. 'Tried to pierce my belly button, but it got infected, and I nearly died, but I did manage a soufflé that didn't drop, so I'd say it's a win overall.'

Emmett and Luna brought up the rear. It might have been wishful thinking but Luna was sure that he was walking closer than he normally would.

'Hey, the carnival is in town, do you want to go tomorrow?' Emmett asked, oblivious to what Luna was feeling about his proximity. It was to be expected, since Luna hadn't exactly been honest about her feelings.

'Absolutely. Sounds fun.' They were almost at The Edge now, the concentration camp sign greeting them hello.

Emmett paused, right below the sign. 'Best summer ever?' he asked, holding up his little finger.

'Best summer ever.'

*

They didn't go to the carnival once – they went every day for a week. by the final night, Luna had eaten so much candyfloss, she was at risk of turning into a ball of the pink and blue sticky stuff.

'I feel sick,' Mae slurred. Her pupils were big. Part sugar, part the fact that she'd been drinking blue WKD vodka. They were on the worst possible ride for someone to announce imminent sickness. A sort of deadly circle thing called the Wheel of Doom, which spun around so fast and tipped upside down. They weren't even strapped in; that's how fast it went. The neon lights of the carnival were a blur, and *Umbrella* by Rihanna was blasting out, pulsing inside Luna's skull.

'Hold it in,' Luna told her, her own stomach mounting quite the protest. Physics might not have been Luna's forte exactly, but she guessed that puke and the gravitational pull of the Wheel of Doom would be traumatising for all involved.

Mae turned her head to the other side and said the same thing to Emmett, where he was plastered into his little booth. As they spun Luna was sure she was being taunted. Tested somehow. Emmett's was the only face she could see.

Luna wasn't sure if it was part of the testing, or if she was quite unwell herself, but Emmett was in slow motion, saying 'no' to Mae over and over. Luna had eaten quite a lot of sugar and drunk some WKD too. It just tasted so much like a fun drink, it made her forget it was bad for her. It also made her forget about the fact that Emmett hadn't said anything about last summer, on the beach. He hadn't picked up the conversation where they'd left off. If anything, he was being extra friendly. Just very, very friendly.

So Luna was using blue WKD and sugar to dull her anguish at the fact. Mae had declared that Luna would make an excellent juvenile delinquent with an alcohol dependency.

Finally, the ride stopped and they stumbled off it. Emmett rubbed Mae's back while she puked in the grass.

Zadie, who didn't appear to be affected by anything, even blue WKD and a mountain of candyfloss, just stood to the side, smirking at her.

'You all right, Mae?' she asked. Mae gave her the thumbs up mid-puke. 'Just training my liver.' This made Zadie smile. Luna was pretty sure that out of all of them, Mae was the only person Zadie could half tolerate.

'Carousel?' Emmett asked, still rubbing Mae's back.

'Definitely,' Luna answered even though her denim skirt was too short to elegantly get a leg over a plastic horse.

'I'm out.' Mae was finally upright again, though a worrying amount of bright blue sick had just poured out of her.

'Come on, Mae, I'll get you some water,' Zadie said. She looked at Luna. 'I'll text if she gets worse.'

Ahmed was off at some family wedding so it was just Luna and Emmett now. He smiled what Luna privately thought of as his friendly smile, small and unanimated. She hated his friendship smile.

'Ready?'

They started to walk towards the carousel, passing the

fun mirrors on their way. Luna caught sight of her distorted body, the mascara that had been dragged to the side of her eyes by the force of the spin on the Wheel of Doom, and the fact that her lips were stained blue from candyfloss. The muscles in her shoulders were pulled out of proportion, more enormous than ever.

Usually, she'd be so embarrassed to look like this in front of Emmett. She was the exact opposite of everything that The Beauty Bible encouraged her to be. She wasn't poised, or refined, she was a literal mess.

'What's so funny?' Emmett asked. Luna had stopped to look at herself in the fun mirror. It was obscene, how bad she looked.

Emmett was next to her now, distorted but still fit. She wondered if he had any idea just how fit he was. Luna saw it, the way girls would look at him. Women, too, sometimes. But since Cadence, Emmett hadn't shown any interest in anyone.

'Are you drunk, Luna?' He smiled.

'No.' She shook her head, still laughing. Maybe she was a little drunk. 'I just look so horrific . . . ' She was fighting for breath now, waving a hand between her and Emmett. 'It's crazy to think that I ever thought . . . I mean I ever hoped . . .' She shoved the same hand over her mouth, even though she was still giggling. Blue WKD must be more potent than she'd realised.

But Emmett was looking at her then, not the distorted crazy version that had super short legs and big shoulders, the real version, the one that still had mascara and candyfloss lips.

Luna hoped that it wasn't pity in his eyes. She thought that she could cope with a lot, so far as Emmett was concerned, but not pity. Never pity.

He tucked a section of her hair behind her ear.

'You're beautiful, Luna,' he said.

For a second, the carnival around them went quiet, like all the air, light and noise of the place had been absorbed by Emmett's words.

What did he mean? she thought again, her brain fully frazzled. And why does he look hurt?

She wanted to ask for clarity, something, anything. But she had no idea how to do that. How to ask for the things that you wanted. Instead, all she managed to come up with was, 'Thank you.' And anyway, she didn't believe him. Not for a second. Of course, she wasn't beautiful.

The carnival came roaring back to life, slamming into them.

'Carousel?' Luna asked. She could only manage short sentences now.

'Okay.' Emmett looked shaken up. Like they'd just been through something together, she just didn't know what. Luna was sure that he was looking at her lips just then. Is this what happens with kissing? This hadn't happened at home, when she'd been kissing Jacob Grangemoor. He had done what any self-respecting sixteen-year-old would do and had sent his friend to ask if Luna wanted to neck him. There wasn't this unending tension.

They didn't talk as they gave their tokens for the

ride – their last of the evening – to Barry in the ticket booth. Barry didn't look to Luna like a man who should be in charge of heavy machinery, let alone a carousel that children could go on. He had gravy down his white vest.

When she slid onto a horse, Emmett followed her. It was a two-person horse, so there was nothing especially untoward about this, but they'd never sat like this. Luna clung to the plastic mane like her life depended on it, feeling almost fevered.

They waved at Earl. The carousel was his favourite ride; he spent so much time on it, Luna thought that he must be immune to motion sickness. One of the evenings this week, she'd seen him sharing a beer with Barry. Earl seemed to be allowed to ride without a token.

In the distance, they could see the sea. It was evening, but the sun hadn't set yet and the sky was orange and pink. Not dissimilar colours to Earl's graveyard painting. The view settled something in her, just for a moment. She felt calmer here, in her core.

'I wish I lived here,' she said. 'It's so gorgeous.'

She felt rather than saw Emmett nod behind her as the carousel started up a merry jingle to say that we're about to move. She could hear Earl laughing.

'It is,' he answered. 'But I can't wait to leave.'

Luna didn't understand why anyone would want to leave here.

They started to move, up and down and forward. The motion pushed Emmett into Luna and she felt him all along her back. An ache developed, right between her thighs.

'I really can't wait to leave,' he said again with feeling, and Luna wished that he'd stop speaking directly into her ear. It was very distracting.

'But what about Earl?' she asked.

'Hopefully, he'll come to visit me. I've got to get away. I want to get away, Luna. You understand, don't you?'

Luna was halfway jealous that Emmett got to conjure his dreams so easily and make a plan to follow them.

'Maybe we could apply to unis in the same cities?' he suggested and while Luna knew on an objective level that she wouldn't just be able to finish college and move to Northumberland right away, the prospect of doing anything other than that filled her with dread. If Emmett wasn't here though, would Northumberland be the same? Was Emmett Northumberland to her? Possibly, she needed to lay off the WKD ahead of conversations like this about the future.

Luna felt ill-equipped for this talk. She was also quite horny.

'Exam results first, and then we'll see,' she told him. 'Plus, we have two years of school left.'

He was so close to her. It was hard to concentrate on anything.

'Exam results first,' he agreed.

'Mum is throwing me a party, you should come. You can fight her off when she tries to kill me for getting a ton of Ds.'

Emmett laughed. 'You won't fail. Is your dad coming back up for it?'

Her dad was doing his usual of staying two weeks and then going home to work. He'd be back at the end of summer to pick them up.

'Nope, Mum has invited Eyebrow Clive. She'll be so cringe around him, I'm warning you.'

'Do you think she'd ever cheat on your dad?'

Luna had thought about it. A lot. Late at night when she was trying to sleep. It disturbed her sketching in her mind.

'I doubt it, but you never know. I think that's just what marriage is like.'

'I don't know why anyone would get married.' They went up and down and round and round. It was a gentle ride, but after the Wheel of Doom, anything was a lot.

'Oh really?' The world beyond the carousel passed in a blur. Luna didn't let on that the entire point of The Beauty Bible seemed to be to get thin and pretty enough to bag a husband.

'Yeah, relationships always go wrong. Even if you really love someone, you'd end up losing them. I bet your mum and dad were friends once.'

Luna twisted around to look at him. He was right there. So close.

'That is a . . . depressing way of looking at things.'

He shrugged. 'It's the truth, though. I'd never risk losing someone important by getting into a relationship with them.'

This felt big. If only her sluggish candyfloss brain could make sense of it all. It was as if Emmett was trying to tell her something. The way he was pressed to her. It was a lot.

'What about sex?' Luna blurted out, even though the most experience she'd had was one single kiss. Emmett must have more. He was sixteen. He was bound to have had more. Luna knew, via Zadie, that he'd lost his virginity to Cadence. She shifted on the horse.

'You don't need to be in a relationship for that, Luna.'

Luna was hot all over, and as the horse stopped moving, she was out of her seat and wobbling down the steps of the ride in a flash. 'Sorry, it's the WKD,' she called over her shoulder when it wasn't that. It wasn't that at all. It was Emmett being close to her, it was him having to spell out how he'd never get in a relationship with her because he was scared of losing her; it was him casually talking about sex. Luna thought she might be done with it all. She wanted to be done with it all.

'Luna, wait.'

Emmett caught up. 'Sorry,' she said, panting and halfway to crying. 'There's been a lot of spinny rides.'

Her phone started playing *Big Girls Don't Cry*, the ringtone she downloaded especially for the summer. It was Zadie, telling her that Mae had been sick again. 'I'd better get her home. Mum will go apeshit if she finds out Mae's drunk. I've got to go,' she said again.

'Hey Luna . . . ' He caught her arm as she turned to leave. 'We're okay, aren't we?' And she thought how Emmett needed this. He needed them to be okay. This is what he was talking about – people leaving him. Luna thought about the dad he didn't know, his mum in prison, even Cadence, who couldn't cope with it all.

'Yeah, Emmett, we're okay.' She swallowed it all down, buried her secret and smiled.

'So, in summary, I think Emmett doesn't want to risk our friendship on something more. Either that or he doesn't like me like that. Which would be fair. But he did say that I was beautiful, so probably it's the friendship thing.'

'It's chicken shit is what it is.'

Luna and Mae were in bed the next morning, a bright blue day peeping at them from beyond the curtains. Mae had them, and her eyes, firmly shut.

'It's not chicken shit, it's perfectly sensible. Think about it: neither of us knows one couple who actually likes each other, let alone loves each other. Aside from Earl and Sebastian, who were in love half a century ago. And even that went tits up when Sebastian disappeared. It makes sense that Emmett wouldn't want to risk what we have.'

Luna was fairly certain that she was trying to convince herself as much as Mae. Part of her even felt a little bad. It was comfortingly familiar, the sense that she had been wrong this whole time. Emmett was probably right. Luna could hear her mum and dad arguing in the kitchen. Chances are, he was absolutely right.

'Do you think they could hate each other just a little bit quieter?' Mae groaned.

'I don't know, and I'm not going to ask.'

Mae tunnelled deeper into the duvet. 'You could just tell Emmett, you know?' Her voice was all muffled. 'That's what I would do.'

'Tell him what?'

'Just be like, look Emmett, I'm in love with you. I'm hot as fuck and you need to stop being a coward and get with me. Or I know, sing "Lady Marmalade" at him. That worked for me once. We could look for a feather boa in one of the charity shops in the village.'

'You are insane. Of course, I can't tell him. He must never, ever know.'

Mae muttered something that sounded like 'your funeral' as the bedroom door banged open.

'Girls. Before your father leaves, he wants to go and see the puffins again, for some ungodly reason.'

'It's tradition!' her Dad called, in a sing-song voice that forced their mum to close her eyes and breathe through her nose for a moment.

'So get dressed so that we can go and see these awful birds for the millionth time.' She shouted the last part back towards the kitchen, directing it at their dad. And Luna thought that Emmett was surely right – because she would never, ever want them to get into a blinding argument about some birds.

Chapter Seventeen

Luna didn't fail.

That's what she reminded herself as she moved around the cottage, a tray of prawn cocktail lettuce boats held aloft in front of her. They'd already started to wilt.

Luna's mum had described her grades as 'perfectly respectable exam results', which was probably somewhere between a compliment and a comment. But perfectly respectable was entirely fine by Luna. Especially since she thought she'd failed. Her dad had texted her 'B good' because most of her grades were Bs.

'I'll take one of them off your hands, Luna.' Ahmed, leaning back against the kitchen worktop, peeled a prawn cocktail boat off the tray her mum had arranged them on.

All around the cottage, little groups of people were gathered. It was like two different styles of art meeting on canvas, and it being all wrong. For instance, there was Earl, paint-splattered and wearing his feather top hat, an artist to his very core, chatting politely to Eyebrow Clive, the most literal man on the planet. Zadie, who, Luna was sure if she were an artist, would be a cubist, was talking to her mum, who would paint vases of flowers and nothing else. It was a mish-mash of friends her mum had in the village, and people Luna knew from The Edge.

'Were you happy with your results?' she asked Ahmed.

He shrugged. 'I have more important things to be worrying about than grades, Luna.'

He folded down a page in his book, *One Hundred Poems to Fall in Love By,* and looked over at Zadie. 'Emmett said that you got a special recognition certificate for Art?'

Luna flushed red, sure that even her stomach was the colour of beetroot. Art was the only subject that she had got the top grade, alongside a certificate to say that she was in the top 3 per cent of candidates.

Luna looked around for Emmett. She wondered if she was ever not looking for him.

'He went into the garden, I think,' Ahmed said, smiling at her.

'I'm not looking for anyone in particular.'

'Sure, Luna. I believe you.'

It seemed that everyone knew how hopelessly in love with Emmett Luna was.

'You know, there might be a way for us to both get what we want,' Ahmed carried on. It was stuffy, Luna needed water. She put down the tray of soggy prawns.

'I don't know what you mean.'

'Come on, Luna. We aren't little anymore. You're sixteen

now, time to start playing with the big kids.' He was peering down at her, completely grossing her out.

'Can you just spit it out, Ahmed? What are you talking about?' Luna's head was starting to ache, a consequence of not sleeping the night before. Or the night before that.

'Try this. You want to get with Emmett.' She neither confirmed nor denied. 'I want to get with Zadie. So how about we get with each other, to make them jealous.'

It was the most ridiculous thing Luna had ever heard.

She started to laugh.

'That would never work.'

'It's actually a classic trope. Works every time.'

Somehow, Luna doubted that this was true. But if there was a chance . . .

'I don't know. Do you even want to kiss me?' she asked.

'You're not hot, but you're beautiful. Interesting. And I appreciate those qualities.' It wasn't quite the compliment Ahmed seemed to think that it was.

Luna didn't want to kiss Ahmed any more than he probably wanted to kiss her, but she was stubbornly stuck in the friend zone with Emmett.

'Emmett probably just doesn't fancy me,' she told Ahmed.

'Emmett is obsessed with you,' he answered simply. 'You forget, I'm here when you're not.'

Luna wanted to push for more info, but she didn't. Still, his words were a balm for her frayed heart.

'Why hasn't he made a move then?'

'Because he's terrified. And this summer especially, he's

comfortable. Too comfortable. He has you right where he wants you.'

Luna didn't like the insinuation that Emmett was using her in some way. She went to defend him, but Ahmed held up his hands.

'I'm not saying that he's doing it on purpose, or for any reason other than fear. I think we just need to jolt him out of it, that's all.'

The party carried on around them. Luna watched as Emmett came in from the garden. His eyes briefly met hers before he moved to whisper something to Earl. Whatever Emmett told him, it made Earl frown. He continued to frown as he and Emmett huddled in the corner, deep in conversation.

'Just think about it, Luna.'

'What here? In my parents' kitchen?'

'No, we'd have to wait for it to have maximum impact. Really hit home. When the time is right, come find me. Let's see if we can put an end to all this longing.'

The time was never right. Or at least, it wasn't for the next five days. Emmett sunk into a dark mood, his first that summer. He wouldn't meet Luna's eye when they talked, but he agreed to let her sketch him. Luna couldn't be sure that it wasn't because that way, they wouldn't have to speak.

'Do you know what's wrong with Emmett?' Luna asked Earl one afternoon in the studio. 'And also, I can't get his eye right – what do you think?'

Earl peered over her shoulder. 'Eyes are difficult, I think. Like a tiny universe on the page. But this is very skilled work, Luna. You're too hard on yourself.'

'All this time sketching an eye.'

'It is very beautiful. You could add more dimension, perhaps, where the eyelid casts a shadow. But still, it is excellent work. You should become an artist.'

It was a thing that Earl kept saying to her. He smirked as he said it.

'It's not real art.'

He held up her pencil.

'What is this?'

'It's a pencil.'

'Okay, but does it know that it is a pencil?'

'Well, no, it can't think for itself. I know what you're doing.'

'Then you will know that so much of the world is subjective. This is a pencil because we all believe that it is a pencil.'

'You can make your point now.' Luna smirked, and Earl laughed.

'Art is what we say it is, that is all. Oh, and Emmett has had word that Tanya will be out this September. I think that he has mixed feelings, as you say.'

Luna thought about the party. About how Ahmed had said that Emmett was too comfortable.

'He's down again,' she said to Earl.

Earl had paused in front of his own work in progress. He frowned. 'He is. I hate to see it.'

'I do too.'

'It will not last.'

'But any sadness is too much, isn't it?'

'You cannot make people happy, Luna.'

Luna knew this, she did. But she was still going to try.

Earl sighed. 'As a young child, Emmett learned that the world is not a good or a safe place to be. That is what he knows. It will take some time for him to see that the world is beautiful too, I think. Until then, we can just be with him, yes? That is enough, I think.'

'You're right. I'm glad he has you when I'm not here.'

Earl waved a hand away. 'He is company to me. I am the lucky one.'

Luna didn't reply. Instead, she continued to sketch Emmett's eye, and quietly marvelled at the tiny universe within it.

It was the last night of the summer and they were at the beach.

'You know, I think I might just wear some shorts,' Luna told Mae. They'd packed their things, and Luna's scruffy denim shorts were on the top of the pile. 'I think I'm done with the Beauty Bible since it's been such an epic fail.'

'Yeah, fair play.' Mae was wearing cycling shorts and a crop top. 'It was rubbish advice anyway. I feel like my eyebrows will never grow back.'

'Same.'

'You should go for it with Ahmed tonight. Because if

something doesn't happen soon, I'm going to walk into the sea. There's too much tension.'

Mae was a big fan of Ahmed's idea. She was annoyed, actually, that she hadn't come up with it herself. 'This sort of thing never fails,' she told Luna.

Her mum, dad, and Eyebrow Clive were in the back garden together. Ever since Dad had come to pick them up a couple of days ago, things had been super polite between them all. Like they were all walking around on eggshells the whole time. It half freaked Luna out. But also, it made a nice change from all the yelling.

Their mum made the girls promise that they wouldn't be back later than ten, and recounted for posterity the story of their being missing persons for eighteen minutes to people who were all there for that eighteen minutes. After this, they were free to go to the beach.

Everyone was there. Earl, Zadie, Emmett, Ahmed. *Ahmed.* He gave Luna a look that said it's now or never, and whatever she thought about the merits of the plan, if they were going to do it, it had to be tonight.

She shuffled over to where Ahmed was sat reading.

'Okay, I'm in,' she told him. He put his book, *War and Peace,* in the sand and sat up straighter.

'Excellent. We need to lay some groundwork. Put your head on my shoulder. Then we can strategise.'

Luna did as she was told. It was quite nice, actually, having someone tell her how to behave. Except, almost immediately, she got a neckache from resting her head on his bony shoulder.

Mae urged Luna on from across the fire. Emmet either hadn't seen them or purposely wasn't looking.

Ahmed picked up Luna's hand and laced her fingers with his as the others talked and laughed. He dropped his voice to a whisper.

'We need to make this count, Luna,' he told her. She swallowed. She had virtually no experience at kissing, which was tragic, she knew. 'We need them to see us as sexual beings.'

'But, I mean, we aren't, are we?' Ahmed was a bookworm through and through, and Luna had no experience at all, bar what she'd imagined.

'Speak for yourself. I've been reading the complete works of Jilly Cooper.'

Luna's mum loved Jilly Cooper's novels.

'It's confidence, that's what women like.'

Luna wanted to answer that she thought that women looked for a lot more than just confidence, but she was distracted by the way Ahmed was running his fingers up and down her arm. It felt nice. How much nicer would it feel if it was Emmett doing that? she wondered.

'Take a walk with me.' Ahmed stood up and pulled Luna up too. 'We're going to the water,' he told the others.

'I'll come,' Emmett said.

'Sorry, Emmett man, we want some alone time, don't we, Luna?'

Zadie's eyes flicked towards them from where she was sitting with Earl and Mae, and she frowned.

'Yes,' Luna agreed, having essentially lost control of her faculties at this point.

'Come on.' Ahmed pulled her away. 'Laugh,' he ordered her as they ran, and Luna let out a shriek of delight that was too loud. She was a puppet now, just doing as she was instructed.

'This should do it.' They were still holding hands, at the water's edge, the waves lapping at their feet. The others could still clearly see them. It was late summer, and the beach was pretty empty.

'We need to frolic a bit. Otherwise it'll look staged.'

Luna didn't know how to frolic, but she jumped some waves. And when Ahmed put his arm around her shoulders as they looked out to sea, Luna thought that the whole thing was . . . awkward as hell.

'You really like her then, huh?' she asked him.

Luna knew her motivation for doing this, but she didn't know if it had ever occurred to her that Ahmed might be quite so hopelessly in love with Zadie.

'With all my heart. She's my soulmate, Luna. My muse.' What a pair of hapless romantics they were.

They'd been down by the water's edge for some time, and Luna had thought about backing out every other minute when Ahmed said, 'It's show time, if you're ready?'

Luna reckoned that Ahmed would make a brilliant novelist one day. He had an eye for this sort of thing, since the sun had gone soft and hazy and they probably looked as good as they were going to look at this point.

For some reason, Luna hadn't given too much thought to the idea of kissing Ahmed. She didn't want to, not really, but she wasn't appalled by the idea. It would be an awful lot easier if she did want to kiss him, an awful lot easier.

'Is he looking?' she asked Ahmed, pretending to laugh again as he fake-splashed her with a wave. Peak frolic.

'He's never not been looking. Come here.' Luna let Ahmed pull her close to him, their feet still in the water, the sun behind them.

Imagine he's Emmett, she thought, as he ran a hand up the side of her face and wrapped it into her hair. 'You have gorgeous hair, Luna.' He didn't mean it. Luna hated her hair. Who wanted ginger hair? But she understood that he was trying to put her at ease, so she rolled with it.

'Thanks, so do you.' She was lame, undoubtedly, but this wasn't real, so it didn't matter. Ahmed just huffed out a laugh and then his lips were on hers. They were cool, cooler than she expected them to be, and for a second, she froze, thinking about all the reasons that this was wrong, but then Ahmed muttered, 'You're fine,' and Luna decided to just go for it.

She flung her arms around his neck and opened her mouth to let his tongue in. She was a bit grossed out since it was wetter and colder than she expected. But it was okay. It was just a kiss.

She pulled away. 'Sorry, no more.'

'That's fine, Luna. I think it worked anyway.'

Luna wasn't sure what he meant until she looked up the beach. Emmett was storming towards them.

'I'll give you two some space,' Ahmed said, kissing her on the edge of her nose. They were back to being friends.

'Hey, Zadie!' he called, starting back up across the beach. Luna just waited, feeling like a duck out of water as Emmett got closer to her.

'What the hell is going on, Luna?' he asked. No hello, no how's it going, just straight in there. For the first time ever, Luna felt angry at Emmett. Surely he didn't just get to come here and question her, did he?

'Well, I just kissed Ahmed,' she said, turning her back to him.

'I know, I saw. Half the beach saw. Earl had to take Mae to the caravan for an emergency macaroon.'

Luna laughed. Trust Mae.

'You didn't mind if half the beach saw you kissing Cadence,' she fired back. Maybe it was the sunset. Or the kiss. Or the fact that Emmett was acting so pissed when he had no right, none at all. Luna felt some of what she kept buried inside her bubbling up. Fighting to be released.

'What has that got to do with anything?'

'Only that it's one rule for you and another for me.'

They were shouting at each other now, stomping about in the sea in a fit of dramatics.

'Or is that how you like it, Emmett? Do you want me to just pine for you the whole time while you give me weird looks and say I'm beautiful one time and then barely speak to me another? Because it's messed up.'

Emmett looked like Luna had hit him.

'No, Luna. I don't . . . I didn't.' He must have understood her then, because he said, 'You *are* beautiful, but our friendship is the most important thing to me ever. I'd never want to . . . you know . . . '

He couldn't get the words out. However, Luna seemed to have plenty of them, all ready to go. Possibly, years of angst were just pouring right out of her right now.

'That's chicken, Emmett, and you know it. What about what I want?' She kept shouting.

'What is it that you want, Luna?'

This is it, she thought. Emmett couldn't say it. He wasn't capable of saying it. It would always have to be her.

Luna took a deep breath. She'd been so brave on this day. Braver than she'd ever been, perhaps.

But she couldn't say it either.

And wasn't that tragic, she thought, that the pair of them were so messed up that neither of them were willing to take the chance? Emmett might have been running away from his feelings, but Luna hadn't exactly been putting it all out there.

'I just want to be honest.' She told him the only words that she could find. And anyway, it was the truth. 'I don't want to spend the rest of my life burying everything I feel. I want to be honest with myself. And with you. It's just . . . hard.'

He was closer to her now, looking right at her. The sun was behind him, giving him a halo.

'You're really important to me, Luna,' he said.

It wasn't enough. It would never be enough.

'You're important to me too, Emmett.'

'I'd hate to ever lose you.'

'You won't. I'm not going anywhere.'

'You're leaving in the morning,' he smiled.

'I know, but aside from that. You'll always have me.'

'Good, I couldn't bear it.' He pulled her towards him, and she went, hugging him hard. She felt the warm press of his body, and she knew that he was crying by the way his ribs shook.

'It's okay,' she told him. 'Things will always be okay.'

The sea tried to move them, dragging them with the tide, and Luna thought that that was how things were with her and Emmett. They were buffeted by the waves, clinging to each other, trying to stay together when there was so much pushing against them.

'I'll be back next summer,' she told him. 'And I'll write.'

He pulled back, his eyes red. 'You promise?'

Luna tried to find a smile for him. 'I promise.'

Chapter Eighteen

NOW

Montmartre in Motion: Oil on canvas. A busy piece, Spencer employs bright colours to create a sense of movement and structured forms, while maintaining a connection to reality. The hues are bright and clashing in ways that heightens excitement. The figures are lifelike and interwoven, pulling the eye from one to another seamlessly. c.2007.

There'd been a time when loving Emmett had felt like the hardest thing that I had to face. Of course, that was when I was a teenager, before things took the turn that they did.

It started with breathlessness. In Dad, I mean. The signs were there, those final summers. And then when he got worse, we thought it was just the fallout of Mum running off with Eyebrow Clive. The shock of her leaving hit him hard. So we thought it was that he wasn't coping, like a helpless, breathless little bird.

The divorce wasn't even done the first time some doctor who wasn't Dr Dave said the words 'congenital heart disease'. And even then, we didn't know how serious something like that would be. But Dad just deteriorated, once he was diagnosed. Like his body, his heart, just gave up. He got thin, he couldn't walk up the stairs. The doctor who wasn't Dr Dave told us that getting a transplant would be an option, but Dad had a rare tissue group. We both do.

There were tests on Mae and me. They showed nothing at first, and we thought we'd escaped it. But then, before I even realised it, before I felt unwell in any way, my heart had begun to fail.

Dad lived for five years after he was diagnosed. I've already had ten. Sometimes I think about how it must be for Mae, watching her dad and then her sister die. I know that I wouldn't cope if things were reversed.

Speaking of which, Mae isn't done with me this night. I settle back against the bed in my tiny hotel room, on the side that Emmett sat on while I napped, and look out at the night sky.

Mae: What do you think he'd do, if he knew?

Me: Well, the generalised response has been to run the fuck away. So I think he'd do that.

It's the truth. I might have pushed a lot of people away after my diagnosis, but plenty had gone of their own volition too. There'd only been Mae. And Zadie. The odd boyfriend who just didn't get it.

Mae: You're on the transplant list.

Me: And how did that work out for Dad? You know what Dr Dave said about my tissue group.

Mae: Dr Dave said we need to stay positive.

Me: I am positive. Positive that I won't get a transplant.

I can't explain it, but living without that hope means in some ways, it's easier for me. Living, expecting to get a transplant that might never come, is worse somehow. I've come to realise that false hope is worse than no hope at all.

Plus, waiting for a transplant is basically waiting for someone else to die. If you think about that for too long, it's all sorts of fucked up.

Mae: I hate it when you get like this. It's unnecessary.

Another thing I've discovered is that Mae can cope with almost anything. But she can't cope with this. I take a breath and lay back on the bed.

Me: All I'm saying is that there's no point in telling him.

Mae: He might stay, if he knew.

Me: Because that's exactly what I want to happen. Guilt him into staying. I wouldn't do that then, and I won't do it now.

Mae: He might have contacts!

Me: He doesn't, Mae.

Me: Listen, it's late, I need to get some rest. Another day walking around Paris might kill me anyway, then I won't have to worry about getting a transplant or not.

Mae: Not even remotely funny.

Me: I think I'm hilarious. It would save us all some time and effort.

Mae: Can't you just even pretend to have an ironic zest for life?

Me: I'm in Paris. With my long-lost love. What could possibly be zestier than that?

Mae: Fine. I suppose that is quite zesty. Love you. See you Friday xx

Me: Love you too. See you soon xxx

I send a Care Bear GIF with a beating heart that's kind of freaky, to reassure Mae that it's all okay. I'm worried about how badly she's coping with this. It's not like it's new information, and the good thing is that so far, she's showing no signs of the myocardiopathy that killed Dad. She's older than I was when the ultrasound first showed that my heart was beginning to struggle. It's a shit choice, but I'd rather this happen to me than her.

So it's not new new. Being added to the transplant list is new-ish, I suppose. It's just another step towards the inevitable. If I think too much about Mae, after, I lose it. Mostly,

I try to do what Earl suggested once, in a conversation I'll never forget. Ground myself in the moment and live it. That's what Dr Dave advocates, too. People have gone mad from the waiting.

There's no way I'm bringing all this misery to Emmett's door. He had his fair share of that as a kid. I need to protect him.

But as I drift off to sleep, I remember that I'd had the same thought twenty years ago. Right before it all went wrong.

The next morning I'm a heady mixture of depressed and excited. Excited to see *The Edge of Always* again, excited to see Emmett, but depressed that it all has to end soon. This is why neutrality is by far the better option; it's much less exhausting than quite so much feeling.

I pull on some leggings and an oversized shift dress with squirrels all over it. I genuinely wonder if I'll have to leave some of my stuff here when it comes to getting my suitcase shut again. I'm taking it with me since I'm going straight to Emmett's hotel after MAM. And fuck, there's a reality I never thought would happen. I'm kneeling on top of the case, winded and gasping when there's a knock at my hotel room door.

'Hello?' I call, assuming it'll be the eager beaver receptionist.

'Luna.' Fuck, it's Emmett. Look at the state of my case! I bet he packs like he's in the Marines.

I quickly chuck my medicine bottles in my bag and then

fling open the door, hearing my case spring back open on the floor behind me.

'Emmett,' I smile, blowing some hair off my face. 'What're you doing here?'

He's holding a bag stained with grease, so you know it contains something good. And two coffees. If it was a thing that we still did, I'd kiss him.

'Just thought I'd bring you breakfast.' He peers behind me into the room.

I make little grabby hands towards the coffee.

'Okay, thank you. Ignore the mess. I don't know how I seem to have more stuff than when I arrived.'

It is, I think, good that I didn't heed Mae's advice to bring a menagerie of vibrators. The only thing that could make the mess more embarrassing is a rogue vibrator amidst the chaos.

Emmett's wearing a dark green T-shirt today that sets off his eyes. It's only a T-shirt, I've seen him in a ton of T-shirts, but it's . . . distracting.

'Shall we have these on the balcony? We've a few minutes before we need to set off?' he says, holding up the pastry bag.

'Yes, definitely.'

We sit outside and watch Paris below us. It's warm, the pastry and the weather, and I think that the loveliness of it all is actually making me more, not less, depressed. Imagine one week you're sitting on a balcony in Paris with the sun on your face, a busy, bustling avenue below you, and the next, you're running an art class in a hospice for people who are dying, knowing that one day, probably soon, you'll die there too.

'Are you okay, Luna?' Emmett asks.

Maybe my misery is written all over my face.

'What? Yeah, I'm fine. Sorry, just got lost in my thoughts there for a second. I thought I'd be desperate to get home, but now I don't want to go back.'

'I thought you loved Northumberland?' he asks, taking a bite of his croissant.

'I do. It's just . . . tricky to explain.'

'Try me.'

And if I was going to tell him, now would be a really great time to. But I'm not. Once people know that about you, they act different. Not that I think that Emmett would behave like everyone else and assume that death is catching; he's a doctor; he'll know that it isn't. But people see you differently, and there's no taking it back once it's out there.

'I guess, sometimes I'm just a bit lonely there. But it's nothing, and I have my Deathers. Hey, I posted last night asking them to look into where that blue door from *The Rubicon* might be. It was Mae's idea.'

I'd checked this morning and there were a couple of comments saying that they were on it. God bless the internet.

I've trailed off, so I finish with, 'Plus, Paris is lovely – who would want to leave?'

He laughs. 'I have that thought every time I go.'

We finish our breakfast in companionable silence. Emmett watches as I tip my face up to the sun, letting it soak into me.

Time is moving at super speed today, I'm sure. One short second I'm checking out of my hotel and the next we're being ushered towards *The Edge of Always*. Mari is meeting us here, and I haven't even thought of what I'll say to her. It's different, being here when it's empty, when the art, not people, take up all the space.

We sit on the same concrete bench in front of the painting as we did two days ago. How was it only that long? Once again, I'm staring at my own face. Younger, full of life, and I'm thinking how it'll still be here once I'm gone. I'm immortalised in this painting and yet I'm looking at a person I barely know anymore, though I'm certain that I had no idea who I was then, either. Maybe some people just never know. We remain enigmas, even to ourselves, our whole lives.

'I had the strangest thought, the first time I saw it,' I whisper to Emmett. I don't know why I'm whispering. There's no one else here.

'What's that?' he asks. He's so close to me. Too close. It's throwing out my senses.

Now that I've started this conversation, I don't want to finish it. But I can't think of anything to say so I just admit, 'I thought for a short moment that Earl had painted both of us.'

Emmett doesn't say anything, but he tips his head to the side and studies the piece some more.

'He definitely did paint you. That much is obvious.'

My face takes up so much of the painting, my hair splayed out around me, caught by the wind I presume.

'Yes, but look in the right corner. There's a shadow, some

of the colours there are greyer. It felt like you, I don't know why. It made me think of you.'

Emmett tilts his head. 'Not so strange, I don't think. I had the same thought.'

'You did?' I'm surprised. I just assumed that I was living in my Emmett-centric world as per. But he nods.

'What is that Earl used to say? That art is about what you feel, not what you see. Well, I feel longing when I look at that. And love. And wanting things to be different. I'd say that's a pretty accurate description of how I felt back then.'

Oh.

Emmett is looking right at me, those green eyes, those eyelashes . . . they'll be the death of me. I think he's about to say something more when Mari, the curator, comes bustling into the space.

'*Ah bonjour*! Welcome to MAM, though you have been here before, yes?'

I'm being kissed by a tiny French woman and reminded of the last time I saw her. Like two days ago, she has many buttons on her suit jacket, they're all gold and shiny.

'*Bonjour*,' I say. 'This is my friend Emmett, he knew Earl when we were younger too.'

Mari looks at Emmett and smiles.

'*Bonjour, madame*,' he says, charming to the last.

'You are happy with the painting?' She gestures behind her.

'Yes,' I say, 'it's brilliant.' I wish I'd said something more impressive, but I feel self-conscious. Does describing a picture of yourself as gorgeous make you an egomaniac?

'Luna is an artist too.'

I shoot a look at Emmett. Why is he telling her that? I'm not an artist.

'*C'est fantastique*. Tell me, what do you paint?'

I can't very well accuse Emmett of lying, so I'm forced to answer in the present tense.

'Er, anatomical drawings. Hearts especially.'

'Ah, I see. They are very technical, are they not?'

I laugh, because that's what I love about them. *Loved* about them, I remind myself.

'Yes, they're incredible really. It's almost like we've reduced them to less than they are, making it seem like all they're capable of is love. They're more than that.'

Emmett is looking at me a certain way. His eyebrows are slightly raised and I know I've said too much. He can tell, I'm sure, that I still care about art. That that's not the reason I gave it up.

'How wonderful,' Mari says. 'And you knew Earl? This is also wonderful.'

It feels good to be talking about something safer.

'We both knew Earl before he was discovered. We saw him paint almost all of the paintings that you have here.'

'Then you are very lucky. I wish I could meet him in real life, yes. I am a big fan of his work.'

I like Mari. She just has this sense of calm self-assuredness about her which is nice. It's making me be calm, too. I'm doing lots of smiles, hoping that it'll entice her to tell me where the painting came from.

'Yes, we were lucky. He was a great artist, but he was a great person too. We're travelling around Paris, visiting all the places he painted,' Emmett interjects.

Mari smiles and laces her fingers together. 'A beautiful way to see a beautiful city.'

'We wondered, though, if you could tell us where this painting came from? We know a collector had his other works, but is it true that this one just turned up?'

Mari gestures to the bench, and the three of us sit.

'The truth is,' she begins and I think that this has been way too easy – she's just going to tell us, just like that. 'The truth is that I have no idea who owned the painting. Everything has come through a broker. A Mr Gregor, I believe.'

'Gregor,' I repeat back to her. Earl's art dealer. There is no way that man is still alive.

'Yes.'

'Okay, but where did Gregor get it from?'

Mari shakes her head. 'I do not know. It took some time to verify.'

Emmett sighs next to me. It does feel pretty hopeless.

'How did you know for sure that Earl, I mean, Spencer, had painted it?'

'The style and the signature mostly. This Mr Gregor had dealings with Spencer before, I believe too.'

'Do you have a contact for Gregor?' I ask her hopefully as she shakes her head and wrinkles her nose.

'We would rather not have dealings with him. He is a drunk, I think you would call him.'

Yep, that's Gregor.

I never really thought I'd find out where the painting came from, but it's disappointing to know for sure that I'll never know.

'It's so odd,' I say. 'To think that Earl sold a painting so long after he died.'

With that Mari looks at me quickly. Reminding me of a meerkat, twisting it's head this way and that between the painting and me. 'Oh no, no, no. We did not buy the painting. Only loaned it. The owner, Mr Gregor said they would never give it up. I don't know. We pay to loan it, but we would have paid much more to buy it.'

So much new information takes me by surprise.

'Wait, what, someone still owns the painting of Luna?' Emmett asks, articulating my thoughts.

'Yes, exactly.' Mari answers.

'But you can't tell us who?'

She shakes her head. 'Mr Gregor would know.'

'But you don't have a contact for him?' The thought of someone that I don't know having a painting of me after I'm dead is strange and uncomfortable.

Another head shake. 'He said he would be in touch. He is very unusual man.'

'Will you tell us?' I ask, talking quickly. 'If he contacts you, you'll tell us?'

'If you like. We have the painting for six months at least.'

I try to do the maths in my head. Maths was never my strong suit, but I know that I'll be cutting it fine.

MAM is open to the public now, and I'm keen to avoid another swarming. But I don't want to go either.

The Answer is Always in the Art.

What answer? What was Earl trying to tell me?

He could have made this a little easier. Emmett is standing next to me, staring intently at the painting.

'Before, when you said Earl would have wanted us to be friends. I think you were right.'

I might be imagining it, or maybe it's wishful thinking, but I'm almost sure that when I say we'll be friends, some of Emmett's smile wanes. That's all we can ever be, though. Because whatever happens beyond Paris, whatever questions remain unanswered, I am leaving. Ultimately, I'm leaving to a place that no one can follow me to. And that's the truth of it.

Chapter Nineteen

So, my suspicions were right – Emmett is rich.

'Fuck me,' I say. He's in a hotel on a wide boulevard. He has a doorman. Poor guy is standing there, sweating in a long coat and hat. The reception looks to be carved entirely from marble, and while my case looked enormous in my tiny room, it seems positively minuscule in Emmett's cavernous hotel suite.

'It's a bit over the top,' he says.

'A bit? It's like a palace. Did you have a rich uncle we didn't know about? Did he die and leave you everything?'

Emmett at least has the decency to look embarrassed. He mumbles something about investments and won't meet my eye. But this isn't normal, is it? For people without generational wealth? For people who work in the charity sector, even doctors?

I'm acting as if I've never so much as seen a hotel room before. I'm throwing open cupboards, peering out the window at the street below. It doesn't feel real.

Emmett has his list of Earl's paintings out again. There's

a neat tick next to *The Weight of Light* and *Longing for Human Connection.*

But we still have *Montmartre in Motion, The Juxtaposition of Life and Death* and *The Rubicon,* the mystery painting of the blue door.

'Which ones did you want to go to today?' I ask Emmett, running my fingers across all surfaces and thinking that this quest still feels as flimsy as fuck.

'I thought we could take a turn around the neighbourhood, since Montmartre is close by, and then maybe go to the spa. We still have tomorrow for the graveyard and it'll give the Deathers a chance to figure out where the blue door is. If they manage it.'

I've never been to a spa. They've always seemed a bit pink and fluffy for my tastes. But this hotel is all rich darkness, so maybe the spa will be the same.

Emmett's still standing by the door, watching me. He's so still, it's unnerving.

My phone buzzes, the medicine alarm.

'Sounds great,' I tell him, walking around the bed to get my case. This could so easily be a 'just one bed' thing, but the just one bed is massive – it's like a small country. Plus there's a couch that's bigger than my bed at home.

'I'll just wheel my case into the bathroom and then we can go walk, then spa. I'll need to buy a bikini to wear in there.'

'I'm sure we'll find something.'

'Great. Great.' I don't know if I'm mentally prepared to see Emmett, my *friend* in the spa. Hopefully they'll give him a massive robe to wear – a head to toe one that covers everything.

But my chest is feeling increasingly tight. Like there's an elastic band around it. I'm half out of breath and it's not even thoughts of Emmett in swimming shorts that's doing it. Everyone assumes that you feel heart failure in your heart, but it's not that. It's your lungs that mostly give up the ghost.

In the bathroom, I open my case, organise my pills for the rest of the day, and then bury the bottles under a chaotic mountain of stuff.

When I come out of the bathroom, I can, weirdly, hear myself. I think that I've gone mad for a second, and let's be honest, Paris would be an excellent place to go mad, but my voice is coming from Emmett's phone.

'In this episode of the Art of Dying, we'll be looking at Neoclassicist Jacques-Louis David. This guy was a true Deather in his day. Heavily involved in the French Revolution, David painted the well-known 'Death of Marat', so it's no real surprise that . . . '

Emmett is pressing at his phone, frantic.

'Sorry,' he says, as my voice cuts off finally. 'It was an accident.'

'You accidentally searched my blog and played an old video?' I'm standing in the doorway of the bathroom still.

'Something like that. You sounded great. I love that you're doing this.'

I shake my head. I want to be annoyed, but there's no fight, no nothing left. 'Just leave it, Emmett. Please.'

He puts his phone in his jacket pocket and holds his hands up.

'Okay, it's away. I won't listen again.'

I let out a breath. I don't talk about the fact that I'm dying in every episode, rarely in fact. But one glance at the comments will show it. There's always some argument about the fact that since I could get a transplant, I'm not technically dying. And then the Deathers who like to philosophise about whether we're all dying. I have a Buddhist follower who's been telling us quite a lot about *anicca*, the idea that life is impermanent. So yes, I might not talk about my death all the time, because who wants to do that? But it's just overwhelmingly death-centric.

'Thank you.' Hopefully, Emmett got fractionally more stupid during our years apart. Otherwise, my behaviour doesn't exactly come across as normal. 'Shall we walk?' I should rest, especially since my chest is so tight, and my ankles feel puffy in my boots as I struggle to get the zip over them. And isn't that a nice image? The last great indignity. Dying with puffy ankles.

'Okay, let's walk.'

I keep going, and as we begin to wander through the streets of Montmartre, it's hard to worry about my ankles. The wide open boulevards make it hard to worry about anything at all. We pass a woman in sky-high heels walking seven dogs, and a group of teenagers who all laugh and talk loudly. A couple kiss against the railings, practically pornographic for the middle of the day. It's so busy.

The Place Saint-Pierre is filled with artists and musicians. There's so much life here, it's confronting. I'm used to keeping my head down, blocking out the world with music, so it's taken me a while to adjust to hearing and seeing everything. I'm full of every colour, reminding myself that whatever happens in the future, I'll be grateful for these days.

'It's easy to think of Earl and Sebastian here,' Emmett says. I agree, this is the sort of place that Earl would have loved. Full of people.

We climb the steps to the white church slowly. And when Emmett offers me his arm, I take it. I silently curse that there is so much climbing in Paris, but the views at the top are worth it. Inside is everything you'd expect from an old Parisian church, dark and gold and moody. I think how much easier it might be if I believed in this version of an afterlife. Not that I believe in nothing, but what I have is intangible and ill-defined.

We stop in a café as I'm exhausted. Emmett goes to order baguettes while I reply to some Deathers. There's a message from Darth Painter.

> **DarthPainter:** Paris suits you Luna. I hope you're having a brilliant time.
>
> **TheArtofDying:** I am, thanks Darth. It's stirring up a lot too, from the past.

Darth isn't online, so instead of waiting for a reply, I hit record for another video.

'Welcome Deathers, to Montmartre,' I talk into my phone, recording a live blog. 'I mentioned in my last video that Spencer studied in Paris and fell in love with these streets. He always said that there was no city in the world like it. I'll link his Montmartre piece in the comments. He was still heavily influenced by Expressionism in this work, so the lines are distorted and the brushwork is mixed, but it's emotionally intense. Earl loved people; he always talked about how interesting people were. It's natural, then, that he'd be drawn to painting places with so many people from all walks of life. I think it says something too, the fact that in his final years, he painted Paris, the place he learned to love art.'

I talk some more about Earl's time at art school in Paris.

'This time had such a seminal impact on his work. Earl liked to mix different styles, experiment. He never subscribed to one school of thought. And you can see that in Paris. And like in Paris, the mixture really worked for Earl, it kept his art interesting.'

I see that Emmett is coming back, so I wrap it up.

'And that's all I've got time for. Have a great day, Deathers. And remember, bonus death points for anyone who figures out where the blue door might be.'

I finish recording and hit upload. Almost immediately, my phone pings. Mae.

> **Mae:** Nice video. You are so falling in love with Emmett during this great romantic quest you're on.

Me: Thanks. And no, I'm not. It's a platonic quest.

I have to keep my message to Mae short because my hands don't appear to be working properly anymore.

Mae: Heard that before.
Me: I don't want my heart broken again.
Mae: Hate to break it to you sis, but your heart is already fucked. Go live a little. What's the worst that can happen?

I'd die of a broken heart, *with* a broken heart. The most tragic (if slightly poetic) death ever.

Mae: What's that quote? People who don't learn from the past are idiots? Tell him you're poorly, tell him you love him stupid.
Me: That is not a quote.
Mae: Should be.

'Hi,' I say to Emmett as he finishes weaving his way through tables, tray laden down with carbs, the Rue Saint-Rustique in the background.

'Hi,' he smiles, putting the tray down. It looks delicious, but my appetite is non-existent.

'What do you think Earl wanted us to feel, coming here?' he asks.

I look around at all the people.

'Maybe he thought we'd become hermits when we were older and he wanted to remind us that there's a world full of people out there.'

Emmett laughs. 'He wasn't wrong, for me at least.'

I sigh. 'Nor me.'

'Do you think that's why we were so intense when we were younger? Because we just didn't like other people?'

I've always acknowledged how intense my feelings were for Emmett. I don't know that I really ever believed that he felt the same way. He never told me that he loved me, though I was sure I loved him.

'I mean, maybe. We were pretty codependent back then.'

Emmett laughs.

'Just a bit.'

'I think we both wanted something good in our lives.'

He nods. 'It terrified me.'

'It scared me too. How much I loved you. Even if I didn't admit it at the time.'

Emmett's gaze is intense. Maybe I preferred it when he couldn't communicate, when he didn't know how, when neither of us did. Now it's all so overwhelming. When really, what's the point? None of it matters. I'm not doing that again, falling in love. Not with Emmett, not with anyone.

It's okay for Earl. From beyond the grave, he can order us to mix with people if he wants, but in my case, it just wouldn't be fair. I gave up that part of my life, which had been pretty underwhelming anyway, once the symptoms of heart failure started. Mae had called me a noble imbecile.

'Why did you stop drawing, Luna?'

I'm looking off in the distance, at the bustling boulevards. It's like he expects that I'll answer, if he just springs the question on me.

'Please don't make me say it,' I half beg.

He looks at me for a moment, no, two, before he nods once and begins to eat.

And watching Emmett tuck into his lunch, in a place that Earl once was, in a place that Earl painted . . . well, it makes me so sad that falling overwhelmingly, terrifyingly in love is off the cards. Falling in love, I think, would be very easy indeed.

I wonder at what point I'll stop being tested. It feels as if my life is one long test, that I'm mostly failing. Because looking at Emmett in the spa, I might not fall in love with him, but falling in lust seems like a distinct possibility.

I found a bikini. I'm only small now. I didn't fall out of love with chocolate or crisps; they're as important to me as ever. But I just can't eat much – it's a part of my condition. It's stupid really, all those years I wasted worrying about not being soft and small, because now all I want is to be healthy and strong. So I picked up a small bikini, declining to try it on because who wants to get naked in a changing room with their ex-boyfriend three feet away? And plus, I hadn't been sure that I'd get my boots off and on again. Stupid ankles.

But since emerging into the spa I've discovered two things. One, that UK size small and Paris size small are two very different things entirely. And two, somehow I find semi-naked Emmett even more attractive than I did all those years ago.

Don't get me wrong, I've always found him attractive. When he was long and thin and gangly when we were teenagers, I drove myself mad with horniness before I even realised what it was.

And he's only improved in the past twenty-years. It's offensive.

He ducks under the water. I'm lying on a lounger on the proviso that I don't want to get my hair wet when in reality I need to keep my ankles up. I know that I should be more worried about how unwell I feel. I know that. But I'm distracted. I was right, it is dark in here. All navy blue and gold with moody lighting, and actually, it's awkward as hell being here with him.

We'd both emerged from the changing room, me clutching my robe like it was the giver of life around my super tiny, string bikini. Emmett had just shrugged his robe off and put it on a lounger. He took one look at me and dived into the pool.

'I'll just chill here then, shall I?' I'd said, propping myself back on the lounger.

And now I have to watch him swim. It's like I said, I'm being tested.

I close my eyes. Emmett had said something about resting. I should rest. It's late afternoon and I haven't rested all day.

I should close my eyes and rest since my chest is feeling so tight. But it's like I can't make myself look away. Emmett swimming is the sun, and I'm a dumb little moth pulled towards its brightness.

'Excuse me, miss, is this lounger taken?' a man asks with a French accent, but not in French, which makes me think that I don't look French enough for someone to speak French to me.

'Yes, sorry, it's my friend's.' I smile and look over to see Emmett half hidden under the water. Only his eyes are above it, watching us like a crocodile.

Rest goddamit! I tell myself.

I don't rest. Emmett comes to lie next to me, and we whisper about how amazing the spa is. I'm possibly talking to his pecs. He looks like a runner to me. He's not stacked or anything, he's still on the lean side. He's pale and there's a small patch of dark hair on his chest. Whatever he's got going on, it does it for me.

Part of me wonders if my heart is struggling so much because it's preoccupied with diverting blood supply elsewhere.

A woman in a spa uniform comes to tell us that we can have our treatments now. Emmett just smiles and says, 'my treat,' but then I think he dies a bit because they show us into a couples' treatment room.

He starts rabbiting in French, and the woman in the uniform looks horrified and leaves.

'She's checking whether they have two rooms.' Emmett looks self-consciously at the two massage beds.

'It's fine,' I tell him.

'I didn't mean to book a couple's massage. I'm not that much of a cliché.'

I laugh a nervous titter but mostly I'm thinking cliché me Emmett, cliché me away!

'Honestly, it's fine. It's a friendly thing to do, right?' I think I'll look back and wonder whether I'm being tortured or treated on this day. Possibly a bit of both.

The woman who looks like she should be on a runway somewhere is back, clipboard in hand, and tells us there is no other room.

Emmett, who appears to be suffering some exquisite pain right now, tells me as much and I reassure him that it's fine. I'll just be over here, half naked with my puffy ankles, literally dying, a couple of inches away from Emmett and his regular ankles.

Two more spa workers appear, armed with towels. This shit is getting serious then. I quickly fill out a questionnaire about my health. I'm not exactly honest. I just assume that if aromatherapy oils finish me off, I was probably a goner anyway.

And then I'm face-down on a bed. I'm looking at Emmett, because I thought it would be more awkward to look away from him. I see now that this was a total error. I should be staring at the wall. I have to look at him while some woman undoes the strap of my bikini top while they hit 'play' on the romance playlist. Clearly, they're going in hard.

It's been so long since someone touched me, I have to look

at him while a woman I've never met runs her hands up my back and across my shoulders. I'm sure she swipes the side of my breast where it's squished into the table.

I watch the same thing happen to Emmett. The way his skin glistens and gives under her thumbs.

It's meant to be relaxing. It's not relaxing.

'You are very tense, yes,' Emmett's masseuse tells him in heavily accented French.

He just sort of grunts at her.

It's amazing to me, the fact that we're here. A week ago, I never thought I'd ever see Emmett again, and now here we are. On some ill-fated mission guided by Earl and his paintings, frolicking around Paris, half naked and in the middle of a couple's massage.

I remind myself, for the tenth time this hour, why going there with Emmett is a bad idea. It's an extensive list of reasons. It should take me far longer to get through than it does.

It's just that watching him all oiled up makes me forget all the reasons. I'm struggling to even remember my own name.

No. Behave, brain. Different countries. Hurt me so bad in the past. Dying.

You know you really are desperate when even the thought of your untimely death doesn't quash the horn.

We're instructed to roll over so at least I don't have to look at him anymore. I do have to lie there while the masseuse drapes the towel over my nipples so that half my breast is hanging out. It's bad form to move the towel, isn't it? It's just a tiny towel. I thought this was a posh hotel. Why do they have such a small towel? It's alright for Emmett, his towel covers everything he needs it to, though he does have his eyes shut. I have more parts in need of covering. I try to shuffle down the bed a fraction, to no avail.

To be on the safe side, I keep my eyes shut for the whole rest of the massage. It's only when they leave us, mercifully wrapped up in towels (could have done with some of these earlier, Cherie) that I open one, tilting towards Emmett just a touch.

He has both eyes open. And he's staring at the ceiling.

'Thank you, that was lovely and relaxing,' I lie.

'Yes, very relaxing. You're welcome.' He sounds like a robot.

'How long do you think we should lay here?' I ask.

'They said to take as long as we like.'

What I do know is that I can't be the one to move first. My bikini top is folded neatly on a little table next to the aromatherapy oils. There's absolutely no way I'm getting up and trying to wrestle it on while Emmett is here.

Emmett sees me looking at my top.

'I think I'll go now, though. You take as long as you need.'

He's out of his towels like Jesus out of the shroud. 'I'm going for a cold plunge.' He tells me, leaving.

I smirk. Maybe I'm not the only one affected by this whole situation.

It does take some wrestling to get my bikini back on. Even my fingers are oily and also, they don't appear to be working so well. I should probably call the helpline. I just don't want to. I just want my heart to hold up for two more days.

I can't escape it, not fully though. I have to go and check my phone. Downside to being on the transplant list is I can't ever really be entirely away from it. I can't ever switch it off.

Anyway, I literally slide into the changing room and check my phone. Nothing except some inspirational quote memes from Mum. The day that woman learned to share from Facebook was a dark day, indeed. Mae had tried to remove her from the family Whatsapp.

Emmett appears to be several cold plunges deep by the time I'm done checking my phone.

I walk over to him.

'How're you doing?' I nudge the top of his arm where it's now freezing.

'Okay,' he tells me. 'Are you done?'

I nod. 'I might just head up to the room.'

He douses himself in freezing water again.

'Be my guest.'

I go to walk away, thinking that we've spent quite enough time in this spa.

'Luna.' Emmett touches the top of my arm lightly. I turn. It feels important. Whatever he's going to say, I think it'll be important. How can I be so close to him? He's right there, and he's looking at my lips. Some sort of lip-based muscle memory kicks in, and I wet them with the edge of my tongue.

'Why did you give up art?'

Tell him, I think. Tell him and he'll kiss you. No, no, no. Bad idea. Bad idea. Bad idea. It doesn't work, and reminding myself that this is a bad idea doesn't matter.

I'm still laser-focused on his lips, shaking my head furiously at his question, but I'm all in by the time Emmett looks at the ground and says, 'I'll see you upstairs.'

And I forgot, how could I forget that there's another reason it will never work between Emmett and me. It's not just my heart that's damaged; he's damaged too. And if memories of the past have shown me one thing, it's that no amount of love can fix him.

Chapter Twenty

THEN

Luna was 16
Emmett was 17

'Excited to be back?' Mae asked from where she was sitting next to Luna in the car.

'Yes. I mean, I think so.'

For the first time in years, Luna was determined to enjoy the summer as Emmett's friend – no more pining. She thought back to what she'd done last year, kissing Ahmed like that, and it felt so wrong. No, Emmett had made it perfectly clear that he didn't want to risk their friendship, and Luna was okay with that. She had to be.

Luna had heard from Emmett this year; they'd written as always. She knew that Tanya was out of prison and clean. She knew that with Gregor's help, Earl had sold another piece, the Montmartre one. She didn't know anything else. More than ever this year, she'd tried to just get on with her life, to pretend that Northumberland didn't exist. Except, of course, it did, and they were almost there.

Her mum and dad weren't speaking. Some argument about the fact that he was here for the whole summer this year, which hadn't exactly made her Mum happy. Luna wondered how many trips to the puffins they'd do.

'I need a break, Jennie. I can't shake this virus at all.'

They'd maintained a terse silence for the whole journey.

It continued as they pulled onto the driveway of the cottage.

'Great drive, everyone – the chat was excellent as always.' Mae was out of the car quickly. Luna waited though, because there, sat in his usual spot, was Emmett.

Her *friend* Emmett, she reminded herself.

That was this summer's plan. The Platonic Plan. Luna thought that it felt significantly easier to remember the merits of this plan when they were several hundred miles away.

'Hi,' she said. She felt scrubbed clean. After the dark year when she was fourteen, and last year's Glam Plan, Luna felt rubbed raw and tingly. Like a blank canvas.

'Hi,' he smiled. 'Need a hand bringing your stuff in?'

'Thanks.'

Luna loaded up Emmett's arms with supplies. She had more artwork than ever this year. If she didn't draw, she started to feel twitchy. Her anatomical drawings were getting better and better. Never good enough, never a replica of the real thing, but she liked the struggle – something about it felt noble.

It still wasn't the sort of art she felt she should be creating, but she accepted now that this was what she was drawn to. If art was always destined to be her hobby, she reasoned that she might as well draw what she liked.

Emmett piled Luna's things in the space at the bottom of their bed while Mae laid down and closed her eyes.

'You okay, Mae?' he asked her.

She waved a hand towards him.

'I have a pressure headache. I've been getting them whenever I'm forced to be around Mum for more than half an hour. Ten minutes and I'll be good to go.'

'Okay. We can go to The Edge – the others are there.'

It was impossible not to want to look at Emmett. But, Luna reminded herself, this was perfectly normal, totally within the bounds of a platonic relationship. They hadn't seen each other for a year; desperately staring at Emmett was a normal way to behave.

She noticed that his hair was shorter than it had been in the last couple of years, the curls were close to his head. It made his face seem sharper, a collection of angles that Luna had never fully registered were forming. Angles that made her heart speed up, left her feeling light-headed. This reaction possibly wasn't within the bounds of a regular, run of the mill, platonic relationship. It was just that when Luna thought about the scrappy boy Emmett had been when he was fourteen, there was none of that left now. Instead, there were darker patches on his chin, where he'd shaved.

It was undeniable: Emmett, the boy who had been Luna's best friend, was no more.

Nope. No. These thoughts were not in keeping with the friendship she was determined to cultivate. Men and women could be friends. Luna thought of her mum and Eyebrow Clive . . . Actually, that was probably a bad example.

They talked and filled in the blanks of the past year as Mae recovered from her headache, and then they were on their way to The Edge.

'I just wondered, Luna,' Emmett started, 'whether you'd like to do something just me and you tomorrow?'

When Luna looked at him, he swallowed. The movement of his Adams apple had her enraptured.

'Like what?' she said eventually, surprised. And also confused. Luna was also a little bit hopeful, though she had absolutely no plans to admit that to anyone, or herself for that matter.

'Like go to Holy Island.'

Emmett knew that Holy Island was one of Luna's favourite places up here. An island that could only be accessed when the tide was out.

The seed of hope that had been planted seconds before began to bloom and grow, like the fragile buds that formed at the first sign of spring. Luna acknowledged her hope, how delicate it was, how lovely it was. She almost wanted Emmett so say nothing else, in case he destroyed it.

'You could bring your pencils. Earl said he'd drive us.'

Luna couldn't imagine going to Holy Island and not drawing.

She held her breath, and when it seemed that Emmett had nothing more to say, nothing that might stamp out her fraction of hope, she answered.

'Okay, then. I'd like that.'

He nudged his hand against her own.

'Best summer ever,' he promised, linking their little fingers. Luna felt it like a spark of electricity.

'I'd like that too.'

Best summer ever, indeed.

Luna was ready for a day on Holy Island with Emmett. Or at least, she thought she was. Last night had felt strange, strained maybe. As if they were collectively holding their breaths, but for what, Luna wasn't sure.

She had to wait an age for her mum to come out of the bathroom but when the door finally opened and her mum emerged in a waft of perfume, she looked her daughter up and down and said, 'You've really grown into your features, Luna.'

Luna decided to ignore the tone of surprise since she was feeling generous. She felt distinctly less generous eating her breakfast listening to her mum and dad bickering. She wasn't sure which she disliked the most: silence or bickering. Neither was particularly fun.

'Must you leave all that rubbish on the table?' Her mum was fussing around Dad's models. 'There's no room for the breakfast spread.'

'Breakfast spread? Why are we having a spread? Just eat toast like a regular person.'

'I told you already, Clive is coming. And I'm on the Atkins. Why can you never support my aspirations?'

'Oh well, if Clive is coming then let's get the silver platters out. I told you, Jennie, I'm not well.'

On and on they went. Luna ate a slice of toast over the sink and listened out for the rumble of Earl's old van. Ever since last summer, when Emmett had lived with Earl, they'd become closer. Emmett said that he thought of Earl as like a grandad, and Luna was sure that Earl saw Emmett as his grandson.

Luna wasn't sure, exactly, how legal the whole thing had been, with Emmett living with Earl last year. She knew about things like social services, and the care system. Her mum had chuntered about how inappropriate the whole thing was. Luna didn't understand why none of the rules seemed to apply to the people who lived at The Edge. Sometimes, Luna imagined that the caravan park was barely real, a place which only existed for her and the people that she loved.

Neither her mum nor dad looked up as Luna said goodbye and darted from the door, grabbing her sketchbooks on the way.

Despite a restless night, Luna wasn't at all tired when she climbed into the back of Earl's van.

'Hi,' Emmett said.

'Hi,' she replied.

'Good morning, Luna. Got everything you need?' Earl asked from the driver's seat. Luna thought he looked smaller somehow. She pushed it from her mind.

'Yep, I'm all sorted.' She tapped the side of her bag with her pencils and notebook in. 'What are you working on today, Earl?' she asked as they drove north towards Holy Island.

'I'll be keeping going with my new piece.'

Earl had shown them his new work yesterday. It was called *The Rubicon*. He'd only just started it, but it was a blue door, probably somewhere in Paris. He'd told them that a rubicon is a precipice, a choice between two paths. So the door symbolised the choices they all had to make. Luna thought it was sadder than his other work, darker and more haunting, but still very beautiful.

'I'm sure Gregor will love it.' Earl's new collector had commissioned another of his paintings since last year, much to Gregor's delight. Luna was worried about the strain on Earl of working towards deadlines, though. He looked thinner, more worn out than normal. Zadie had mentioned a lingering cough.

'My dad's got that as well,' Luna had answered. 'There's a bug going around, I think.'

Now, Luna was distracted by the view from the van's window. She loved crossing the flats towards Holy Island and imagining that everything they were driving across would soon be beneath the sea.

'The tide starts to come in at 3pm,' Earl told them. 'I'll come back for 2.30, shall I? Make sure we have time?'

Two thirty was five hours away.

'That's great, Earl,' Emmett told him.

'Yeah, thanks for driving us, Earl.'

They waited while Earl coughed.

'This blasted cough,' he said finally, pulling into the island car park. 'So annoying.'

'Maybe you should have a rest today?'

'No, no, I'll be fine.'

Still, Luna and Emmett didn't move.

'Are you sure?'

'Yeah, we can come back with you if you like?' Emmett offered.

Earl waved a hand at them. 'No, no. None of that. Now go and have fun. I'll see you both later.'

They clambered out of the van and waited while Earl turned around and drove off. And then it was just them. Luna and Emmett on an island that felt like it was the end of the world.

'Beach?' he asked.

'Beach,' she agreed. They set off towards the north of the island, where the quieter beaches were, passing a couple of cafés on the way.

They were the first people there, walking along the grassy shore that reached down to the sand, the sun and the sea stretching out for miles ahead of them. Luna always wondered what it must have been like for the monks who came to live on the island centuries ago. They must have felt like they were on the very edge of the universe.

Luna felt like that now.

Neither of them spoke for a while, and Luna had the same sense that she did last night, of joint breath-holding.

'You know, Earl told me something this year,' Emmett said eventually. His voice was clear but he twisted his hands around and around. His shoulders were up, just a touch.

'Oh yes?'

'He said that with him and Sebastian, it wasn't about love. Not first and foremost. It was about friendship.'

'Did he? How interesting.'

Every part of Luna's body lit up. Like a million tiny fires lighting beneath her skin. She couldn't quite believe what she was hearing. She didn't dare believe it. Surely, she must have the wrong end of the stick. After all of these years, all this longing, it couldn't possibly be this easy. Things weren't easy, at least not for her. At least not this.

'He's been giving me all sorts of lectures, about emotional maturity.'

Luna knew that Earl was the only person who could get away with talking to Emmett like that. He was the only one that Emmett would listen to.

'That's cool.' Luna picked up a shell, rubbed the bumps of it under her thumb. It would be a good one to sketch.

'Did you know Mae wrote to me this year?' Emmett asked. At that, Luna stopped walking. She did not know this. Mae was an open book – she didn't keep anything from Luna. She'd even told Luna that the whole situation with Ahmed and Zadie was completely hopeless because Zadie liked girls. Though Luna was sworn to secrecy on the matter.

'No, I didn't know that,' she told him. 'What did she say?'

They'd stopped walking.

'She called me a coward.'

Fucking Mae. 'Wow, Emmett, I'm sorry. You know what she's like,' she babbled. 'You're not a coward; you're sensible. You're right. I've been stupid. Emmett . . . ' she said, though she'd no idea how to finish the sentence.

'Luna, let me just say what I need to, will you? I've planned the whole thing. I need to get it out, now. This is hard for me. Talking like this.'

'I know.' And Luna did know. It was hard for her too.

'What I'm saying is, well, I never should have got with Cadence, or anyone, because she isn't my best friend. You are. And I've been so scared of losing you, but Mae and Earl, and even that stupid kiss with Ahmed, they helped me to realise that I'm going to lose you. If I keep being scared. I want more. If you do too. I want us to be more than friends. If you want that too.' His whole speech, Emmett is fidgeting. Shifting from foot to food, balling and unballing his fist.

Luna didn't care because surely, this wasn't how it was meant to go. Teenage boys didn't come out with whole speeches. They lunged at you, tongue first.

It was just confusing. Luna had spent the whole year trying to tell herself that they should just be friends.

She was about to say no. A tiny dark part of her thought that it would be good for him to find out what it's been like, to be the one doing all of the longing. So much longing. But they were by the shore, and a huge wave came and soaked them.

They were both laughing then and Luna thought how

ridiculous it was that she'd even consider not giving into this; she'd wanted this for so very long. Maybe the whole time. Emmett was laughing and Luna thought that she could do this for him, she could make him laugh and be happy and it would be the greatest thing in the world. They were running away from the water, her trainers completely drenched. Emmett's too.

They ran up the beach and Luna got a stitch but Emmett grabbed her hand and then they running together. The beach was still deserted and when they stopped running, Emmett said, 'I worry I'll be no good at this. I don't know how.'

She didn't let him finish. Instead, she said, 'Please, yes, do it,' and 'I don't care' and Emmett seemed to know exactly what she meant.

The kiss was tentative at first. Scary because they both knew that they were crossing some sort of threshold. Emmett's mouth was warm and wet as it slid against her own and Luna thought that this was the most wonderful thing in the whole world. As long as she lived, she thought she'd never top this moment. She put her hands on his chest, just because she could, and felt his heart beating hard beneath his T-shirt.

'How are you so calm?' he asked her.

'Because it's you and me.'

'I'm sorry.' Luna didn't know why Emmett was apologising.

'Don't be.'

The truth was, Luna had probably been in love with Emmett her whole life.

Once they started kissing, it was really hard to stop. Luna couldn't quite believe that this was happening, in this place on the edge of the world. The first flick of his tongue made her sigh in a way she'd never done before. She hardly recognised herself.

They walked along the shore some more, carrying their shoes, the ruins of the priory in the background. They sat on the grassy bank so that Luna could draw, but they ended up kissing instead. Luna was amazed to find something that she enjoyed more than art.

It was just that, with art, she felt it in her hands, maybe her heart too, if she really thought about it. But kissing Emmett, well, she felt that everywhere. She was warm all over, and it made her skin more sensitive to the breeze. Her hands trembled a little and even the tips of her toes felt tingly. How miraculous, she thought, that she could feel so much, just from a kiss. She wondered at the marvel that her own body could create such sensations.

Emmett kissed her again, and this day, this moment, this hour, felt timeless, like the island.

'I wish we could stay here forever.'

She meant in this moment.

'We *will* leave. But we'll go together.'

'Would you come back, once you've finished uni?' she asked him. 'They need doctors here.'

'I can't. I think I'll be different, if I can get away. It's this place that makes me unhappy.'

Luna thought she'd be different if she could stay.

'Don't ask me to stay Luna, please.'

'I won't.'

She would never ask for more than Emmett could give. She promised herself that. There was so much more that she wanted to say. She already had a sense that what she had with Emmett was wonderful, but frightening too. But it was impossible to remember why it was so frightening when Emmett started to kiss her again.

'We'd better head back to the car park,' he said eventually.

Luna didn't want to go – some small part of her worried that this would stop as soon as they were anywhere else. It still felt fragile, just like it had when Emmett had asked her to come here yesterday. But of course, she didn't want to get stranded on the island either. Once the tide was in, there was no way off. Only a handful of people lived here full time.

Her worries eased somewhat as Emmett held her hand as they walked back to the car park.

'This should be harder?' he said, lifting up their interlocked fingers. 'We've been friends forever.'

'I know, it should.'

It didn't feel weird or hard, though. For Luna, it felt exactly how it was supposed to feel. She expected it to feel like fireworks, or sparks, and it did, it did feel like that. But it was also . . . calm. It felt right. The Platonic Plan had been a disaster, but honestly, Luna didn't care one bit.

They were waiting in the car park. It was after three and there was no sign of Earl. It was hard to be, like, super worried about this. Especially when Emmett was still holding Luna's hand, running his thumb backwards and forwards over her knuckles. It was hard to remember why she worried about anything, ever, when he did that.

Emmett called Earl.

'It's just ringing out,' he said, a slight frown between his eyebrows.

'Maybe he got distracted painting,' Luna wondered out loud.

'Yeah, it's probably just that.'

The kernel of worry that she'd been determinedly ignoring started to take hold as the car park emptied around them. Emmett walked up and down constantly now, trying to get hold of Earl.

'Still nothing.'

They looked out over the flat sand that stretched between the island and the mainland. The road that ran directly down the middle of it. Already, water was creeping towards it.

'Should we set off walking?' Luna asked.

'I don't think we'll make it.' Emmett shook his head. 'Earl said the tide started coming in at three. It's almost four now.'

Now Luna really was worried. Not particularly about being stranded, but about Earl. It was just so unlike him to not be somewhere he was meant to be. He was always there.

'I think we should set off,' she told him. 'To check that Earl's okay. We can run for it.'

Emmett looked out at the road, the way the water wasn't at all far from it.

'We have about twenty minutes. Come on.'

They set off at a run.

Out here on the road, watching as the tide ebbed its way determinedly towards them felt an awful lot less safe than back in the car park. There were no cars around.

'How's your swimming?' Luna asked, trying to keep the worry out of her voice.

'Let's not test it, shall we?'

Luna was hot, sticky and exhausted and they weren't even halfway. Plus, the tide was right there, at the edge of the road.

'I don't think we're going to make it.'

She really was panicked now. It was more persistent than the tide, the panic.

'We need to get as close to shore as we can.'

They ran even faster. Luna thought half hysterically that she'd rather run than swim. Where on earth was Earl?

Up ahead, the sound of an engine. Luna looked up, sure that it must be Earl. Except it wasn't, it was her . . . dad.

They stopped running, confused about why Luna's dad had come for them. She felt sick from the running but also from the worry that something might have happened to Earl.

'Dad, what are you doing here?' she asked as he came to a stop next to them. She and Emmett climbed in, buckling in as her dad did a million-point turn on the small sliver of road that wasn't taken over by the sea. He sped away, and some insane part of Luna thought how her mum would laugh to see that he could drive fast, he just mostly chose not to.

'Dad,' she prompted him again when he didn't say anything.

'Earl's fine,' he said and Luna deflated like a balloon with all the air let out of it. 'He had a funny turn and he's in hospital. He told the paramedics that you were here. But they're letting him out later. He'll be home soon.'

'Can we go to see him?' 'What sort of a funny turn?' Emmett and Luna asked questions at the same time.

Her dad waved his hand. Luna thought for a second he was the one who looked ill.

'Just old age. He's fine, though. Said there's no point in visiting. By the time you got there, he'd be on his way home.'

'Are you sure?'

'Absolutely,' her dad smiled. 'Now how was the island? The buttresses on that priory are some of my favourites, I have to say.' He kept talking, and Emmett linked his little finger over Luna's in the back of the car. But the little kernel of worry she had about Earl, well . . . it didn't completely go away.

Chapter Twenty-One

Earl didn't come back to The Edge that day.

Or the next.

The five of them, Luna, Emmett, Mae, Zadie and Ahmed, kept a sort of vigil by his caravan. Luna had picked her fingernails down to nothing, and Emmett's hair was sticking up at all angles. She didn't reckon that any of them were sleeping, but Luna was certain that he wasn't. He just paced and paced, full of coiled-up energy. In one of his darker moods.

Tanya emerged from her caravan one morning with a black eye and a split lip, her first in several months, and Luna thought that without Earl, they were falling to pieces.

'I'm going to see if he's back,' Luna told Mae first thing a couple of days later.

'I'll come.' She threw herself out of bed. She hadn't slept. Since the day on Holy Island, she had been euphoric that Emmett liked her liked her, finally, but also terrified that it would all go wrong.

Mae had responded to the news that Emmett and Luna

had kissed with 'about fucking time'. She'd been calling Emmett her brother-in-law ever since.

'We're going to check on Earl,' they told their mum in the kitchen. She was staring with disdain at their dad's models.

'I don't know, girls. It just feels like you're spending a lot of time down there. It can't be good for you. It's not right, the things that happen there.'

'It's because Luna just can't stop shagging Emmett,' Mae said without missing a beat. 'There'll be babies all over the place if we don't get her on the pill stat.'

Her mum went puce.

'She's winding you up, obviously,' Luna added. 'Though I don't know why she'd do that.' She looked pointedly at Mae.

'The reaction is just priceless.' Mae shrugged.

'I don't know why you bait her, what if she hadn't let us come?' Luna muttered to Mae as they walked towards The Edge. 'Then I wouldn't have seen Earl or Emmett today.' They were all frayed around the edges. Luna didn't feel like she had much energy for Mae and her ways.

'Please. Have you seen how much time she's been spending with Eyebrow Clive this week? She doesn't care where we go so long as we're not bothering her.'

'True. Shit, do you think she'll have an affair?'

Mae raised one eyebrow. 'With Eyebrow Clive? I doubt it. She just wants to make Dad jealous so that he wants her again.'

'Grim.'

'I know. But it's the truth. That's how marriage works.'

They reached the gates of The Edge. It was slightly overcast for a change; Luna pulled her jumper over the ends of her hands.

Emmett was sitting outside his caravan, alone. He stood up when he saw them and Luna thought that however worried she was about Earl, Emmett felt it ten times as much.

'Hi,' he smiled, dark and weary until he was kissing her good morning. A sad and desperate kiss and Luna wanted it to take away all of his hurt.

'It's early, people, let's keep it clean. What's the news on the big man bro-in-law?' Mae asked him.

Emmett's sad smile brightened somewhat.

'He's coming home today,' Emmett whispered. 'Sorry, Mum had a bad night but yeah, Fred, you know with the horse?'

They nodded. They did know Fred with the horse; Earl sometimes walked his dog. 'He's going to pick him up later. Not on the horse obviously.'

Relief made Luna feel almost light-headed. Maybe everything would be okay.

'That's great,' she said, kissing Emmett back, hard, pouring everything she had to give into it. 'I knew he'd be fine.'

'Course he will.' Emmett smiled properly, finally, into her lips.

'Yeah.' Mae smacked both of them on the back. 'He'll outlive us all, Earl. I'm always right about these sorts of things.'

*

It took some time for Fred with the horse to get Earl back to his caravan. They waited there all day, joined by the others, until eventually, Earl was home.

Luna wasn't sure how she expected Earl to look. Not really. She'd never been around someone who was sick, but she just assumed that Earl would be wearing his usual shirt and hat. The fact that he was in pyjamas and slippers made it very hard not to confront the fact that Earl looked . . . well, he looked like an old man.

'He *is* an old man,' Mae told Luna when she'd asked her if she was worried later that night. 'He's in his eighties.'

Mae was right. Even if no one seemed to know for sure how old Earl was, he'd been an old man the whole time Luna and her family had been coming to the cottage. It came as something of a shock to Luna, the reality that while she had been ageing over these summers at The Edge, so too had the people around her. And that included Earl.

Once he was home from hospital, Earl became the centre of all their plans that summer, as if through collective will alone, they could get him well again. Ahmed took out several books from the local library, ones that he thought Earl would like, and stayed up late reading to him every night. Luna heard Zadie mutter that it really was a pity she didn't fancy boys.

Zadie and Mae took over the baking, conjuring up ever more elaborate treats to tempt Earl, who seemed to have left his appetite at the hospital.

The only person who didn't seem worried about the fact that Earl looked to be getting more, not less, poorly, was Emmett.

Luna had been worried that Earl being sick would force Emmett to sink even deeper into his darkness. The sort where he spent a lot of time looking out to sea and asking what the point of it all was. But instead, Emmett had responded with such forced optimism that that in itself had become a cause for concern for Luna.

They were sitting tucked in against the edge of the cliff, having left the others with Earl. Emmett's hand was in Luna's hair. She was gripping the front of his T-shirt, doing her best to anchor them in this moment.

Between her parents and Earl, they didn't get a lot of privacy, so there'd been no time at all, really, to play out the various scenarios that kept running on a loop through her head, the worries about Earl and Emmett battling for dominance. Like right now, Luna wanted to, she didn't know, touch Emmett all over, but she was so worried that he didn't seem to realise how unwell Earl was. She made herself break the kiss, but it took a few seconds of breathing deeply before she was ready to talk.

'Do you think Earl's getting better?' she asked him, tiptoeing into the conversation. She wasn't able to help kissing down the side of his neck.

'Yeah, absolutely, he is.' Emmett tilted his head back, and Luna kissed a path across his Adam's apple.

'It's just . . . ' She pulled away again. Emmett's cheeks were flushed, and his eyes were glassy. 'He didn't eat any of those muffins Mae made; you know cherries are his favourite.'

Emmett frowned at that, only for a second, before he schooled his features into a neutral smile again. 'Maybe he just wasn't hungry. It's normal after you've had a chest infection to lose your appetite a bit. Don't worry, Luna.'

He reached for her again and Luna went. She wanted so badly to believe him.

'You're sure?' she asked.

This time, Emmett had no trouble summoning a bright smile. 'Absolutely, Earl will be back to his old self in a couple of days, you'll see.'

Earl wasn't back to himself in a couple of days. And Fred with the horse had to take him back to hospital more than once. Luna was no expert, but she was fairly certain that Earl had more than a chest infection.

She wondered, on an evening in the dark, if this was the price she had to pay for being happy with Emmett. As if there was some cosmic, karmic force in the universe that said that in order to have so much happiness, pain had to come from elsewhere. There was Earl and there was her mum and dad. Mae had seen their mum sneaking into Eyebrow Clive's house one day when their dad was on a long trip to the puffins. Luna felt sure that their dad knew too. Like Earl, he seemed grey and heavy. Her dad had always been a big bear of a man, and now to Luna he looked to be shrinking.

So she should feel guilty if her happiness was causing all of this pain. The uncertainty pushed her closer to Emmett. He was the only thing she was sure of, and she wanted to grab hold of him tight. She worried that she wouldn't survive if it ever ended.

'We should stop?' he said.

'What, no way, carry on.'

Emmett laughed. They were on his bed, and he was laid on top of Luna – the very last thing she wanted to do was stop.

'Your mum might come home any second. Plus, we told the others we'd be back at six. It's seven already.'

He meant from Earl-watch. They had a rota and everything, though Earl (and Emmett) maintained that they didn't need one.

'Alright fine.' She sat up and straightened her clothes as Emmett rolled off her.

They walked, hand in hand, towards The Edge, and Luna thought, again, how easy life would be if she could just stay. Leaving felt like abandoning Earl and Emmett more than ever this year, and she didn't want to do that. She wanted to stay and keep them all happy and safe.

'I'm just going to go and water Miss Compton's plants,' Emmett said. Earl being sick had made them all realise just how much he was doing for the other people who lived at The Edge. Miss Compton had gone to visit her son, and apparently, Earl always watered her plants when she was gone, so now they had taken over, along with a whole host of other stuff that Luna had no idea that Earl was doing.

'Okay.' She kissed him. 'I'll see you at Earl's.'

Luna walked the rest of the way alone, calling hello to people sitting outside their caravans.

She didn't even think about knocking; they'd never knocked at Earl's.

She found him on the sofa, reading a leaflet.

'Where are the others?' she asked him and watched, panic-stricken as he tried to hide the leaflet behind a sofa cushion. It was too late, though. And now, Luna was crying.

How to tell your loved ones you have cancer.

'I sent them to the beach; there is no need for this vigil.'

'We're just trying to take care of you.'

Earl's caravan was full of artwork, stacked against cupboards and piled on the little table, and Luna was furious. It felt like her blood was lava. She was furious and she didn't even know what or who she was furious with.

Luna couldn't stop the tears, once they'd started, and Earl knew that she'd seen the leaflet. He tapped the sofa next to him and Luna went, stupidly crying big stupid tears, even though people survived cancer all the time? Didn't they?

'The leaflet did not cover this,' Earl told her, pulling it back out from behind the cushion.

'Emmett will be here soon,' she told him. She didn't know exactly why she said this. Except that already she wanted to protect Emmett from this. Earl nodded and tucked the leaflet away again.

'It will not be so quick, little Luna. This is what the doctors say. Once Emmett has left, they think.'

'You have to tell him,' she said, still unable to believe that this was happening. How could this be happening?

'Not yet. After his exams. Once he has gone.'

It seemed to Luna that some of the air had left the caravan. Why was it so difficult to breathe?

'But that's next year!' she said, half gasping. 'You can't keep this a secret until next year. It'll be obvious.'

Earl chuckled. 'People believe what they want to believe, little Luna. And Emmett wants me to be well. I will have no big treatment, just enough to keep it at bay for now.'

For now. Luna felt sick.

'But why?' She wasn't sure exactly what she was asking. Why not tell Emmett? Why is this happening? Why can't things just *be* good and *stay* good?

Earl answered the first of her questions.

'Emmett has a chance to get out of this place, Luna. To be free of his childhood. If he is ever to make his way back here, he must be allowed to take that chance and go. How could I live with myself if I were the person who stopped him, hmm? No, I think we must protect him from this.'

Luna wanted to tell Earl that nothing mattered, it didn't matter, that Emmett should know. But she also agreed, this would destroy Emmett. What if it did rob him of his only chance to get away?

'How . . . how can we manage?'

'We will live in this moment, the same as we always do, Luna. This is the way of things, is it not?'

She didn't answer. She couldn't. It shouldn't be the way of things.

'Do not tell him, Luna. I am asking you this one thing, yes?'

There was no time to reply because the caravan door was opening and Emmett was bundling through it. 'Hi Earl . . . Luna, what's wrong?' he asked, stopping dead in the little caravan kitchen.

'I, er . . . oh I was just thinking that . . . ' Luna floundered but she had nothing. Nothing other than the fact that Earl was sick. The fact that he was dying.

'Luna and I were talking about *The Arnoflini Portrait* and how while there are many secrets in it, it is still a beautiful piece.'

Luna had no idea what *The Arnoflini Portrait* was, but there and then she made the decision to do what Earl had asked and save Emmett this heartache for as long as she could. Maybe she was doing it for herself, too, in some way. So, she said, 'It's just really emotional.' This wasn't the first time that Luna had lied to Emmett. She'd lied about her feelings for so long. And she'd thought that nothing, nothing could hurt more than those lies. She knew now though that she was wrong. This was the lie that hurt the most.

Earl nodded, satisfied, but Emmett said, 'Okay,' really slowly, and then laughed in a way that said, 'Artists.'

They spent the rest of the evening outside the caravan, towards the cliff edge, looking out at the sea. Zadie plaited Mae's hair and Emmett, Earl and Ahmed played cards as the sun set. Luna kept looking at Earl, half expecting him to just disappear one second, half wondering how it could ever be possible that he just wasn't there.

Luna had never thought about death. It seemed to her like a foreign country, something far away and distant. She knew that it worried Emmett. He'd seen it more than her. When you had an addict as a parent, it became something of an inevitability.

But now, she was being forced to confront death. And it struck her as nonsensical. How could it be that a man who had so much love and energy to give, more than maybe anyone else she'd ever meet, could one day not be here. Where did it go when he goes? All that love and energy? It seemed unfathomable.

She wished that she could stop the passage of time. Or, better than that, she wished that she could go back to how things were before she knew this awful thing. She would keep Earl's secret to protect Emmett. And she'd keep the secret Mae had told her, about her mum and Eyebrow Clive. She thought about the secret thoughts she had about herself. The ones that told her she'd fail. She thought that all of these secrets might well have a way of coming for her. She knew for certain that she couldn't outrun them forever.

Chapter Twenty-Two

NOW

The Juxtaposition of Life and Death: Oil on canvas. Spencer's use of colour in this piece is extraordinary. The interplay of light makes the scene almost pulse and shimmer, adding a breathing quality to the composition. The brushwork of the tree cascades across the canvas, as if it is alive and in flux. c.2007.

I settle onto the bed in Emmett's room, the aromatherapy oils making me almost light-headed.

I'm flicking mindlessly through the comments on my blog, just like I'd do at home when I want to escape my own thoughts. I click on my profile and see that my followers are still going up.

I'm never going to be a social media guru, I'm not even close to being in influencer, and I wouldn't want to be. I wasn't lying to Emmett when I said that initially I just wanted a place to vent, and talk about the art that interested me, after my diagnosis. I guess that deep down, I'm hoping that I'll find an artist who's solved it. Death – what happens after.

I read once that humans have evolved to live with death because we simply refuse to believe that one day it'll happen to us. It's one of the reasons why living with a life-limiting condition is so tricky. We don't like to be confronted with our own mortality.

I'm bone tired, weirdly horny, and also now depressed. Which is a heady mixture.

I have several Instagram messages. One from Darth saying that he can't find the blue door. I'm disappointed, since Darth seems intelligent. If anyone had found it, I'd have expected it to be him.

I scroll and reply to some more when a message from Vincent, one of my earliest followers, comes through. I jolt upright.

VincentVanGetOutOfHere: I think I found the building!

I reply right away.

TheArtofDying: What where? How did you find it?

VincentVanGetOutOfHere: AI. It only took all night and day.

Vincent has Parkinson's disease. His muscle spasms make it difficult to sleep.

> **TheArtofDying:** I could kiss you! Great work.
>
> **VincentVanGetOutOfHere:** There's more.
>
> **TheArtofDying:** Do tell.
>
> **VincentVanGetOutOfHere:** It's an art studio. They have a class on tomorrow night, life drawing. It could be that Spencer actually went there to paint.
>
> **TheArtofDying:** Wow, imagine that.

Even as I type it, I'm thinking that I could go there. I could draw in a place where Earl likely was. If drawing was a thing that I did anymore.

Vincent has sent a link! It's to the art studio and I can see it then, the same bright blue façade of Earl's painting.

> **TheArtofDying:** Brilliant work!
>
> **VincentVanGetOutOfHere:** I live to serve our leader.

'Guess what!' I tell Emmett the second he walks through the door, tiredness and unwelcome horniness gone. 'A follower found the door in *The Rubicon*. It's an art studio, and they have a class tomorrow night.'

'What, no way?' Emmett looks like a man who has endured several cold plunges. His hair is flatter than normal, sticking to his head. In my excitement at Vincent's discovery, I'd forgotten that Emmett and I are staying in this hotel room tonight. Together. In separate beds, but together still. 'Are you going to go?'

'I don't know. They have a life-drawing class on tomorrow night, but it's been so long since I drew anything, I'd be all crappy.' This, I think, is as good an excuse as any.

Emmett walks over and sits next to me on the edge of the bed.

'You don't have to go. Not if you don't want to.'

Emmett has asked several times why I don't draw anymore, so it's unexpected, the ease with which he gives me an out. I think about how it would be to not go. To just let this opportunity pass me by, float away into the distance never to be seen again. It would be easier to return to neutrality, without living through this experience, I'm sure of it.

I think of the door. Choices. I could maybe just look at the building. That would be enough. Maybe.

'I'll think about it,' I tell Emmett.

He nods and then says, 'We can go to the graveyard in the morning, if you like.'

'I do like.' I feel so tired though, and my chest is tight. I think I'd better take Dr Dave's advice and rest. Which is how I find myself on the giant bed in Emmett's room, surrounded by a small mountain of food and watching *Escape to the Chateau*.

It's like a very vivid depiction of every childhood fantasy I ever had.

It's comfortable and familiar and I think about how easy it would be to slip back into this. I catch Emmett looking at me from the other side of the bed and wonder if he thinks the same thing. He might. But, as a sudden tightness in my chest steals my breath, I remind myself that I can't have this. I couldn't have it then and I can't have it now.

I can't have this with Emmett, but I could have art. I could bring art back into my life, however long or short that may be. It's this thought which makes me reach for my phone, in the darkness of the Parisian night. It's this thought which makes me scroll to the website of the art studio with the blue door, and it's this thought which makes me book a place on the life-drawing class.

As I lay back down, I realise that I'm smiling, that I want to have things to look forward to, like I did when I was younger and I felt excited about each summer. I'm not like that anymore, but maybe just for tomorrow I can be.

We're in the Pere Lachaise cemetery. It was one of the last things that Earl painted, *The Juxtaposition of Life and Death.*

'It's amazing here.' I spin on the spot, my eyeline in every direction taken up by huge tombs, some decrepit and decaying in a particularly Victorian type of way, others new, with stained-glass windows and pictures of the dead. Everywhere, there are trees. Flowers and grass spring up from the ground, or else force their way through concrete, demanding to be seen.

'It's a great cemetery,' Emmett agrees. He has *The*

Juxtaposition piece up on his phone, seemingly determined that we can find the exact place that Earl painted.

'This way I think.' He sets off and we pass through the heart of the cemetery, which is full of people. Some like Emmett, hold their phones ahead of them, others have a map. If there's a significant person's tomb, a little cluster of tourists gathers around it. Like Oscar Wilde's; even though a wall of glass protects it after someone hacked the penis off the angel there, there's still a massive group of people. One or two of them seem to be weeping.

Needless to say, it takes us an age. Partly because I'm stupidly slow as per, but also because I insist on stopping to look at so many of the tombs.

'This place is bigger than my actual house,' I say, peering at a particularly large one covered in moss, which no one is looking at. I wonder how easy it is to get a spot here; maybe Mae could come and chuck some of my ashes in one of the massive family crypts where they must have space. I want the rest of me in the cemetery at home, the same place where Earl is.

It's a sobering thought, and frankly it's a testament to the brilliant cemetery that I've only just started to think that one day, and soon, people will be walking past my grave, wondering who I was. I see a bad photo of someone stuck to the front of theirs. Mae knows that only great photos are allowed.

I take some pictures for the Deathers.

'Everything okay, Luna?' Emmett is ahead of me, holding his phone up to the horizon as if it's a compass.

I take a breath. 'Yeah, absolutely fine. How're you getting on?'

I lose him momentarily as a group of Japanese tourists, all wearing little red caps, cut between us, following a man with a flag.

'This tree.' He comes back for me and points to a tree at the front of Earl's painting; it's unusual, with a twisty pale trunk. 'I think it's over by that far wall. There's some wall in the background, see.'

It's not well defined, but there is a wall in Earl's painting. There's a sense of perspective; I don't think the tree is right by the wall.

'I think it's just a bit in front of it. Let's have a look.'

We keep walking, more urgently now that we're close to the spot Earl painted.

'It's there,' I say, hurrying, in the loosest sense of the term, towards the twisty tree in the distance. 'What do you think Earl wanted us to realise, by coming here?'

'I don't know. But look, that's it.'

We arrive at the point that's obviously in the painting. We're on the outer edges of the cemetery here, and the tombs are much smaller. Normal headstone-sized, almost. It's quieter here too, away from the other tourists, more peaceful.

'Do you think Earl was here?' Emmett asks, and I think he must have been, since he remembered it so well.

'I think so.' We stand then, our hands almost touching, and I know that both of us feel closer to Earl than we have done so far. I don't know what Earl was trying to tell us, if we're even doing what he instructed when he said the answer is always in the art, but it feels good, being somewhere he was.

'Look,' Emmett says, nodding his head towards the gravestone under the tree.

I move closer to get a proper look and I realise then what it says:

SEBASTIAN LACOMBE
19TH SEPTEMBRE 1928 – 27TH AOUT 1951
ARTISTE ET REVEUR

'What's *reveur*?' I ask Emmett, staring intently at Sebastian's grave.

'Dreamer,' he answers. 'Did Earl ever tell you that Sebastian died?'

I shake my head. 'Earl never said anything except that they got one summer together, and then he disappeared. Maybe he knew, after all, that Sebastian was here, if he painted it?'

'He must have done. I didn't know his surname before.' Emmett is tapping into his phone, his eyes scanning whatever he finds before he hands it to me.

'Sebastian Lacombe is buried in the Père Lachaise Cemetery in Paris. A talented young artist who was already making a name for himself in the post-war years, Sebastian succumbed to TB at the age of just twenty-three. His grave can be found . . . '

'Earl must have known he was sick – you don't die from TB quickly,' Emmett says.

'Or maybe he wanted to believe that Sebastian was well. Maybe it was easier to think he disappeared, rather than accept that he was dead.'

Emmett looks down at me, blocking out the sun for a moment.

'That makes sense.'

'Why do you think that he wanted us to come here though – if that's what he even wanted?'

'I don't know,' Emmett shrugs. 'Maybe he wanted to remind us that life does end.'

Oh Earl, I didn't need reminding of that.

I look between the grave and Emmett. The life that's in the painting isn't the greenery like I've always assumed – the trees and flowers and moss that butt against the graves here – it's the love between Earl and Sebastian.

'I think it's the fact that love means death. Like they're two sides of the same coin. It's what he suggested to me about beauty and decay too. You can't have life and love without death since death is what makes it all so special.' It's been so long since I felt that life was special; it is really, though, if you think about it. 'I think he was telling us to take the risk.'

'Luna.' Emmett has turned to face me. 'I know you want to be friends, and I understand. I never did deserve you, even back then, but if you could find a way . . . I don't want us to spend the next twenty years not knowing each other. I want more, but if you want to be friends, then, please . . . '

Emmett is visibly suffering when I reach up and plant a gentle kiss on his lips. I don't know what makes me do it. There are so many reasons I shouldn't be doing it. But being here, and thinking how one summer of love sustained Earl for a whole lifetime, it makes me realise that it doesn't matter if my life is short, we only ever have this very moment anyway. And in this moment, I want to kiss Emmett.

He's momentarily stunned and I think for a second I've made a terrible miscalculation but then he's pressing his lips to mine, firmer and more insistent. And maybe it's a weird thing to be kissing so passionately in a cemetery, possibly in whatever afterlife might exist we're going straight to hell, but I'm breathing hard and feel light-headed when we pull apart.

'Luna,' Emmett is close to tears, 'I thought I'd lost you.'

'I can't promise you a future,' I tell him, meaning something different from what he thinks. Maybe we'll only have these two days, and so be it. Two days is better than nothing.

'I understand.' He doesn't, but at least I've given him some fragment of truth.

We walk back to the hotel slowly, pressing close on the metro and holding hands along the boulevard towards Emmett's hotel. Holding Emmett's hand is like trying on an old worn jumper that you lost for years and then rediscover. It just fits so well. We haven't agreed to come back here, we've hardly agreed anything, but I notice that I'm the one leading the way. If I only have two days, I want to press as close to Emmett as I can.

We pass through the lobby of the hotel in a daze. I don't know how we get to our room.

I do know that I go and stand in front of the mirror, the

full-length mirror. A part of me wants to check that I'm still really here. That I'm whole, since I feel so otherworldly all of a sudden.

Emmett appears behind me. An apparition in pale blue.

'Luna,' he says and standing behind me like that, we just fit together. I see that. I've always seen that. We shouldn't. It shouldn't work. He's preppy and I'm not. He's disciplined and I'm chaos. He's tight and sinewy and I'm soft and small. We shouldn't fit together. But we do.

I feel my heart in my chest and I think come on, please don't give out on me now. Please give me this time, as Emmett brushes hair from my shoulder and trails a finger slowly up the side of my neck, leaving a trail of goosebumps in his wake.

'I thought I'd lost you,' he says again. I shouldn't let him believe that he can have me. For so many reasons, all of which are escaping me right about now. Especially when he leans down to kiss the path his fingers just took.

Suddenly, I'm desperate, I make a desperate sound, but Emmett seems determined to go slow. He's torturing me basically, and I'm letting him.

His eyes meet mine in the mirror.

Yes, okay, I'm letting him.

He eases the strap of my dress down on one side while he continues to trail kisses wherever he wants. I'm light-headed with lust, dizzy with desire. Apparently, I turn into a poet when I'm turned on.

The other side of my strap comes down, and my top just gives up any pretence of staying up and flops down at the front. I clench and unclench my hands, itching to cover myself up, but Emmett is making soothing noises and so I give in to it all.

The edges of my vision go dark again.

I'm literally going to die from lust. Mum will disown me. Nope, not the time to think about Mum right now, not when Emmett's hands are working their way down my chest and I'm just watching them in the mirror.

There's a thin sheen of sweat on my skin as Emmett's hands continue their torture; he's back to kissing my neck and I think, you know what, if this is how I go, then so be it. What a way to die.

I can't take it anymore. I need to turn around to kiss him properly. I want to press myself so close to him that I'm impossible to dislodge.

I can feel my pulse, it's erratic. Just give me a little more time, I think. Let me have this day, this night. But then Emmett is on his knees in front of me, and I'm watching him in the mirror. It's illicit and gentle and so stupidly sexy all at the same time. And for the first time in a very, very long time, I give over my body, willingly, trusting it, tentatively at first and then with more conviction. I give over my body to Emmett.

Chapter Twenty-Three

The hotel room comes back to me in fragments. The heavy curtains, the dark floor, the huge lighting, the mirror.

The mirror.

I can see myself in the mirror. I'm on the floor, sprawled out like a rag doll. I hate the fact you can see my ribs, but there's also a naked Emmett which I love. I think I blacked out for a moment there, and now my chest is rising and falling quickly, as I start to panic.

'Nice of you to rejoin us.' Emmett rolls on his side to face me, and I'm rewarded with a great view of his arse in the mirror. My mouth is dry though and I'm still feeling shaky. Emmett realises a fraction of a second after I do that I don't feel good. My pulse is rapid, beating hard in my head.

'Luna,' Emmett frowns, 'is everything okay?'

Not really, the edges of my vision are blurred.

'I haven't taken my meds yet,' I tell him, blinking quickly, trying to count my breaths. 'My pill box is in my bag, could you maybe bring it?' I say, settling back against the pillows that he drags off the bed and props under my head.

I hate feeling like I'm broken.

'Hey, it's okay.' A still-naked Emmett hands me the pills and a glass of water. Since I sort them into a box that has times of the day on it, it doesn't say what the medicine is for, but still.

'That's a lot of medicine for someone who had glandular fever,' Emmett says, kneeling next to me and putting the back of his hand on my forehead as I knock them back like the pro that I am.

'It's like vitamins and stuff.' I don't even sound convincing to myself and I think, tell him now, you idiot! He's here, helping, he's a doctor, he can help.

But I'm leaving tomorrow. That's all we get. And information like this, it fills up space and time. There's no shying away from it. It would take all of everything.

'I feel better already.' Emmett puts a blanket over me.

It's true, I do. Maybe I did just need to rest.

I want to get back to feeling sexy. Emmett is still naked, and I'm only human after all, but there's just no natural segue back from squeezing someone's nipple and then moments later handing them a giant pill organiser. What do you do next?

Emmett obviously doesn't know either; he's just kneeling next to me, looking stressed. There's a vein on the side of his forehead that wasn't there before.

'Hey, it's fine,' I tell him. 'I feel fine, relax. Get in here.'

He gets more pillows and comes to lay next to me on the floor, brushing my hair back off my face. 'You're okay,' he tells me. 'I'm okay.'

I mean, I'm not. And the weight of the constant lying settles over me as Emmett kisses my forehead.

My eyes flutter shut as the kisses carry on; it's gentler this time, softer. Sometime later we make it onto the bed at last; I think I want to take this moment and stretch it out for all of time. As Emmett moves above me, I think that I want this to never, ever have to end.

My body is in a sort of constant battle between being excited and just wanting to go to sleep. An afternoon of sex with a long-lost love and a couple of mild cardiac episodes will do that to a person.

'I booked the class,' I tell Emmett. He has his head buried in my hair where I'm laid over his chest.

'You're tired,' he says, 'you don't have to go.'

'It's my last chance – the final point in the quest. Now or never.'

He is silent for a beat. And then he's moving.

'Come on then, we'd better go.'

It feels like Paris itself knows that something big is happening. The stars seem especially bright. The streetlights glow with extra warmth. People laugh louder, or else chatter in cafés with more vividness. It's like the city knows that there'll be a choice to make, and soon. Or maybe I'm projecting, looking for things that aren't really there.

'Are you okay to wait and eat after?' Emmett asks. I think he's become a feeder in his old age. He's obsessed with feeding me.

'I'm fine, honestly. I'm too excited to eat.'

We're walking slowly now, the pace dictated by me and my pitiful body. Emmett knows where we're going, so I try to remind myself to take in the streets as we pass them until we arrive at a small, nondescript building.

'It's here,' he tells me, halfway down some regular Parisian boulevard. The blue door. The final thing that Earl painted.

The door is old, worn. The stones around it are crumbling, their edges no longer sharp.

It's the same as at the cemetery – the feeling that Earl was here, in this very spot. I can feel him urging me on, pushing me forward towards the door.

Inside, the lights are on, but the windows are frosted. Emmett doesn't move.

'Maybe this is where they met?' he says.

'I think so too.'

'I'll see you in a couple of hours. I have my phone – call if you need me?'

We'd swapped numbers earlier, self-consciously and quietly. I hadn't wanted to think about the fact that I'd have a means of always contacting him now, if I needed one.

'Okay, but are you sure you don't want to come in?' I ask. For a man who just had sex twice, Emmett seems heavy, weighed down in a way that reminds me of the past.

'No, this is for you. Go, and I'll see you soon.' He leans down and kisses me, gently. It feels like the intimate gesture that it is, and his being in such close proximity addles my senses and makes me wish with everything that I have that things were different.

By the time I push the door open, Emmett is already gone. I'm greeted by a bright room, people sat around the middle of a space where a stool is covered with a white cloth.

'*Bon soir, madame*.' A man with an expansive beard comes over to me. He's pencil thin and wearing a stripy suit.

'*Bon soir*, I have a booking, for the life drawing . . .' but before I even manage to finish half a sentence, the man lets out a string of very loud, very French exclamations. I'm almost certain that I just heard every French swear word going.

'It is you!' he finishes.

'Er . . .'

'Louis! LOUIS!' Another man, this one in every way diametrically opposite to Louis, appears in a Hawaiian shirt and cargo shorts. 'The model is ready, she will wait no longer. *MERDE*!' The man in the Hawaiian shirt also spots me.

'We must talk after class,' Louis tells me, before he and the guy in the shirt have a whole conversation about me.

I can't interrupt them because a model is walking through the space now, a white dressing gown draped loosely over her shoulders.

And then there's a naked woman on the stool. I stumble towards one of the spare easels. I'm having some sort of out-of-body experience; it's all just happening so fast. Obviously I'd signed up to the drawing class, but didn't I realise that I don't do that anymore? Drawing makes you feel free, but I'm not free. I'm trapped inside a broken body.

The model arranges herself into an artful position, one knee raised, which she rests her elbow on and her chin on her hand.

And yet . . . I'm in front of a blank canvas. I can hear Louis and the other man still arguing in the back room.

I must look like a startled deer who has never so much as wielded a pencil because the person next to me, who is head to toe in neon pink Lycra, leans over and says in heavily accented English, 'Is just a little fun, yes?'

I nod, grateful even as stress claws at me, pulling me towards the blue door and away from here.

She gives another encouraging smile, readjusts her tiara and then sets to work.

Fun.

Some people are inclined to think that artists are a bit snooty. And probably some of them are. But I love artists. Artists might be lots of things, but they are rarely boring.

It's weird if I just sit and stare at the model without drawing.

I could just do a little. I didn't think that I could come to Paris, and here I am. I didn't think that I'd ever see Emmett again and look what happened there. In Paris, anything is possible. So yes, surely I can survive one art class. I mean, I'm light-headed, and my heart is pounding, but I think it's the paint fumes. Hopefully, it's the paint.

I pick up a pencil, far more my medium than paint, and try to ground myself in the moment. I'm somewhere that Earl was. He might have painted in this exact spot.

I look between the model and the blank canvas.

Everyone thinks that with life modelling you're all thinking the same thing – that there's a naked person in the room – and maybe some people are, but I've never felt like that. I've always been excited to capture the realness, or as close to it as I could. That's what I've always loved about art. No matter how good at it we are, we can never fully capture the human experience. Even the most accurate depiction of a human form is just that, a depiction. And yet we keep trying.

It's probably another reason why I quit art, though. Because who wants to study the human form when my own is so persistently lacking?

I try to push the thought from my mind, focus instead on the model – the shape of her back as it curls over, the rise of her knee. I'm trying to sketch it out, to let myself bleed into the ebb and flow of the scratching of my pencil. I'm out of practice, and my swollen hand is cramping; it makes each stroke fragile, delicate and lovely, and I think that's it, isn't it – no matter how fragile we are, we're still lovely. No matter how thin the line between life and death becomes, no matter how much some of us might feel like we're straddling both worlds, the living and the dead, so long as we can make art, we are life and life is us.

Louis, now back and with a lit cigarette hanging out of the side of his mouth, raises his eyebrows and nods as he walks past behind me. I don't draw for approval, though, you can't – it's too subjective.

Earl taught me that art is what we make it. I see art

everywhere, or at least I used to. Art magnifies the human experience. That's why I stopped.

I've been trying to make my life as small as possible.

Maybe that's been the whole point of this thing. Perhaps Earl's art was never about beauty, or fun, or people, or death, or choices for that matter. It was about feeling something, anything, this whole time.

And I do feel, as I draw. I feel the wonder of a blank canvas becoming full, the marvel that we can do this. Humans can make art and know that they're making art. It's pretty miraculous if you think about it, that as a species we can make anything interesting, just by looking at it a little differently.

I'm so full, yet it's a flicker of a moment before the time is up, and the model is putting her robe back around her. I hardly even recognise my drawing. It's an outline. 'There's a hollow emptiness; this is very intriguing,' Louis says, and I realise he's right. I've done a lot of shadow and shading on the outside, but I've left the inside completely blank. 'Darkness,' he finishes. He pronounces his s's as z's.

It's possible that I've just drawn my trauma, but I don't have time to dwell on it because a man in a lilac suit is coming towards me.

'Excuse me, miss, but do I recognise you?'

'No, I don't think so,' I tell him, hoping that we're not about to have a repeat of MAM here.

'I thought the same thing,' a woman pipes up. She's wearing a poncho; she looks like a giant bat. 'From the Earl Spencer piece. She is a lot like you.'

'Oh, do you think so?' I'm not entirely sure what to say, so much for flying under the radar.

'Yes, yes, it is you. Your hair is very unique. How fascinating.' The woman is really close to my face. 'Did you know Spencer?'

At this point the other artists are heading our way, all peering. I take it they've all been to the new exhibit.

For a moment, before the fear sets in, I feel pride for Earl. All these artists know who he is. It's amazing, I wish he was here to see it.

'Yes,' I say proudly, my heart beating a heavy beat, even though my voice is shaky. 'We knew him when we were children.'

The crowd make all the right cooing noises.

The pink lady claps her hands together really fast several times. 'I must interview you. The man behind the artist.' She holds his hands up to make a square. 'I can see it now. You will give us the inside scoop.'

'Interview me, what for?' I look and feel quite alarmed.

'Rise Art. It is my little, how you say? Magazine. We were the first to cover the exhibit.'

Rise Art. That's the link that Mae sent me. The art world is small.

I don't have time to reply, though, because Louis is urging me into the back room. His partner is there, looking sullen. The air is thick with smoke, which really isn't good for me. It's basically a storage cupboard we're talking in, with art leaning against every inch of wall.

'Gregor said you were very beautiful,' the man in the Hawaiian shirt says, and I think he's very grumpy for a person wearing a shirt with palm trees all over it. Amidst the smoke, it takes a short second for my brain to realise what's happening.

'What, Gregor, as in Earl's broker? You know him? What can you tell me about the painting?'

The shirt man throws Louis a dirty look and makes a pft sound, but my mind is racing. The painting. Gregor. Rise Art. It's as if all the pieces are there, but they won't fit together and give me the answer I need.

'But Gabriel, she is in the painting.' The way Louis pronounces his t's in English makes him sound more French than if he were just speaking French.

'This does not matter. We made a promise.'

'Look,' I interrupt as Gabriel and Louis continue to throw dark looks at each other. I direct my plea to Gabriel – he seems to be the one I need to convince here. 'I'm not well.' (I'm not proud about pulling out the dying card here, but tell me that you wouldn't do the same). 'I don't know how long I have. Before the worst happens, I just want to know who has a painting of me. This person obviously knew Gregor, and Earl, and I'd like to talk to them while I have the chance, that's all.'

'Oft, she is dying. This is a tragedy.' That's Louis.

'Non, she is too old for it to be a tragedy. Only sad.'

My heart rate is going berserk and it goes dark for a second, just at the corner of my eyes.

'Mademoiselle?' Louis asks.

I shake my head. 'Sorry, I'm fine. But is there anything that you can tell me? Anything at all?'

Louis and Gabriel exchange a look and then Gabriel lights another cigarette.

'Gregor swore us to secrecy,' Louis starts. 'Insufferable man, bragging about his new Spencer.'

'Did he tell you where he got it from?'

'Yes.' Louis does a chef's kiss. 'He had a name, but I forget it too.'

Gabriel puffs out a plume of smoke and mutters something in French.

I've started to sweat, claustrophobic in this cupboard. I'll take anything that they can tell me. I don't think I realised, until now, just how much I want to know.

'I would want to know, Gabriel, if someone had painted me,' Louis says.

'Who would paint you, you overblown . . . '

Gabriel starts swearing up a storm.

'Please,' I interrupt. 'Anything you can tell me.'

'All we know is this.' I'm looking directly at Louis now, urging him on. 'The owner of the painting was not French. He is like you, English. Gregor says it was someone who knew Earl well, like a grandfather to him. That's what Gregor said.' He laughs. 'Apparently, he has this painting for a long time. And to think that there was another Spencer and none of us knew.'

'Wait, what, the owner of the painting knew Earl?'

'Yes, Spencer left it to him, after he died.'

The rest of Earl's estate, not that there was much back then, went to TB research, which makes sense now. But I can't get my brain to compute what Louis is saying. It really sounds like he's saying that Emmett had the painting all these years. But that can't be the case. Because he would have told me, wouldn't he? He wouldn't have pretended like he had no clue where the painting came from when he had it the whole time. He wouldn't lie to me like that, would he?

I leave the gallery in a haze, messaging Emmett and telling him to meet me back at the hotel.

I don't know what I'll say to him. I don't even know how I feel about being lied to. All I know is that, finally, I might get some answers about *The Edge of Always*.

Chapter Twenty-Four

'How was the class?' Emmett asks as the door to our hotel room clicks open.

I'm sitting on the edge of the bed, feeling ill at ease. The hotel, the money he seems to have, it must have come from loaning the painting. Mari said, didn't she? That they paid to loan it. He's been keeping it from me this whole time.

'Good,' I tell him. My stomach clenches tight. Dr Dave would tell me to eat. I just don't feel like eating.

Emmett comes to sit next to me and I think, he knows that I know! He must do. He can tell that something has changed.

'Why did you stop drawing, Luna?'

I take a breath in and out, ready to tell him that I'm not answering that.

But I'm already doing so much lying, we both are, and though it's necessary, it doesn't make me feel good.

'It reminded me of everything that I've lost,' I tell him. Finally.

He breathes out. I'm not sure I realised that he was holding his breath. 'Luna.' he's crying. So am I. 'I'm so sorry, Luna.'

He's apologising for what happened when we were younger. But I don't want to talk about that again. Really, what does any of it matter?

Or maybe my oxygen levels have plummeted, and I'm not making any sense.

'I know you are,' I tell him, putting my hand lightly on his forearm. It feels like there's an electrical current, and it's running directly from me to him. 'It's not about that. Just Dad and . . . you know. I'm really tired. I'm just tired . . . ' I trail off. Emmett doesn't know what's wrong with me because I can't tell him. I wish I could, though. I wish I could go back to when we were younger, the summers before everything happened when I felt like I had a purpose, a direction, even if it was the wrong one. Or maybe it was never like that; maybe I'm looking back through rose-tinted glasses. Perhaps life is just relentlessly hard.

I don't know if Emmett too feels the shift between us. Or maybe the air tonight really is supercharged.

'We need to talk, Emmett,' I venture, trying to steady my voice.

'I know. Where do we start, though?'

'Where it began. With the painting.'

He nods.

'The people who ran the gallery – they know Gregor.'

Another nod. He wipes his eyes.

'Okay.'

I feel breathless again. Have I taken my meds tonight?

'They said Gregor told them that the person who had *The*

Edge of Always knew Earl. Gregor said he was like a grandfather to them. That this person was left it after Earl died. Who do you think that might be, Emmett?'

'You know.' His eyes are red, his face tear-stained. I'm battling with myself, desperate to take away his hurt.

My vision starts to go blurry. Emmett is lying to me, but I'm lying to him too. How did we get it so wrong?

'They said that this person had the painting for a long time. I can only presume that they sought out Gregor because they knew he'd had dealings with Earl in the past.'

I'm so woozy, I can't catch my breath. Anger and regret, a maelstrom of darkness takes me over.

'Luna.'

'I presume that person would be quite rich now.' I make a show of looking around the hotel room. 'Having loaned a famous art museum a genuine Spencer.' My voice is hoarse.

'I'm sorry.' His voice cracks. 'I wanted to tell you.'

'I don't understand. Why didn't you, Emmett?'

'Luna!'

It's flashing before me then, a montage of our final summer together. A series of freeze frames, each more devastating than the last. The guilt. Regret at everything I lost. Is my life, filled with regret, flashing before my eyes?

Maybe it is.

In the blink of an eye, it's over. Around me, everything is black.

Chapter Twenty-Five

THEN

Luna was 17
Emmett was 18

Driving up the A1 for the final time felt to Luna like crossing some great gulf. Not so much a bridge between childhood and adulthood, but more like an abyss.

At the end of summer, she and Emmett would be going to university, just not the same one since Luna didn't get into their first choice. Distance shouldn't have been a problem for them. They were used to distance. But it seemed to Luna an indication that things were going wrong. First Earl and the lie, and now this. When her brain wouldn't let her rest, when not even drawing worked to calm her mind, she imagined how it would go down, what he would say when it ended. It was like she was torturing herself. She wondered how normal this was.

Luna had convinced her mum and dad to let them all go to the cottage at Christmas and they'd had Christmas with

Emmett and Tanya. Eyebrow Clive had popped round, completely pissed, and Earl had been there too. He didn't look any worse than he had done last summer, so that was something in Luna's mind.

Mae nudged Luna with her knee.

'Ready for the best summer ever?' she asked.

Luna laughed. It felt impossible to think that this summer could be the best summer ever. The final summer ever, maybe. Whatever happened, Luna knew that the summers in the cottage were the times when she'd grown up. She'd been shaped by her time up here with Mae, Earl and Emmett, buffeted by the wind and the sand.

'We're here, girls,' their mum said from the front seat. Luna tried to push her worries away, stomp them down, and hide them in a cupboard somewhere because there was Emmett, waiting on the step as always. All those years Luna wanted to go to him, and now she could. He wrapped her in his arms, and she breathed him in deeply.

'Not here, Luna, it's unseemly.' Her mum brushed past them.

'God yeah, you two make me sick. Hi big bro.' Mae punched Emmett on the top of his arm.

'You gave me a dead arm!'

'That's what I was trying to do.'

'Fuck Mae,' he muttered. 'You look . . . '

He trailed off. Luna knew what he meant. Mae was gorgeous. She just sort of grew into all her features overnight. People stopped to look at her, that's how stunning she was.

'It's totally unfair, right,' Luna complained, when really, she loved that Mae had turned out so beautiful. It flew in the face of everything their mum warned her about. Plus, she let Luna draw her all of the time.

'You're both beautiful.' Emmett kissed her.

'Not here – Mum will have a seizure. I'll bring your stuff in, Luna. Come back and save me later.'

Luna hugged her sister. She was hugging her more and more these days. The thought of leaving her at the end of summer made Luna want to grab hold of her and not let go.

'Yes, yes. I'm truly amazing. Now go – escape before World War Three breaks out.'

They could hear their mum and dad arguing in the kitchen.

'Come on,' Luna said, holding on extra tight where their hands were linked. 'Is Earl in the studio?' she asked, trying to keep her tone light.

Emmett shook his head. 'He's had that chest infection again. He's just resting in the caravan. Is your dad still poorly?'

The knot of worry that Luna seemed to carry around with her at all times grew tighter.

'Yeah. I think it's the stress of arguing with Mum the whole time. Mae says that as soon as she's eighteen, they'll split up. She thinks they're staying together for me and her at this point.'

'That's crap.'

'Yep.'

'How's your mum?'

Emmett shrugged. 'Okay, mostly. She's going to stay with her sister for a couple of weeks, later in summer.'

'That's cool. We can have sleepovers. I'll paint your nails and curl your hair.' Luna laughed to cover the awkwardness of talking about sex without talking about sex.

'My hair is already curly.'

They were kissing then, pushed up against the wall of the gardens in the centre of the village. Luna felt the scratch of the rough brick against her back.

'We don't have to *do* anything,' Emmett said.

'I want to,' Luna rushed out, and they kissed some more as a low-burning heat worked its way up her spine. 'I really want to,' she told him, pressing her forehead against his.

They spent some more time scandalising the local tourists before walking finally to The Edge. Luna felt that the caravan park looked more run-down this year, as if Earl's health was tethered to it somehow. And if The Edge looked decrepit, so too did Earl.

'Little Luna,' he smiled. He was sitting outside on a reclining deck chair, a blanket over his legs. Zadie and Ahmed had taken up positions on either side of him. Ahmed closed a poetry book.

'Hi guys.' Luna tried to smile, zeroing in on Earl. He looked sick, really sick, so much worse than he did at Christmas.

'Thank fuck you're here,' Zadie said, standing up and stretching. 'Maybe this one will cheer up a bit now.' She nodded her head towards Emmett. 'Is Mae at the cottage? I think I'll go and call for her.'

'Yeah, she's there. Go save her.' Zadie saluted and sauntered off, sucking on a red lolly that had stained her lips extra pink.

'What a tragedy.' Ahmed looked after her. 'Did you know that Zadie was a lesbian, Luna?' he asked.

'Yes, and I don't really think it's a tragedy, Ahmed.'

Not in the same way that Earl dying is, Luna thought, but didn't say.

'No, I suppose not. One day, I'll find someone else, I'm sure.' Ahmed stood up too, ready to begin that search right now. 'I'll leave you guys to catch up. Nice to have you back, Luna.'

Then it was just the three of them.

'How're you feeling, Earl?' Luna asked, sitting down in the space that Ahmed had just left.

'Much better now, little Luna, don't you fret. I'll be back on my feet soon.'

'It's really knocked him, but we've turned a corner now, haven't we, Earl?' Emmett was chipper. He fussed around Earl, tucking his blanket in, and Luna thought that maybe it was only because she knew what she did that it seemed completely obvious to her that they were dealing with more than a chest infection. Earl was so thin. His eyes were bright, but they were the only part of him that Luna recognised.

'Yes, almost better now.' Earl caught her eye and smiled sadly. 'But enough about me. Tell me about you, Luna. You will carry on drawing, at law school? I should be very sad if you stopped. You must promise me?'

'I promise.'

The afternoon stretched into evening, and it was comfortingly familiar, being together here, in the place where Luna had grown up. She sketched Earl in his chair, with Emmett next to him and at the end of the night, she gave Earl the drawing.

'I will treasure this, Luna.' He folded it and held it to his chest, and Luna felt that her heart might break. 'You have a gift.'

Emmett smiled and kissed Luna on the forehead. Luna had never known him to be so persistently upbeat.

When Emmett left, with money from Earl to get them fish and chips, which Earl wouldn't eat, Luna tried again to speak to him about Emmett.

'I'm really worried about him,' she said.

'I am making some preparations,' he paused, 'for after. This brings me peace. It is my choice, to protect him from this, and there is still some time, Luna. It will be better for him not to see the end. He has seen too much death already.'

'I worry about you both,' she answered.

'Do not worry about me, Luna. I am painting still; I have you and Emmett around me. And the others. I find that I am quite content. This is, as you say, the natural way of things. Only art lives forever.'

No one ever told Luna that growing up felt like sitting on the edge of this cliff, looking out at a future as uncertain as the seas. But for now, in this moment, they were here. And maybe that had to be enough.

'Luna, Mae, we need to speak to you both.'

Luna would have had a bad feeling about this, but her life was already so full of bad feelings, she didn't have space for more.

Her parents were at the cottage dining table. Their constant arguments had really taken their toll on her dad this year; he'd never really got over last year's virus. Now, his ginger hair was grey and wiry at the sides.

'What's up?' Even Mae seemed to realise that something serious was about to happen as she and Luna slid onto the other two chairs at the little round table.

Her dad twisted his hands together. Her mum sat up straight and said, 'Well, I may as well just come out and say it. Your dad and I are getting a divorce.'

The word hung in the weak morning light. Possibly, Luna should be upset. Possibly, she should feel something negative about this. But all she felt was relief. Sheer relief. Her parents' unhappy marriage had loomed large across her childhood. Every fun event punctuated by their sniping at each other, every happy day finite.

'Okay,' Mae said.

'Okay?' her Mum repeated back.

'I mean, you guys haven't exactly been a picture of everlasting love all these years. We thought you'd do it years ago.'

Luna's dad began to cry, silent tears that made Luna feel

something about this. It was pity. For everything they'd all been through over the years. Not together though, never together.

'We may need to sell the cottage,' their Mum said, and that one really did hurt.

The three of them, their dad, Luna and Mae, all began to speak at the same time. Protesting.

'We agreed not to decide anything until we've spoken to solicitors, Jennie. There might be a way for me to keep it.'

'You can't sell it,' Mae argued. Luna didn't say anything. She knew that it was all too perfect. She was learning that she couldn't have the things that she wanted.

'Michael, you barely spend any time here, why do you want it?'

They began to argue again, but the anger in Luna's mind drowned them out, a cacophony of negativity that made it impossible to think of anything other than how it felt as if everything was ending. And there was nothing that Luna could do to stop it.

Chapter Twenty-Six

There was no one home. Luna had turned eighteen yesterday and now there was no one home.

'It's not good enough.' Emmett looked around at his caravan. It was late, but the sun hadn't set yet and the big window let in a sort of orange glow.

'It's perfect,' Luna told him.

And maybe she was being selfish, wanting this when everything else around them was falling apart. Or maybe that was why she wanted this so bad. She wanted to be so entwined with Emmett, to let him into her body in the hope that nothing could tear them apart.

'Should we?' Emmett nodded his head towards his bedroom. 'Or we don't have to. If you've changed your mind.'

'I haven't,' she told him, touching his arm lightly.

They didn't spend a lot of time in Emmett's bedroom, for obvious reasons, so it was interesting for Luna, getting this insight into him. There were two single beds, one filled with neat piles of his stuff. Mountains of textbooks, clothes, that sort of thing. He pulled the little curtains closed over the small window. It only made the room slightly less bright.

Luna swallowed, wondering if she should say what she was about to. She decided that it was an evening for being brave.

'Emmett, I know you have, but I've never done this before.'

He stopped by the curtains, a knee on his bed. 'You haven't? We don't have to do anything, Luna.'

'I want to. I just wanted you to know.'

Now it was his turn to swallow. 'We can go slow, and like, stop at any time. If you want to.'

'I know.'

'Even if you think we can't stop. We can.'

'Thanks Emmett.' Luna took a step closer to his bed.

'Thanks for trusting me.'

'Always.'

Emmett was standing in front of her then, running the backs of his knuckles up her arms. They both watched, fascinated as a trail of goosebumps followed his move.

Then he was sliding his hand into Luna's hair, kissing her, slow at first and then deeper, more persistent. Luna always thought that sex was fast, frantic. But Emmett was making it seem like they had all the time in the world. And even though they didn't, Luna wanted to believe, just for tonight, that they did.

'Can I take this off?' His hands were running along the bottom of her top.

Luna breathed in, but nodded.

Top off, it was her turn. Admittedly she was much less patient than Emmett, she had his T-shirt off and on the floor in seconds.

Luna had seen Emmett without a shirt on a million times. But it was still novel that she could touch him like this. Flatten her palm and run it up his side and across his peck, where there were a couple of hairs.

He followed suit and when his hand brushed over Luna's nipple under her bra, she started to shake.

Really, it was a miracle that her legs were holding out.

'Turn around,' Emmett told her, and oh, that was easier. It felt so nice, the way he kissed the back of Luna's neck, along to her shoulder, where he nudged her bra strap down. And then the other side. Then her bra was gone and his hands were snaking over the top of her shoulders and down.

'Is this okay?'

Luna made a squeak that she hoped conferred agreement. This was better than okay.

'You're so beautiful, Luna.'

Luna wanted to laugh, because she wasn't. She'd never been beautiful, but as Emmett turned her round and then helped her out of her shorts and knickers, she felt beautiful.

It was like an out of body experience, being naked in front of Emmett. Like, how did they get here? Luna realised that while she was naked, he still had most of his clothes on. It made her feel extra naked, but he was sitting on the edge of the bed, pressing kisses to her stomach now, and she was a bundle of nerve endings, incapable of speech.

Emmett guided her round to lie on the bed and Luna watched, enraptured as he took the remainder of his clothes off. He had to let her draw him, that's what she thought. She'd never capture how gorgeous he was, but she'd die trying.

As he knelt over her, she thought that this must be it, but they weren't there yet. There were more kisses, in places that Luna never dreamed anyone would kiss her. A soft groaning that Luna realised was all her. She was so loose-limbed and away with it that she felt like a fragmented bundle of feelings by the time Emmett pushed into her.

It was uncomfortable, for a short second, and he was whispering into her ear until she relaxed, welcoming the feeling of being so full. It was delicious, the low unfurling of heat in the bottom of her stomach.

'Does it feel okay?' Emmett asked.

'Don't . . . stop,' was all Luna could manage in reply.

That encouraged him and he pushed faster, harder. Luna clung to his shoulders like they were a life raft in the middle of the ocean, thanking some higher being that one of them was so fit. They rode the wave of it together and Luna wondered, genuinely, why they hadn't just been doing this the whole time.

When it was over, Emmett rested on top of her, pressing gentle kisses to her forehead.

Her thighs ached.

He turned his face towards her and she brushed a loose curl back off his head.

'What did you think?' he asked, starting to move as Luna pulled him back on top of her. She liked feeling his weight.

'I think I loved it,' she told him, alarmed to find that she was close to tears. It was just a lot. Surely she'd crossed some sort of a threshold here. She'd had sex, her, with Emmett.

He kissed the wetness away from the side of her eyes, murmured that it was okay, he had her. Asked if she was okay over and over. And when she told him that she was, for a brief, fleeting second, she let herself believe it too.

Luna wanted to tell Emmett that she loved him. They hadn't said it. But Luna knew she loved him.

She didn't say it.

'What will you do, if they sell the cottage?' Emmett asked her.

They were laid on Emmett's bed, Luna's head on Emmett's shoulder.

'I don't know. Dad said he wanted it, so maybe there's still a chance . . . ' She didn't really believe this to be true.

'It's fucked up.'

'I know. It's weird, once we're adults it's like we're meant to just be responsible for our own decisions, but how do you leave it all behind?'

Summer would be over in a week. Luna didn't know what would happen, after.

'I don't know.'

'I guess you try and learn from it?' Luna wondered. She did know that she didn't want a relationship like her parents had. She wanted what she and Emmett had, where they were everything to each other. Or he was everything to her, at any rate.

Emmett laughed. 'I've learned not to become a heroin addict alright.'

'And I've learned that dark eyebrows are like catnip for middle-aged women.' Luna said this because she didn't want to say what she really felt.

Emmett laughed again. 'Ah well, at least we have each other.'

She rolled over to face him, traced the outline of his eyes, his nose, his lips with her finger.

'At least we have each other,' she repeated back to him and hoped that it would always be true.

'Should we go check on him?' Luna asked sometime later.

Earl had been in the studio that afternoon working on what, Luna didn't know. He was so frail.

He was meant to message when he was done so that Luna and Emmett could walk and get him, bring him back in his wheelchair.

But it was late now. They'd lost track of time and they hadn't heard from him. Outside the window, blue lights started to flash. Luna knew that something was very wrong.

'What's that?' Emmett asked.

'An ambulance, I think.'

They got dressed quickly. Luna tried to ignore the sick feeling. Earl had to be okay; he said he'd be okay for a while longer.

But when they got outside and found Zadie, Ahmed and Mae all huddled together, Luna didn't think that something was very, very wrong, she knew it. They were crying. Luna didn't understand. Why were they crying? And why was Zadie holding Emmett back? Why wouldn't she let him go to Earl?

There was a noise in Luna's ears, like white noise. It buzzed and wouldn't let her hear anything. But she could see people talking; half the caravan park had come to see what was going on.

'He'd been sick for ages.'

'Fucking cancer.'

That was Fred, the one with the horse who had picked Earl up from hospital last year. He'd taken his cap off, was holding it in front of his chest.

'What do you mean?' Emmett asked. He'd twisted round to speak to Fred. Next to him, Mae and Zadie were white as ghosts.

'Picked him up from oncology myself last year, didn't I? Poor sod.'

There was no time for any more questions though, because the ambulance people were backing out of the caravan then, carrying a stretcher.

'Why is the blanket over his face?' Luna heard shouting and then realised that it was her. 'He won't be able to breathe.' They were all fighting to get through then, while some doctor who'd been summoned told them that there was nothing anyone could have done. That he likely died earlier this evening.

Luna was sick right there in the grass but she still didn't believe it.

It was an awful, awful thing, shock. It refused to let you believe what you knew to be true, dragging out the pain of not knowing.

But right then, Luna couldn't believe it. She just couldn't accept that Earl, a man who lived a life with so much colour in it, was gone.

Chapter Twenty-Seven

They were sitting around the kitchen table in the cottage. It was late, and the night felt extra dark to Luna.

For once, her mum hadn't fretted when they'd turned up at the cottage. She'd taken one look at them all and wordlessly let them come inside; another person not surprised by the news that Earl had been dying. Her dad must have told her, Luna supposed. He'd been asleep on the couch but now he nodded and squeezed Luna's shoulder as he went towards the bedroom.

Everything was falling apart.

'He didn't look like himself. I thought people looked like themselves when they died,' Mae said. Mae and Zadie had gone to check on Earl, and had found him on the floor of the caravan.

A seizure probably, the on-call doctor had told them after the ambulance left, a result of brain metastases from primary lung cancer.

Emmett, who had barely said a word until now began to mutter, 'How didn't I know? I didn't say goodbye,' over and over for a while after that, before lapsing into silence again.

Now he sat, staring at the wall. Not drinking the cup of tea that Luna had made him.

She wondered whether it would be better to come clean now. Rip it off like a plaster. Get it over with and admit that she had known, and if she'd just been honest, Emmett would have been able to say goodbye.

'Luna, are you okay?' Zadie asked her. Luna wasn't crying; she thought there'd be more crying. 'Sorry. Stupid question.' Zadie had an arm around Mae.

She couldn't even reply.

'I wonder why he didn't tell us,' Mae said. 'It's not like him, to keep a secret. We could have helped him.'

'It'll have been because of me.' Emmett wouldn't stop walking. Up and down the little kitchen he went. Never stopping, his fists balled tight at the side of him like he was about to punch something, anything. 'It'll be me,' he said again. 'He won't have wanted to upset me and now I'm the reason no one got to say goodbye to him. I'm the reason he didn't tell anyone and just dealt with this all on his own for a whole year. I'm so fucking selfish, so selfish.'

'Mate, it wasn't you,' Mae said. 'You can't think that.'

'It was though.' More walking. 'It's obvious. He probably didn't have treatment so I wouldn't know how sick he was. He'd be here now, if it wasn't for me.' He punched the stone wall and Emmett was swearing and grabbing onto his hand. It was everything that Earl hadn't wanted to happen.

And Luna knew that she couldn't let Emmett believe all of these horrible things that he was telling himself. For the first time since Earl died, she found her voice.

'He was planning to tell you.'

Her words were quiet but their effect in the kitchen was immediate. Everyone stopped talking and waited for her to say more.

'What do you mean, Luna?' Emmett asked. A question that sounded like a warning.

Big fat tears rolled down her cheeks now. They dripped off the end of her chin and she didn't care.

'He wanted to wait until you'd done your exams and left. He was going to tell you when you'd gone. There was no treatment; there was never anything that they could do. It was because he loved you so much. That's why he didn't tell you. He wanted you to be free to go.'

'Shit,' Zadie said. 'You knew?'

Luna nodded.

'Then fuck, why didn't you tell me, Luna?' Emmett asked at the same time that Mae said, 'How long have you known?'

'A year,' she admitted, thinking that it wasn't quite the same as ripping a plaster off. More like letting all the blood drain out of you, slowly. 'Earl made me promise that I wouldn't tell you. You'd have done the same; we'd all have done anything he asked.'

She felt all of them pull back from her. Maybe she'd lose them as well as Earl. Maybe it was what she deserved.

'I would never have kept something like that from you,'

Emmett said. He was quiet, but somehow that was worse. It'd be easier somehow, Luna thought, if he shouted.

The door to the cottage slammed and in the silence she knew that he was gone.

Zadie and Ahmed too.

It was just her and Mae now, in the kitchen.

'You stayed,' Luna said.

'Earl wouldn't want this,' Mae answered, crying too. 'And anyway, I fucking love you, you idiot. It'd take more than that to get rid of me.'

Luna knew then that Emmett didn't love her. He'd never told her that he loved her, and she'd never asked that of him. She'd promised herself, after their first kiss, never to ask for too much from him and maybe that was as good an indicator as any that her love was fleeting and fragile, like a butterfly with a broken wing. Beautiful but doomed at the same time.

Because Luna wasn't certain about much, but one thing she had always known to be absolutely true was that Emmett would leave. He'd go, leave her and Northumberland. This, he had told her and now it was come true. Emmett would go and chances were, he'd never, ever come back.

Chapter Twenty-Eight

NOW

> **The Rubicon**: Oil on canvas. Believed to be close to Spencer's final work, this is his most pared-back piece, evoking silence and stillness. Yet the colour of the door is still rich and varied, with elements of texture. There's a sense of calm here and acceptance. c. 2008

All I remember are the blue lights – the rapid French, the whirling of the helicopter and the lurch as it left the ground. When I come to, fully, in a bright white side room, there are three things that I know to be true.

1. I'm alone.
2. I'm home.
3. The end will be here, and soon.

I don't press any button to let them know I'm awake. My limbs are heavy, but I'm surprisingly alert, like my brain knows that our time is almost up, and it's decided to really take in every sound, every colour, every speck of dust that the sunlight captures. Perhaps this is what Earl meant, all those years ago, when he said that before we die, he imagined that we experienced an explosion of technicolour. I'm seeing the world in high definition at last.

I sit. Feeling the steady beat of my heart. Letting the weight of Emmett's absence settle over me. He lied to me about the painting. I was lying to him too, of course, just like I did all those years ago. The sex. I don't suppose any of it matters now. He must know how unwell I am. There are no secrets. Not anymore.

There's a print on the wall. A David Hockney. Beneath it there's a quote:

The world is very, very beautiful, if you look at it.

The door opens, and I turn my head as Dr Dave comes in, smiling.

'Ah, Luna, you're awake,' he says as Emmett follows him into the room and my poor, battered heart squeezes, just for a second.

'Where's Mae?' I ask, eyes darting between the pair of them.

'She's in the waiting room. I'll tell her you've come round in a moment.' Dave sits on the edge of the bed. He's about to tell me I'm going to die, I know it. And Emmett will hear it too and oh . . .

'It's okay, Luna,' Emmett says. 'It's okay.'

What's okay? Our fight, the fact that I'm about to die? None of that is okay.

'Emmett tells me that you had a bit of a funny turn in Paris,' Dave says, looking down at some notes.

I clear my throat. 'Yes, I, er, I fainted. I hadn't felt well for a few days.'

I look away guiltily from Emmett, where he stands by the door.

'And you'd been taking your meds?'

'Yes, but not always at the right time. I was too caught up in Paris, you see.'

'Paris does tend to have that effect on people.' Surely, Dave isn't going to round off this conversation with, 'And by the way, you have two days left to live,' is he? That would be odd, even for his cheery disposition.

'You had an infection – we're giving you antibiotics. We'll keep you in for a couple of days of observation but with rest and fluids, you should be able to go home early next week.'

'Home,' I respond dumbly.

'Yes, home. I presume you don't want to live at the hospital.'

'No, definitely not. Thank you, Dr Dave. I thought you were going to tell me that . . . you know . . .'

He smiles. 'No. Though obviously, the situation remains serious.'

I look guiltily over at Emmett as he manages a faint smile.

'But you're not going anywhere quite yet. A heart might well become available.'

Emmett must know then. He must know that I've no future.

I swallow and nod. 'Thank you again,' I say as Dr Dave goes to leave.

'Don't thank me. Emmett did everything that he needed to do. Even paid privately for an air ambulance.'

An air ambulance from Paris to the north of England. I'd have to sell a kidney to be able to afford that. Not that anyone would give me a great deal of cash, even on the black market, for one of my organs.

'I'll leave you two to it,' Dr Dave says as he leaves. 'I'll ask Mae to give you ten minutes, shall I?'

'Yes please, thank you, Doctor.' I'm not looking at Dr Dave as he leaves, though. I'm looking at Emmett.

As soon as the door clicks shut, he's on the bed, his hands around mine as I say sorry over and over and over.

'I'm sorry I didn't tell you – I didn't want to ruin our time together. I'm sorry I lied to you about Earl. You must hate me.'

'Luna . . . ' Emmett's thumbs are wiping away her tears, then his. 'I have never hated you. I never deserved you, not then, not now.'

I sniff and shuffle further upright in the bedding.

'But I didn't tell you I was sick, and it's exactly the same as before, when I didn't tell you about Earl.'

He's shaking his head. 'It isn't the same as before. Don't think that. I knew Luna, I already knew.'

That makes me pause. I sit back to look at Emmett's face. He's aged a year in the last day. The skin under his eyes is paper-thin, and his lips are cracked, like he's been out in the desert, starved of water.

'What do you mean, you knew?'

'I knew about your blog.'

'When?'

'A couple of months. You linked it on your personal Instagram. It was an accident, I think – you took it down quickly. I'm letting on just how often I looked you up on social media here, aren't I?'

'I did the same,' I admit.

'It means I knew. It was why I loaned MAM the painting. I wanted to reach out, but I didn't think you'd come just for me. I knew you'd be there for Earl. He loved you so much, Luna.'

'And I loved him, we both did.' Emmett's words are finally sinking in. He knew, this whole time, he knew.

'I wanted to give you the opportunity to tell me yourself. I didn't want to pressure you. I was so annoyed when you walked up the Eiffel Tower. Course, I didn't know exactly how extensive the myocardiopathy was, but I knew you shouldn't have been doing that. I kept asking why you didn't draw anymore.'

He knew. He's still talking.

'I just knew that I had to see you. I've always been selfish, I still am, especially when it comes to you.' He looks at the floor. 'I'm DarthPainter, by the way.'

That makes me laugh. A half-hysterical laugh that cuts through the room like a bolt of lightning.

'You caught me messaging you, in the hotel room. That's why I was on your blog.'

I'm lost for words, caught somewhere between shock and awe.

Maybe I should be angry that Emmett didn't tell me the whole truth. But there's been so much hidden, so many half-truths, so mostly all I feel is relief that it's all in the open. Plus, he knew, and he's still here. I might not know what the future holds, but for now, he's still here.

So instead of getting angry, I squeeze his hand as the door flies open.

Mae.

'You're alive.' She's on the bed in a fraction of a second.

'Did you think I wouldn't be?'

'I thought you'd just fainted, no big deal, until someone,' she makes a face at Emmett, 'freaked out and spent five grand on a private air ambulance.'

'You didn't?' I ask him.

'I wanted you to be under the care of your regular cardiologist. Plus, I'd already called Dr Dave and the air ambulance before we met in Paris.' He does look guilty at all of this. 'Since we're being honest,' he finishes.

Mae is looking at Emmett with something close to shock and awe. There's another knock at the door. Zadie pokes her head around.

'Is she okay? Is she alive?'

'Hi Zadie.' I wave at her.

'Emmett, long time no see. Thank fuck you're still with us, Luna.' Adult Zadie is much like teenage Zadie. Very cool.

'Did you tell everyone that I was dying?' I ask Mae.

''Fraid so. Mum is on her way too.'

'She isn't.'

'Yep. But me and Zade have a plan to distract her anyway.'

Zade.

'You do?' Mae smiles at Zadie as Zadie leans over and kisses Mae on the forehead.

'Wait, Zadie is who you've been hooking up with?'

Mae smiles, and some deep part of me relaxes. Maybe she'll be okay.

'On and off for about twenty years now, I'd say,' Mae laughs.

'On now, though,' Zadie finishes.

'Definitely on. It should distract Mum from your helicopter trip over the English Channel, I think.'

I feel full to bursting, I'm so happy. The Hockney print swims behind watery eyes.

'I'm so happy for you both,' I sniff. 'So happy.' I try to smile, but it's difficult since I'm still crying. 'Why didn't you tell me?'

'Just figured it might rub salt in the wound if I was all happy with my teenage crush and you were still determined to be desperately sad for all of time.'

I reach up and hug Mae – she's always had the biggest heart. Emmett might be the love of my life, but so is she. 'But now Emmett's back, everyone's happy.'

I don't look at Emmett. We haven't discussed it. I don't know what the future holds, for me or us. It's still the case that I'm dying unless I get a transplant. It's still the case that his job takes him far away. It's still the case that he's spent his whole life running away from Northumberland and the darker memories it harbours for him.

There are loud voices in the corridor outside my room. Zadie stands up. 'I'll leave you guys to it,' she says, slipping out of the door before Mum and Eyebrow Clive come through it, old and frail, and I think about how much I've hated them over the years. People who aren't good age just as much as people who are, I suppose.

'Luna, you're awake,' she says in a prim tone, scanning the room, her eyes settling on Mae.

'Yes, it's just an infection. I'll be home next week.'

Mum nods and her shoulders relax just a touch. I wonder if, in her own way, she does love me. Or maybe it's just something she's incapable of.

'We saw Zadie in the corridor just now. I didn't know you were all still in touch? Leave it alone, Clive.'

Mum is straightening my already straight blankets, while Clive picks up and puts down anything that's loose in the room. He's holding a sick tray when Mum snaps at him.

'Zadie's my girlfriend now,' Mae announces.

Mum lets out a sigh.

'I always said it, didn't I, Clive, that Mae would turn out to be a lesbian? And she's so beautiful, too. What a waste.'

It would be neat to say that we had some sort of a heart-to-heart here, a great big family reconciliation where we said all the things that have been left unsaid for so long. But maybe that's not real life and things don't always get wrapped up neatly, because we don't do that. There's no collective clearing of the air. We just carry on. Because maybe it's okay for our relationship to just be okay.

I don't know who laughs first. I have a horrifying feeling that the giggle I hear might have come from Eyebrow Clive. But then Mae is laughing, I'm laughing so hard that I have to lie back down, and Emmett is smiling.

Finally, Mum is laughing; I don't even know what we're laughing about anymore. Probably the fact that life is so ridiculous, if you think about it. It's often hard, and it's often completely absurd until it isn't, until it's over. So maybe the trick to it all is to laugh as much as you can, as hard as you can, until you really can't laugh anymore.

'So this is it, you're leaving then?' I ask Emmett. We're standing on the edge of the cliff, our cliff, though there's no caravan park behind us, but the sea crashes into the rocks, and the wind . . . it's just like it was twenty years ago.

I can't think of another reason for Emmett to bring me here, back to the beginning of the end.

'You know,' he says, looking off in the distance, along the cliff, 'this is what I think Earl painted, this scene. Behind the portrait of you, I mean.'

I nod. I've thought that too. 'Except The Edge was the caravan park, not a cliff edge. I like that we're maybe the only people who knew that.'

I hadn't told my Deathers that, not in the blog I'd uploaded after I got out of the hospital a week ago. Mae and Emmett had taken turns watching over me at the cottage, but I'm better now, or relatively so, so it must be time for Emmett to leave again.

'I think maybe it had a double meaning.' He looks out at the sea. 'You know, it seems daft that I hated it so much here. It's really beautiful.'

It is, I've always thought so. It's early morning and there's a hint of autumn mist across the ground – the gradual winding down before winter.

'You didn't hate the place, just your situation.'

'I was angry.'

'You were super angry,' I laugh. 'But you had good reason to be. What you went through, Emmett, it wasn't right. I knew that, but I didn't acknowledge it. Not properly back then. I thought I could make you better, but it doesn't work like that.' He's turned to face me, and the way my hair blows out behind me, it's precisely what it was like all those years ago. I brace myself for what he's about to say, sure that the pain of it will be etched onto my heart forever.

'It wasn't easy for either of us. We neither of us had enough love from the people who were meant to love us the most.'

I look out to sea. It still comes with a side of guilt, the thought that my childhood was *lacking*. After all, I was incredibly privileged in lots of ways. But two opposing things can both be true. I was privileged and deprived at the same time.

'I never told you, did I?' Emmett carries on. 'What happened that night I left the cottage, after Earl died.'

I shake my head, waiting for him to talk.

'I just sort of stumbled around at first. I was so confused, like I couldn't believe what had happened. I didn't want to go to The Edge and see Earl's caravan, and I couldn't come back to yours, so I went to the studio in the garage eventually. You know Earl walked home that night he died? I've no idea how he managed it. But he must have left the garage door unlocked. That was when I saw the painting.'

I'm crying again.

'It was so beautiful. Even then, when I was so angry, and stupid with it, I recognised that it was a beautiful painting. There was a note with it too. For me.'

'A note?' This is new information. Emmett reaches into his pocket and pulls it out, gripping it hard against the wind.

'Can I read it?' I ask him.

He nods and hands it over.

Emmett, I am leaving you this painting – let it guide you home. You will do extraordinary things, Emmett, of this I am sure. No one, I suspect, will write about me. But if they do, I hope they say that you are my most outstanding achievement. When you are ready, go home, Emmett. My boy, I will see you in whatever awaits us on the other side. EJS.

I'm sobbing now, for everything we lost, and everything we could have had but didn't.

'He wanted you to come home,' I say, eventually.

'He did. But I don't think that he meant to Northumberland.'

Emmett wipes his thumbs across his eyes and then reaches to do the same for me. It's such a tender gesture.

'I never told you how much I love you, Luna. How much

I have always loved you. I didn't know what to do with it back then, because my love for you has always been so huge. Like, right from when we were five or something crazy like that. That's what Earl was trying to show me. The answer to the question is *you,* Luna, you're my home. And if you're here, then that's where I will be. Right here, with you, if you'll have me. Will you have me?'

I am ... devastated. These are all the things that I've always wanted Emmett to say. And now he's said them, it doesn't matter. None of it matters because though I'm well in this moment, we both know that I'm almost out of time.

'But Emmett, I'm not well, you know I'm not well. I don't know how long I have, but it can't be long.' I mumble a few words about tissue type and transplant, which absolutely no one should have to say during grand declarations of love.

'I'll never have children,' I tell him. 'It wouldn't be fair.' I mean, because I wouldn't be around long enough to see them grow up.

'That's not my priority, you are.'

'No, Emmett, you don't understand. I'm dying. I'll be dead soon. There's no point, we're too late.'

Emmett has turned to face me, but I can't look at him. It's just like before – I need to let him go. It's the right thing to do. The thing that he desperately needs, if he's even to have a chance at happiness. I tell him that.

'You have to go, Emmett. Go back to your life, forget about it here. Meet someone else. Settle down. Have a wonderful, brilliant life.'

I think I've convinced him. I sound convincing, even to me, when my words are breaking my already broken heart and crushing my soul. Here's what I know. Earl told me that beauty cannot exist without decay, that life can't flourish without death, but sometimes, death isn't poetic. It isn't beautifully tragic. It's just sad. And I can't bear the thought of all the sadness. I can't face it. Dying alone is bad, but with Emmett it would be unbearable.

'I'm not going, Luna. My life is with you. That's the way it was meant to be. That's the way it has to be.'

'But Emmett, you're not listening to me.'

'Whether you're alive for a week or a year, Luna, I want to be there for it. I don't care how much it hurts after. I don't need protecting anymore because I'm not the same person that I was then. I don't need saving, Luna. I'm already saved.'

All I manage is a sob. It could be true. Maybe Emmett doesn't need saving.

'You deserve this, Luna. Let yourself have it. Let me love you, please.'

At his words, the wind takes whatever reservations I might still have, lifts them up high above the cliffs and blows them away. Of course I want this, I've always wanted it.

I'm laughing then, crying happy tears finally. 'You made me go on a quest to Paris when you knew the answer all along,' I laugh.

'Of course. I just wanted to spend a week in Paris with you. I love you, I love you, Luna.' He's holding the edges of my jacket then, and I'm pressing my lips to his to taste the sea air on them.

'I love you, Emmett.'

'For always?' he asks, through more kisses.

'Absolutely,' I agree. 'For always.'

Epilogue

RISE ART:
ARTIST LUNA ROTH PASSES AWAY, AGED 56

Tragic news in the art community this week as Luna Roth, the artist known for her vivid anatomical drawings and advocacy of transplant support, has passed away. Originally from Derby, Luna spent some of her childhood in Northumberland, and it's there that she met Earl Josef Spencer. Their fates remained entwined long after his death, since Spencer's final piece, *The Edge of Always*, was a portrait of Roth.

Alongside creating her art, Luna hosted the incredibly popular blog *The Art of Dying* until her final weeks. We know that her Deathers will miss her dearly.

Luna's sister, Mae Childs, told Rise Art, 'Luna was a brilliant person. In her art, she tried to capture things exactly as they were; the details were amazing but she always knew that it was impossible. She used to say that the whole thing was a test, because even the most accurate art couldn't capture the beauty of the real life. I'll miss her so fucking much, but I'm so happy that she got to spend her time here, making art in the place she loved with the people she loved.'

Luna leaves behind her husband, Dr Emmett Roth.

Rise Art sends our condolences to all who knew her.

ONE YEAR LATER

Emmett

'Hello, is this thing on?'

'Yes, it's on, idiot – just talk into the camera,' Mae shouts at me from the kitchen.

I cough, self-conscious. Luna always said that having a community online was easier than speaking to real people, but it seems to me that talking into a camera is no easy thing at all. I shift on the couch, extremely self-conscious. I think of Luna, how she did this almost right up until the end, and I'm struck with admiration for my brilliant and brave wife.

'People should see death,' she'd told me. 'It shouldn't be hidden away.' It makes me think that if she could manage that, then I can manage it now.

'You're doing great.' Millie, Zade and Mae's daughter, now almost an adult herself, is standing next to her mum, smiling and urging me on.

'I know it's been some time since there's been an update on this blog.' I look down at the notes scribbled and resting in my lap, though I don't much need them. 'That's because, well, I haven't been able to face it, until now, you see. And if anyone doesn't know who I am, I'm Emmett, er, Emmett Roth. I was Luna's husband. I *am* Luna's husband.' I'm still wearing my ring; they'll have to prise it from my cold, dead hand before I take it off.

'I wanted to come on here for a final update, and for some misguided reason I thought that a video would be easier.' I laugh self-consciously and then sit up a little straighter. 'Firstly, I know that you all cared about Luna. And so I wanted to tell you that she died peacefully, having had many more years than she expected to have, thanks to an organ donor. People and families who donate organs are some of the most selfless I know. To show extreme kindness during a time of loss takes a special kind of courage. I know Luna believed this, too. I wanted to thank you, Deathers, for the kindness you showed her. She was rightly proud of the community that you all built here.'

That part felt okay. But the next part is the bit I'm dreading. I glance behind me, to where *The Edge of Always* hangs in our living room in the cottage. And keep going.

'I also wanted to say something about Luna. And Earl, actually, since I never even went to his funeral. I couldn't cope with it all, you see.' My voice breaks at one of my biggest regrets. 'Yet they both made such an indelible mark on the world, I want to recognise that.'

'Keep going, loser,' Mae tells me. She and Millie are both watching me now, from the edge of the kitchen where Luna and I lived for over twenty years.

'Luna and Earl were artists. I don't think I truly knew what that meant until I lived alongside them. Being an artist, I think, is not something that you do; it is something that you are. They saw the world as a place of beauty, and they lived fearlessly. Not always of course, but most of the time. They were so brave. In death, too, they cared more about the way that their death would affect others; me, specifically. I don't know what I've done to deserve that love, but I carry it with me every day.'

I have to stop to cry a little. It's not as much as in the early weeks and months, but it's always there. A sadness that tugs at me and won't let go.

'I never got to tell Earl how much he meant to me. He was a parent, a friend, a great artist, and it was an honour to know him. He never stopped taking care of me, even when he was dead.'

I pause for a moment to remember Earl and everything he was.

'And Luna, my love. I told her so many times how much I loved her. She was a brilliant person, the brightest thing in the world to me. I choose now to be grateful for what we had. Who else can say that they met their soulmate when they were five? I loved Luna then and now, and all the times in between. I'll never not love her. Always is made up of a million moments, and in every one of them I will love her.'

Another pause. More sobbing that will need editing out.

'Earl told me, and Luna showed me, that life isn't meant to be lived on the edge. You're supposed to plunge into it, submerge yourself in all it has to offer, live boldly and bravely.' I look over at Mae and Millie, who reminds me so much of Luna. 'Because death is the price we pay for living a life filled with love, and it is worth it. Always.'

And at the last, Luna saw a flash of colour so bright it was almost blinding – the colour of love. She flew high towards that light and embraced it.

Acknowledgements

Each time I sit down to write one of these, I feel completely overwhelmed by just how many people I need to thank. It's a humbling experience, one that always reminds me that even in an endeavour as solitary as writing a book, we are never even close to doing it on our own.

My first thanks go to the brilliant readers, book groups, and book sellers who have championed and supported my work along the way. It is my great privilege to have met so many wonderful readers (Yorkshire Reads gang, I'm looking at you!) We'd be nothing without you guys. Thank you, thank you, thank you.

To my agent, Mads, it is genuinely a joy to work with you. You are so clever, so passionate, and so supportive. I am lucky to have you as my agent. If my writing career ever crashes and burns, it's here in writing that the fault will be entirely mine.

Editors new and old, Misha and Molly, thank you both for everything you've done for *The Edge of Always* and my other books. There is no way I'd have four (four?!) books published without you. Molly, I so appreciate that you've always had time for me. Thank you for your guidance and friendship. I'm going to miss working with you so much. Misha, I'm so excited to see what happens next!

As always, I have to thank the wider S&S team. SJ, India (thank you for this gorgeous cover!), the S&S authors who are all so lovely. My beautiful publicist Harriett, thank you so much.

Thank you to the Royal Literary Fund for your support. This novel simply would not exist without you.

Writing friends, I would lose my mind without you all to help me through this (I'm likely losing my mind anyway, but that's on me). Mira, Jane, Julie, and everyone who has read early drafts and sent quotes for me, you're a lifeline in this career. Emma, by your own admission, your messages might be the ramblings of a madwoman, but you're my madwoman, and I like you just the way you are.

Non-writing friends, too. You are all so supportive and so lovely. Thank you, Vicky, who read a rough draft of this and said that it was my best one yet.

Thank you, Dr Peter Wilmshurst, for taking the time to answer my many questions about heart disease and transplants, and for reading an early draft for me. Luna's story is all the more authentic for your input and expertise. It goes without saying that if it isn't, it's entirely my fault!

To family, Mum, Dad, Evelyn, and those who feel like family, Penny and Paul, your support has never wavered. Thank you. Mum and Dad, can you watch the kids for me?!

Dan, what can I say? Like Luna, I thought I'd spend the rest of my life alone. Like her, I didn't need to. Some people are just good, and you're one of them. Most of all, thank you for bringing me a cup of tea every morning. Of all the little insignificant things that you do, that cup of tea is the most significant.

And lastly, my children. Elodie, Hugo, Kit, and my bonus children, Phoebe and Freddie. Every acknowledgement I've ever written has begun or ended with you all. That's because to me, you are the beginning and the end of everything. Every single story that I write, they're all for you. I love you.

Read on for a sneak peek of Rebecca's uplifting and emotional novel.

Available now

Simon & Schuster

Wikipedia

Beyond Baton Rouge
Article

Beyond Baton Rouge was an American pop punk band formed in 1990. For most of their career, the band consisted of vocalist Lola Starr, guitarist Ashton Vain, bass player Shawn Accrington and keyboard artist Prunella Sage. The band were managed by former music producer Jimmy Nickle for Universal Music Group.

Beyond Baton Rouge had several hits, including 'Storm Inside a Teacup', which sold over 100,000 copies and topped the billboard music charts. After their first album, *Don't Ask Me To Sing Softly*, went platinum, *NME* described the band as a 'completely fresh new sound'.

In total, Beyond Baton Rouge had seven top ten hits between 1990 and 1994. Their last single, 'Eyes Full of Wonder', was their only song penned by Starr herself. Released six weeks before the band split, it debuted at number one in the US charts and in five other countries to become their fastest selling single.

In March 1994 the band were due to perform in Vegas. Lola Starr never appeared on stage. She disappeared entirely from public life and was never seen again.

Prologue

'Lily.'

I jolt upright. 'I'm awake. Totally awake. One hundred per cent not asleep right now.'

Dad's laugh is a soft chuckle. A shadow of the deep belly laugh it used to be. The machines *beep, beep, beep* around him. Fucking hell, I can't believe I fell asleep.

In a flash I'm out of the uncomfortable hospital chair, the type with the tall backs that are completely straight. I'm tucking in Dad's blanket, topping up his water. I'm not even fully awake yet, but I'm folding pyjamas like my life depends on it. Anything to distract me from the fact that Dad's breathing is this raspy shallow breath. The sort that sounds like it might give out at any second.

'Lily.'

Finally, I glance up at him. We don't look the same at all, for obvious reasons. But I've always liked the fact that Dad's eyes are slightly too big for his face, just like mine are.

Now, Dad's eyes are even bigger in his face. And there's a deep line between his eyebrows. Stupid line.

'You don't sound too good. Shall I press the button?' I ask him, my finger poised over the big red button behind his hospital bed. Me and that red button are very well acquainted.

The line between his eyebrows disappears. 'Sit down, Lily, love. It's okay.'

There's a beat where I don't move. I think about arguing with Dad that things are really not okay. In fact, okay is lightyears away, in some far-flung, distant galaxy. But you don't argue with people who are dying. So instead, I deflate and find myself back in the uncomfortable chair. I reach for Dad's hand as he takes a few shallow breaths.

'You know how proud I am of you?' Dad asks, and for a moment I'm too distracted by the feel of all the bones in his hand. The way his skin feels paper thin there. Like he's literally disappearing in real time.

'Course I do, Dad.' I'm not even pretending or trying to make a dying man feel good. Dad has been, by any definition of the term, a great dad. Both my parents were literally everything you'd want in a parent. Kind. Caring. Unfailingly proud. And oh, look now, I'm going to cry again.

'And your mum, too, I know she'd be so proud of you.'

Another hand pat. 'I know, it's okay.' Thinking about Mum doesn't do anything to stop the surge of tears; in fact, it sets them off with a vengeance. Mum died when I was eighteen and it's just been me and Dad ever since. Being my parent should come with a health warning: *side effects may include untimely death*.

'There's something I need to tell you,' Dad says, the background a symphony of beeping. His face is scrunched up in worry.

'Hey, whatever it is, it's fine.' I squeeze his hand again.

'Don't be angry, Lily.' Dad has to stop talking. I hold the oxygen mask up to his face while he catches his breath. I wait, trying not to fidget, until he pulls it away himself. 'Lola called.'

For a moment we're both completely still. It's as if I'm outside my body somehow, watching us both frozen in time. Can you have out of body experiences when you're still alive? Maybe not. But Mum, and now Dad and Lola too . . . it's just too much.

Finally, I speak. 'I'm not angry, I'd never be angry, but, er, when did . . . when did you speak to her? Recently?'

He shakes his head. 'Years ago. You'd just turned eighteen. She called. Wanted to speak to you.' Every word costs him.

There's no need to load up the calculator on my phone, or even have a go at doing the maths in my head, because Mum died two days after I turned eighteen. So, I know exactly when Lola called. Eleven years ago. It feels like all the air has left me, as if I'm the one who needs that oxygen mask resting on Dad's chin.

I mean, as deathbed confessions go, it shouldn't be all that shocking. To find out that the person who gave birth to you called hoping for a quick chat. But the thing is, it *is* shocking. Because I haven't seen Lola – my birth mother – in close to thirty years.

'Do you know where she is?' I ask.

Dad nods his head.

'There's a letter. It's with my will. Read it after.' Neither of us need to consider what *after* means. Dad coughs so bad that I cajole him into putting the oxygen mask back on. I tell him not to worry about any of this right now, that it's not important. It's hard to care about the woman who never wanted you when you're losing the last person who always has.

'I'm sorry I never told you. We were both going through a lot. But it was wrong. Everything I did was wrong,' he says through the mask. I won't lie, it has an air of Darth Vader about it.

'Shush. You didn't do anything wrong. Don't think about that now.'

The absolutely last thing I want is for Dad to have regrets.

'You should reach out to her. After,' he says.

That fucking after again.

'If that's what you want me to do, I'll think about it.'

He closes his eyes.

'I know you're lying.' Half his mouth is tilted into a small smile.

'I am not!' I protest. Even though I definitely was lying. I can't see any good reason for finding Lola, none at all.

'Just read the letter, Lily, promise me.' His eyes are open again. Bright blue, piercing in the way they hold my gaze.

I take a deep breath.

'Okay, I promise. I'll read the letter. Don't worry about that now. Just please, don't worry about anything.'

* * *

Discover more from Rebecca Ryan

Available now

Simon & Schuster